BITTERSWEET HARVEST

THE WEIGHT OF THE PLOW

Book II of The O'Shaughnessy Chronicles

by HAROLD WILLIAM THORPE

LITTLE CREEK PRESS™
A DIVISION OF KRISTIN MITCHELL DESIGN, LLC

Mineral Point, Wisconsin USA

Little Creek Press®
A Division of Kristin Mitchell Design, LLC
Mineral Point, Wisconsin 53565

Editor: Carl Stratman
Book Design and Project Coordination:
Little Creek Press

First Edition
Volume II in The O'Shaughnessy Chronicles
October 2013

Printed in the United States of America

For more information or to order books:
Harold William Thorpe: e: haroldthorpe@hotmail.com
or online at www.littlecreekpress.com

Library of Congress Control Number: 2012944434

ISBN-10: 098964314X
ISBN-13: 978-0-9896431-4-6

Front cover photo: ©Lincolnrogers | Dreamstime.com
Back cover photo: ©Gerald Senger | Dreamstime.com

DEDICATION

This book is dedicated to my wife, Lynn, who has
done far more than her share of house and yard
work so that I have time to write my stories.

ACKNOWLEDGEMENTS

I thank Marilyn Hein for her counsel and editorial suggestions.
Carl Stratman, a Little Creek Press editor, pushed me to do better
and offered many ideas that guided the development of this story.
And I thank Little Creek Press Publisher Kristin Mitchell and
her staff for their direction and support each step of the way.

INTRODUCTION

I call the O'Shaughnessy stories Family Fiction. Will, Mary, Sharon, Ruby, Catherine, Gusta, and Jonathon are fictionalized versions of Laura Annette Fitzsimons's loved ones, but the experiences, interactions, and persuasions are the way I imagined them happening. All other family members and characters in *BitterSweet Harvest* are fictitious and any resemblance to the living or dead is purely coincidental. Although the names are different, those who have read Laura's memoir, *From High on the Bluff*, will recognize the villages of Ashley Springs, Hinton, Willow, and Logan Junction. And anyone who has read Laura's book will relive in comprehensive detail the many events she described in that memoir.

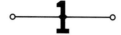

February, 1936

Will O'Shaughnessy knew his mother was worked up when he saw his father's sleigh lurch up the driveway. Gertrude O'Shaughnessy's finger marched in rhythm to her mouth as she dressed her husband down. Thomas didn't argue. He tipped his flask and looked straight ahead.

Gertrude hopped off the sleigh. Mary tried to intercept her, but Gertrude raced past her daughter-in-law and grabbed Will before he stepped off the porch. "You're really going through with it?" She grasped her son's arm and twisted him toward her. "You know what your grandfather thought about your business judgment."

"Didn't I prove him wrong?"

"You sold some cars. I'll give you that. Why'd you leave?"

"I always wanted to—"

"Father said it's those new fangled ideas you learned at the university—don't make sense in the real world."

"I worked hard selling and repairing cars, I—"

"He always said that schooling would come to no good."

"But—"

"He never forgave your leaving him in the lurch, going south to see that uppity black man when he needed you at home."

"George Washington Carver uppity? Dr. Carver knows more about crops than anyone I know."

"What could a black man possibly know? Father said you're not tough-minded enough for farmin'. It's not an eight-to-five job, you know, and you don't have weekends to laze around either. Farmin's seven days a week, sunup-to-sunset work."

"I grew up a farmer."

"You grew up a hired hand. You won't have your grandfather and father to direct you and your brothers to help. I hope you don't expect your girls to pitch hay and milk cows."

And that worried Will, too.

Thomas sat calmly and fondled his flagon while Gertrude huffed back to the sleigh. Then she turned back to her son. "I almost forgot what I came for. Mary's mother called. Said Heinzelman's circus will be in Cedar Rapids next month."

Thomas lowered his flask and spoke for the first time. "Do you think Jesse might be with them?"

"I don't know, Dad." Will saw the pain in his eyes. "There's no time for it now. I've got a farm to build."

Will watched his father's horses turn and slowly move down the drive.

"Sounds as if her nose's bent out of shape," Mary said.

"She was bound to find out. She's upset because we didn't tell her first."

Will O'Shaughnessy knew Wisconsin history, and for a while at the university, he thought he would be a teacher. But he grew up a farmer. All he ever wanted was his own farm. And now he'd get the chance, but the words, "you're not tough enough," echoed through his mind. And now that he'd have to build his own farm, his grandpa's words stung all the more. If, as custom dictated, that grizzly old bastard had given Will his farm, he'd be well established by now.

But was he tough enough? When he lay awake at night, Will worried. Had he quit his automobile business too soon? Did he run away because it had become too hard? The thought that Grandpa might have been right haunted his waking hours and fueled his nightmares.

◆·»»»·««««·◆

They began moving day in the rolling hills of Southwest Wisconsin, crossed the Military Ridge, and then slowly descended crests and valleys toward their new home on the Wisconsin River. Their route paralleled that of Chief Black Hawk's trail a hundred years before when he had desperately guided his small band of refugees away from a United States militia that always lingered close behind. The chief had led his families along a circuitous route to the Wisconsin River where, in an effort to save his people, he fought a valiant delaying action. Although seventy warriors were killed that day, most of the women and children crossed the river.

Will knew that Black Hawk had fought for the lives of his families. He felt a similar desperation, and he hoped to protect his family's welfare with the same fervor shown by that ill-fated chief. The farther they traveled the more anxious he became. The land they traversed that morning seemed better suited to the Native American warrior than to a would-be farmer. Trees, brush, and undergrowth clogged their way. Even if the growth could be cleared, could a horse hold a plow on these steep slopes? Sharp valleys that guided meandering streams to their river destination seemed ill-suited for tilling. And Will knew how a valley stream could flood and wash away a newly planted crop.

After traveling all day through these ridges and valleys, Will, his wife, Mary, and his daughters—fourteen-year-old Sharon, twelve-year-old Ruby, and ten-year-old Catherine—arrived at the Wisconsin River bottom, where they were greeted by a fog so thick that Will had to leave his sleigh and lead his team by their halters.

At dusk a breeze swept down from the bluffs and cleared the fog away, and then he saw it: a plain, double story house with double-hung windows. They rode another ten minutes and turned onto a long, snow covered drive. A black and white English sheepdog caught his daughters' attention when he barked his greeting.

"That must be Teddy," Will said. "Old Mr. Barnes said he'd be waiting. He wouldn't leave his home when Barnes lost it, so he stays here to greet visitors." Will held his horses. "Whoa, Ted, Ned." He tossed the reins down. "He said we could have him. Said he'd not feel right making him leave the only home he's ever known."

"He's ours?" Catherine said. "We can keep him?"

Catherine's cat, Emily, arched her back and hissed so loudly that Teddy backed away, but not without a subdued protest.

"He's a fine host," Sharon said. "He hardly objects to ill mannered Emily."

"Emily, behave yourself," Catherine said. "This is Teddy's home, and you're a guest here. Remember that, young lady."

The girls jumped from the sled and approached Teddy who sat back on his haunches and offered a paw. "See, he wants us to know we're welcome," Catherine said. "A real gentleman."

"Mr. Barnes says that we'll always be safe from rattlesnakes with Teddy around," Will said. "He says he's the best rattlesnake scout on the river."

"Ugh, I hate snakes," Catherine said. "We didn't have poisonous ones at Ashley Springs."

"There are poisonous snakes here," Will said, "so you'd better learn to recognize them and keep your distance, too. It's never a good idea to tangle with something that's quicker and meaner than you."

"I'll never leave the yard without Teddy," Catherine said. "Never, never, never."

"That's good advice for all of you," Mary said. "Too bad there's only one Teddy."

Four sleds full of furniture and household goods slid down the slush-covered drive. "We've got work to do," Will said. "I'll help the men unload." He turned to his wife. "You and the girls go inside and tell them where to put things."

It was as basic as most Wisconsin farm houses, but maybe a bit bigger, with five rooms downstairs and four up. The house had a covered wrap-around porch and a front and back stairs. The front door, on the north side of the house, opened into the living room. Will supposed they'd mostly use the side entryway into the kitchen as it provided a vestibule to keep hats, coats, and boots. The south-facing kitchen opened up into a dining room to the north, which was next to the large living room beyond. Off the living room, a parlor opened into a small bedroom with a southern exposure. The bedroom had a locked door that accessed the back stairs and an enclosed porch.

Mary immediately claimed the downstairs bedroom, saying the girl's legs were young enough to tromp up the stairs each day. And she also claimed two of the smaller upstairs bedrooms to store her excess Ashley Springs furniture and other keepsakes that she couldn't bear to discard. Fortunately for the girls, the two larger bedrooms faced the south where they would get winter sunlight, and because they'd have to room together, Ruby and Catherine claimed the largest room in the upstairs.

Moving in was the easy part, Will knew. The hard days were ahead. His automobile business had floundered during these terrible Depression years. And all across the country people were in despair, trying to eke out a living. Could he make it as a farmer?

2

Will had purchased a small riding horse, Lyda, to complement his bigger work horses: Ted, Ned, Fanny Too, and Mabel. But without cows in his barn, he didn't feel like a dairy farmer.

"McCarthy'll be here today with our first cows," Will said.

"That man gives me the shivers," Mary said.

"He's more flamboyant than we're used to. He seems to know his business, though. He's finding good cows."

Will had just mopped the last bit of pancake syrup from his plate when he heard the truck coming down the drive. He stepped from the house and scanned his farmstead while he waited for McCarthy to back his old Dodge through the open gate toward the barn door. The large barn stood fifty yards from the house and was enclosed by a fenced barnyard. Will would milk his cows and house his calves and horses downstairs, and he'd store hay in the loft above. The barn, a chicken house, an open sheep shelter, a small granary, and a large machine shed formed a semicircle around the end of the driveway. A tile-sided silo stood alongside the barn. And a windmill guarded a large water tank on the far side of the buildings. The driveway that McCarthy had just driven down raced fifty yards from the main road to the railroad tracks, meandered another fifty yards northward, looped around his house, and stopped at the outbuildings.

Will could see the two big black and white cows through the truck's openings. With the delivery of these first animals his vision was almost complete. When Finian jumped from the cab, Will couldn't help but smile. The man hadn't changed much, not even for a workday. Although he was a bit dusty, Finian was as bright as ever: his emerald green, swallowtail jacket was complemented by a plum purple fedora, a shirt the color of sweet cream, matching breeches, and buckle-top shoes.

Will helped unload the two Holsteins and inspected them closely before herding them into the barn. He liked their size, and their drooping bags promised high production.

"Do you have the records on these two?" Will said.

"Good cows," Finian said. "Should give thirteen quarts or more per milking." He handed an envelope to Will. "That's what these records say. Says they're healthy, too"

"Let's see, you've got ten more to deliver. I could use another four. Do you know of any?"

"Fella's selling down Cuba City way. I'll be delivering a bull into Iowa next week. Why don't you come along? You can take your pick of his herd."

"Iowa?" Will thought about his mother's message, about Heinzelman's circus, about Jesse. "Is it anywhere near Cedar Rapids?"

"I'll be going to Marion. It's right next door."

⊷∭∭⊷

It was still dark when Will heard the truck backfire. He had said his goodbyes the night before, had been dressed for half an hour, and paced the entryway in anticipation. When he heard the engine's chatter and the brake's squeal, Will thought about his recent repair business. When he jumped into the cab, the sun's first rays peeked through the window and lighted Finian's attire, and Will forgot all else.

"Morning, Will," Finian called. "Like to start early when I'm hauling cattle. Never know what the day will bring. Gotta drive slow with a load." Gears ground as Finian forced the stick into first gear. "Can't have them too bruised when I get there. Sure hate it when I have to bring them home again."

Finian pushed the stick toward second gear, and Will winced at the sound of metal on metal. Finian clutched, hit the gas, let up, clutched again, and the gears meshed. "Old girl's a bit touchy."

"You shoulda brought her in before I got out of the business."

"Oh, she's good for another ten thousand. You said it's more than cows taking you south this fine morning?"

Will told the story of his disinherited brother, and the irreparable rift that had created.

"So you're going looking?"

"I want to help if I can. Though heaven knows, he tries my soul."

"Never had a brother." Finian pulled a huge hanky from his hip pocket and snorted into it. "Have you had breakfast, my man?"

"I didn't want to wake the kids this early, so thought I'd go without this morning."

"There's a diner down the road, at Belmont. Fries a mighty fine egg. Toast and bacon, too."

They bounded along at thirty-five miles an hour. It would be a long day. The bull staggered from side to side and blared his protests as he bounced off the panels, reminding Will that there were worse places to be than this smelly, uncomfortable cab. Will adjusted his vent so that fresh air whipped past his face. Finian was a likeable enough fellow, but there was more than his flamboyance that made Will a little nervous.

"Did you hear about Paddy telling that he'd killed his wife and buried her in the back yard?" Finian said.

"I can't say that I have."

"Well, at first, no one took him seriously. Then when they didn't see the poor woman for a week, the constables began to search. After a day's digging without finding a body, they gave up. At which time Paddy called his mother-in-law's house and said to his wife, 'Molly, I spaded the yard this morning. You can come home and plant those potatoes now.'"

"Only an Irishman. Did you hear about Father McCrery's trip to Chicago?"

"I didn't."

"He visited the Archdiocese and saw this big, red telephone hanging from the bishop's wall. 'What do you use that for?' he said."

"'Why, that's a direct line to the Lord, but I don't use it often. It costs a hundred dollars an hour.'"

"'I've got one like it myself,' Father McCrery said. 'But in Ashley Springs, it's a local call.'"

"You gotta get up mighty early in the morning to best Father McCrery," Finian said.

"He's a good man. Makes me wish I'd stayed with the church. He's broad-minded about it, I must say. He admits I got a good woman."

The brakes squealed and Will grimaced when Finian missed the entrance to the Good Morning Diner and the truck bounced over the curb.

"I can taste those eggs already," Finian said. "I hope my favorite waitress is here."

Will felt better with a full stomach. The morning inched along, speeded a bit by an endless telling of stories and complaints about politics, religion, and the economy. After stopping near Cuba City and selecting four prime Holstein cows, they agreed to stop back to pick up two of them on their way home. Finian would come back later for the remaining two. They drove on to Cedar Rapids. Finian dropped Will off at the southern edge of town where Heinzelman's Circus was beginning to reach toward the sky. "I'll be back in a couple hours," he shouted as he ground the gears. "Tomorrow morning I want to visit Sykora's at the Czech Village. My mouth has watered for a poppy seed kolace ever since I left Ashley Springs." He waved as he eased his truck forward.

Will shrugged and walked towards the activity. A passel of workers pulled a huge canvas tent in preparation for raising it. Men and women straightened ropes, pounded stakes, and a man led a harnessed elephant across the open space toward the flattened canvas. A huge man wandered from one group to another, shouted instructions wherever he went. Will asked where he could find the owner.

"Mr. Heinzelman? He's in that trailer over there." He pointed to the far side of the grounds. "That's his office."

Will wove his way through the busy workers to the trailer, and pounded on the door.

"Enter at your own peril," a gruff voice called out.

When Will slipped inside, he was greeted by a smile and a hearty handshake.

"Lookin' for a job?"

"Not today," Will said.

"How can I help you?"

"That giant out there said you're the owner?" Will said.

"The Madagascar Colossus?"

"Is he really from Madagascar?"

"Naw. He's from Peoria, but that won't draw customers. He does command attention though. What can I do for you?"

"I'm surprised you're setting up Saturday afternoon. I'd think you'd want the whole weekend."

"This early in the year we're not very efficient. Our new roustabouts haven't learned the ropes yet. I knew we couldn't set up in time to do two shows today, so we scheduled one tonight and two tomorrow. A trial run for the season." Heinzelman took a pack of cigarettes from his vest pocket and shoved it toward Will. When Will shook his head, he flipped the pack upside down, tapped it against his wrist, and slipped a smoke out. "We'll do better." He dragged a match down his pant leg and raised it to his cigarette. "Either that or get a new crew." He took a long draw on the cigarette. "How can I help you?"

"I hear that you have a maimed veteran working for you."

"I did have, but that was a long time ago. Not anymore. Why do you ask?"

"He's not here?"

"I'd rather not give information to just anyone."

"He may be my brother."

"Sorry about him."

"Why's that?"

"I let him go, but I shouldn't have. I thought he was a child molester when, a few years ago, I saw him with a little girl back in Hinton. I was wrong."

"What happened?"

"Three sisters. I thought I'd caught him red-handed. We'd had complaints. But it wasn't him."

"Those were my daughters."

"Don't blame me. The culprit's in the state pen."

"I think he's my brother, Jesse. Jesse O'Shaughnessy."

"He's a bad one."

"Bad one? I thought you said—"

"The other one. The one we caught red-handed."

"But my brother?"

"He played the puppet man." Heinzelman lowered his head. "My people miss him. He didn't have much talent, but he was a likable guy. Tried real hard. The kids loved his show. He liked them, too. That worked against him, I guess. When I saw him with your little girl, I exploded. Kicked him out before we reached Lincoln. We'd had complaints, you know."

"He was innocent?"

"As a newborn lamb. The weekend—if I remember right we were in Olathe—our bearded lady caught a roustabout with a little girl. Little weasel of a guy. He used his puppy to draw them in. She almost tore his eyes out when she caught him with that girl. Just a mite of a thing. He'd have lost his manhood if we hadn't pulled her off." Heinzelman shook his head as he got off his chair. "Shoulda let her at him. I felt terrible about Jesse."

"Do you know where he went?"

"He probably picked up with another outfit." Heinzelman opened the door. "I better check on the Colossus." He led Will outside.

"Mind if I mosey 'round while I wait for my ride?"

"Go ahead. You might wanta talk with Mildred and Louise. They knew Jesse best." He pointed toward a trailer at the edge of the grounds.

The trailer looked too small for two people. Then when Will entered, he saw that the two were one. Siamese Twins, joined at the upper torso. Will was startled at first, but he tried to not look surprised. "Hello ladies. I'm Will O'Shaughnessy. Mr. Heinzelman said I should talk to you."

"I'm Louise," one said.

The other said, "I'm Mildred."

"Glad to meet you ladies. Mr. Heinzelman said you knew Jesse. The puppet man."

"That was terribly unfair," Mildred said.

"Unjust," Louise added. "Mr. Heinzelman made a terrible mistake. Jesse didn't do it. I knew he wasn't guilty."

"He was a kind man, one of the kindest I know, but fearful though," Mildred said. "He didn't want to make anyone mad. He took lots of abuse."

"I knew Jesse," Will said. "He was... was a friend." Will wasn't sure why, but he was hesitant to say brother.

"I'm so sorry," Mildred said.

Together, Mildred and Louise reached for Will's arm.

"Did he drink? I mean, did he take alcohol?"

"I don't think so," Louise said.

"You know that he used to, Louise." Mildred frowned at her sister. "But not at the end. Most everyone carries a flask 'round here."

"He tried to stay sober," Louise said, "for the kids."

"He loved the children," Mildred said. "He learned all kinds of tricks to make them laugh."

"Do you know where he went?"

"He didn't say what he'd do," Louise said. "I suppose he's drifting."

"I don't think he went home," Mildred said. "He hated his brother." She looked genuinely sad. "He never said why."

Louise winced. "That's a bit strong, Mildred. I don't think Jesse had an ounce of hate in him."

"Well, he sure didn't like him much. His brother must have been an awful man."

Will turned toward the door and left without saying goodbye. He didn't want the women to see the tear on his cheek.

He wandered the grounds, but spent most of the next two hours watching elephants raise the big tent. He marveled at their easy gait and obvious strength. Unlike his horses, they moved with a slow confidence, a quiet, persistent shuffle that yielded to no obstacle.

At six o'clock, Finian pulled up to the grounds, now emptied of workers but full of tents. "Hop in," he said. "Let's find some food. I'm hungry."

"Do you know a place?"

"I've heard that Tiny's, down on the river, fries a great T-bone. They say it's reasonable, too. Let's give it a try."

Now free of its weight, the old Dodge truck bounced along the macadam road.

Tiny's was a converted dining car anchored on a length of railroad track. When they stepped inside, Will saw a huge man at the cash register and supposed he was the owner. He didn't know how the man could maneuver through quarters so tight. But when Tiny led them to their table at the end of the car, his agility surprised Will. For a man with a belly like a cow catcher, he moved like a ballerina. He barely acknowledged Will but seldom turned his gaze away from Finian. Will supposed it was the flamboyant clothes that caught his eye.

Tiny set two glasses of water before them. "What can I get you gentlemen?" he said in a gruff voice.

"I hear you cook a mean T-bone," Finian said.

"Best Iowa beef available. Our specialty," Tiny said.

"Then bring us two, with all the fixings."

"No," Will said, "I'm outta steak money nowadays. A slice of Iowa ham, if you will, sir."

"Bring him a steak," Finian said. "This one's on me."

Will began to protest, but Finian would hear none of that. "Don't worry, my man, I'll take care of it." He snapped open his cloth napkin. "Worth the price for a day with a Wicklow man."

The steaks, sizzling off the grill, overlapped their plates. "I'll bring the baked potato right out," Tiny said. "Sure you don't want a salad?"

"No salad," Finian said. "We'll leave the greens for your Iowa steers." He sliced a piece of meat, stuffed it into his mouth, chewed for a moment, then said, "This is pure corn-fed delight. Yes, siree. Might as well toss those greens. Cattle like this wouldn't want them either."

For the next fifteen minutes the only sounds heard were the clinks of metal against china, the chomping of teeth on meat, the smacking of lips, and a few oohs and awes. Will mopped up the juices with his last piece of bread. "It takes a good meal to silence two Irishmen for its eatin'," he said.

Finian leaned his chair back and rubbed his ample belly. "A good Cuban cigar would hit the spot. Didn't I see a box at the counter?"

"I'll buy," Will said as he pushed off his chair. He'd give his stogie to Finian.

"No, siree. I'll take care of this. Just you watch." Finian strolled to the counter. "Tell us the damage, my good man."

Tiny stepped around the counter to face Finian, who had lifted two cigars from the tray. Will could see that Tiny was suspicious. "Be five dollars."

"Would you throw in two good cigars?"

Finian started to shove the cigars into his vest pocket.

"For another fifty cents."

"Two bits each? That's highway robbery. I pay a dime back home."

Tiny shrugged. "Two bits here."

"Would you flip for them?" Finian took a coin from his pocket.

"What'll you put up?"

Finian pulled the fob that looped down his leg and lifted a watch from his trouser pocket. "All I've got is this beautiful timepiece." He turned it in his hand so that sunlight streaked off its surface and caused Tiny to blink. "Far more valuable than two cigars."

"Nice lookin' piece," Tiny said.

"You like it? A fine watch, ten jewels. Tell you what." He flashed the watch. "I'll flip you for this pretty little pocket watch against two cigars and the steaks."

When he held the coin out, Tiny grabbed it from Finian's hand. "Let me see that."

Will had a good look as Tiny turned the coin. One side showed a lady, her front as bare as the Venus de Milo with breasts every bit as perky. And when Tiny turned the piece over, Venus's bare rear looked mighty attractive, too.

"It looks pretty good," Tiny said with a smile that matched his ample girth. "Thought you had a two-headed coin. Everyone's trying to weasel meals these days." He scowled toward Will. "Makes me mad as hell."

He turned back to Finian. "Against that watch, you say?" He leaned over to inspect the timepiece that Finian pushed toward him. "It's a nice looker." He held out his hand. "Okay, shake on it."

"I'll even let you call," Finian said as he shook the man's hand.

"Heads," Tiny said.

Finian lifted the watch toward Tiny's eyes once more, paused, and with his other hand flipped the coin high in the air. It bounced once off the counter, twirled for an instant, and then fell flat, the lady's bare rear apparent to all.

"You lose. Sorry, my man," Finian said as he snatched the coin off the counter. But it slipped from his fingers and fell to the floor, right between Tiny's two oversized shoes.

Finian grabbed for it, but Tiny's foot was quicker.

"Let me see that coin," Tiny said as he reached down.

Finian grabbed Will's arm and edged backward toward the door.

Tiny turned the coin in his hand and saw a rear on both sides. "Hold on," he shouted and reached behind the counter.

Will froze when he saw the gun in Tiny's hand, but the cashier ignored him.

Tiny stared at Finian who, by now, moved fast in the other direction.

Will pulled a five dollar bill from his pocket and threw it at Tiny's feet, and when Tiny stooped to pick it up, he turned and raced towards the door.

When he reached the opening, he heard a gunshot, and the doorsill exploded overhead, showering splinters down upon him.

Finian moved faster. For such a short-legged fella, he sure could run.

While Will circled the truck's rear and raced around the far side, Finian dived through the open window.

Will grabbed the handle, but by the time his foot was on the running board, the truck lurched forward. There was no double clutching this time, just grinding gears and squealing tires. Will pulled himself into the cab, but before he sat down, he heard a metallic ping, and the back windshield exploded, leaving Will and the seat covered with glass.

"I don't think that man likes us," Finian said as he sped away.

"You could have gotten us killed!"

"The man holds a grudge." Finian shifted into high gear. "Not much of a shot though. Glad he's not shooting rock salt from a double barrel. That sure do sting."

"I'll never play cards with you."

"Just a little sleight of hand." He shook his head. "I never dropped one before. I shouldn't have shaken the man's greasy paw."

"You tried to cheat him. You coulda got us killed."

"Can't cheat an honest man, Will."

"I don't think I'd want my honesty tested, not with you dealing. Let's get away from here."

"Glad you threw that fin. It gave me time to get out the door. I owe you." He grabbed Will's arm. "Some fun, hey?"

Will wanted to get away from town, to get away from Finian. But it was too far to walk, and he still had those cows to pick up.

"We'd better head for Wisconsin and get those cows," Will said. "He may get the police out."

"Can't do that."

"You can't do that?" Will grabbed Finian's shoulder.

"It'll be dark soon and I don't have headlights. I saw a lane outside of Marion that we can hide in overnight. We gotta get back here early, though, no later than five-thirty."

"Back here? Are you crazy? We'll head due east at sunrise."

"After I stop at Sykora's. If I don't get there early, those poppy seed kolaces are bound to be sold out."

He should have thrown the man out of his truck and driven north to get his cows. Finian may get his kolaces, but Will wished he'd stayed home. It was bad enough getting shot at, but worse still, where could Jesse be? He must be a desperate man in this land of despair.

3

Will pressed his nose against the window and saw only white. No horses or wagon or sign of his girls. He hadn't expected this spring storm, and Ruby and Catherine were out in it. When Catherine and Ruby had said they wanted to work with the animals and not stay inside and help Sharon with the housework, Mary was skeptical. But their youngest daughters were adamant, so she relented. As he watched snow whip around his buildings, Will began to regret that decision. "I'm going to saddle Lyda and go look," he said to Mary.

The girls had hitched Fanny and Mabel early that morning and left to pick up four boxes of chicks at the post office. The sky had looked clear, and there had been no reason to suspect bad weather, but this wasn't the first late winter storm that Will had seen. Wisconsin weather was always unpredictable.

"They probably stayed in town," Mary said. "I'm sure they'll be okay."

"It's terrible to be out in this storm."

"I'll call the post office to see if they arrived." Mary picked up the phone and cranked one long turn, the operator's signal. She waited a moment, and then returned the phone to its cradle. "The phone's dead."

"The lines must be down." He grabbed his coat and hat off the rack and reached for his boots. Ready to face the storm's worst, he rushed through the door but turned back. "Mary, I may need some blankets."

When he got outside, he called for Teddy. "Come along, old boy, put that nose to work."

Will rode into a wind that whipped snow at him until his lashes were crusted and his face numb. He pulled his scarf over his nose and held it there with one hand, but he couldn't keep the wind from whipping it aside. He didn't dare push Lyda fast because the footing was slick. He tried to stay between the fence lines, and for a while they were there.

When they disappeared under the drifts, he reined Lyda in. Teddy, running ahead, seemed to know where to go. So Will, with a flick of the reins, moved his horse forward and followed his dog between the piles of snow. The wind increased by the minute. He hoped his girls had the sense to stay in town. They'd never been out in a blow like this.

Will leaned into the wind, peered into the driving snow, and saw nothing but white. He strained to see something, anything, and finally saw a large object ahead. As he inched closer he could see that it was an old hay loader. He knew that his neighbor had left it there when it broke down at the end of second crop hay. He'd been out a half hour, and he hadn't even made it past the Jacobs' farm.

Lyda wheezed as she inhaled the frigid air, so Will dismounted and led for a while, Teddy trotting along beside him. It wouldn't do to exhaust his horse before he found his girls. His insides churned when he thought about them. He walked faster, but that slowed his progress as his boots slid back a half step for every one forward. He plodded on until he saw a horse coming at him. At first he thought it was his imagination, that he'd been in the cold so long that his mind was playing tricks. He brushed the snow from his eyes, and when he neared, he could see a rider. Mabel and Ruby? Teddy raced ahead with an enthusiastic yip. When Will heard his dog's name called, he knew it was Ruby. Where was Catherine?

"Ruby, are you okay?" He wrapped a blanket around her and she pulled it tight.

"Catherine's back at the wagon. We broke a runner." She pulled the blanket over her chin. "Hurry, Dad, find her. I'll be okay. But hurry."

Will could see that Mabel was still strong, and Ruby, the wind at her back, seemed able enough to make it home. But little Catherine? Out there alone. He remounted Lyda and hurried forward. At first, Teddy hesitated, and then he started to follow Ruby.

Will called after him, "She'll be okay. Come along. I may need you out here."

He'd ridden only a short time when he saw Fanny coming his way. But she was alone. Had Catherine fallen off? Was she under the snow? Will grabbed Fanny's lead and turned her, pulling her along, but he slowed and scanned the drifts for signs of life. He whispered, "Lord, don't let me pass her by." He hoped that Teddy's nose was as good as Mr. Barnes had bragged.

When he saw the wagon ahead, he dug his heels into Lyda's sides and tugged the lead rope. "Giddyap. Hurry, Lyda." He didn't see Catherine.

Had he missed her? It wouldn't take long for this snow to obscure a downed person. Will jumped off Lyda, raced to the wagon, and found his youngest daughter curled tight against two boxes of chicks. The only voice he heard was the cheeping that came from within. He could see that Catherine had piled snow and straw around the boxes and tried to heat the baby chicks with her body warmth. Will climbed into the wagon and crawled to her. "Catherine." Teddy jumped up beside him and began licking Catherine's face, doing his part to bring life back to his little mistress.

When Will moved her, she opened her eyes. "Catherine, are you okay?"

Catherine moaned and tried to sit, but she slipped back down. Will saw that her face was flushed and her nose, cheeks, and ears were beginning to turn whitish gray—a bad sign.

Will rushed to Lyda, grabbed the blankets off her saddle, and climbed back over the rail to Catherine's side. Her clothing was dry, so he wrapped her in the blankets, hung the chick-filled boxes over Fanny's harness collar, took Catherine in his arms, and lifted her from the wagon. He then mounted Lyda, cradled Catherine between his arms, and talked to her as Lyda and Fanny, the wind at their backs, trudged toward home with Teddy leading the way.

"Don't sleep, Catherine. You've gotta help with the horses when we get home. While I groom Fanny and Lyda, you go to the grain shed and get some feed."

He knew this was nonsense, that she was in no condition to do anything. He had to get her into the house and warmed. Her face looked so pale and she was so lethargic. He had to keep her awake.

⊷⊷⊷

"You're a lucky girl, Miss O'Shaughnessy," Dr. Snyder said. "Another half an hour and we could have lost you."

"My fingers feel all tingly and my toes are numb," Catherine said.

"You've got a touch of frostbite, young lady, but you'll be okay."

He turned to Mary and Will. "Keep her bundled and warm until tomorrow." He lifted her red hands that still showed a white flush at the finger tips. "But her hands will be sore for a few days."

His anxiety over his daughter relieved, Will's thoughts turned to Fanny, and he was heartbroken. His lifelong friend hadn't survived the day's ordeal. The cold and exertion had been too much for her old heart, and she'd collapsed and died before he could remove her rigging. Fanny wasn't just a horse. She had been his confidant and a source of comfort during his hardest times. He knew that she'd lived far longer than he had any right to expect, but he sobbed while he stripped the rigging from her lifeless body.

"The chicks?" Catherine said. "Are they okay, Mom?"

"We lost 'bout half, but we'd not have any if it wasn't for your heroic efforts, young lady." Mary leaned over and kissed Catherine on the forehead. "Ruby's agreed. The chicks that survived are yours. The money from their eggs will go into your college fund. How's that, my dear?"

Catherine looked toward her father. "Oh, Daddy, I'm glad we saved some, but I feel terrible. I never thought it'd be like this. Maybe I'm not cut out to be a farmer."

"You saved those chicks, Catherine. You did what every good farmer does. You thought first about your animals."

He couldn't bear to tell her about Fanny, not yet, not until she'd recovered. Her day had been hard enough already.

W ill knew that Catherine was feeling better when she begged to attend the Good Friday church service.

"I just have to get out," she said. "I've been cooped up in this house forever. I'll die if I have to stay inside another day."

Will was flabbergasted when Mary said, "I'll have Dad bring the new lamb into the entryway." He knew that Mary never allowed barn animals in the house, but she shrugged when he feigned shock.

"Just this once, my dear." She turned back to Catherine. "Now don't go expecting to turn my kitchen into a petting parlor."

Fanny Too, hitched to the buggy and straining at the traces, nickered when Will walked toward the house with a newborn lamb in his arms.

"Don't go thinking you can come in too, old girl. Mary says just this once. To calm Catherine, you know."

Fanny Too stomped her foot on the frozen drive and whinnied again, louder this time. Will supposed she wasn't convinced.

Will couldn't say Fanny Too's name without adding "old girl." Habits die hard. Besides, she looked so much like her mother that sometimes he imagined Fanny was under the reins. The memory of his old friend weighed heavy on his mind. He remembered how he'd shared his innermost desires and fears with her during those days, so long ago, when he was courting Mary. He thought how together they'd endured the hard times with his father and brothers. And he remembered how her enthusiasm had waned whenever they'd visit Frank. Will took solace in knowing that Fanny's last job on earth was to help with the rescue of his daughter.

The storm had been an unexpected ordeal, but Will felt a sense of relief. With the delivery of the last two Cuba City cows his herd would be complete. He couldn't wait to see all sixteen of his black and white cows milling around his barnyard, bawling to be relieved of their frothy white burden. Good milk cows were the key to his future, and although Finian may be a bit odd, he was a master at finding good cattle. Will would soon have the sixteen grade A cows, twenty sheep, and twice as many chickens. Mary wanted hogs so she could keep smoked hams and bacon into summer, but Will was adamant. Ever since the day he pulled his grandfather's mutilated body from the hog pen, he refused to go near a pig. And he wasn't about to reconsider now. Steers were out, too. He hated the idea of taking their manhood. So he sold his bull calves. Prices were too low to waste hay raising them to maturity.

Catherine was so taken with the new lamb that she scarcely noticed their departure for church. After a cold winter and spring, Will loved an outing with Fanny Too in the lead and Mary by his side. The warm sun buoyed his spirits and the reins felt good in his hands.

Fanny Too leaned into the traces when she saw two horses and their buggies tied to the church's hitching post. Not many drove horses these days. Oldsmobiles, Chevrolets, and Fords lined the drive in front of the church. Will didn't miss those cars, not one bit. He still preferred hitching his horses to gassing-up a Model A. Will tied Fanny Too to the post and helped Mary, Sharon, and Ruby off the buggy. The service was about to start, so he knew they'd have to take a front pew.

Will's face burned under Reverend Rosner's austere gaze. He looked from the minister to the announcement board and then back at the minister whose eyes seemed to stab into his soul. "Today's scripture, Matthew twenty-six: verses thirty-six through fifty-six, Christ at Gethsemane." Will knew it well.

"What man shows strength?" the minister said. And that question coursed through Will's mind, a question he had struggled over his whole life. But Grandpa knew the answer, and the old bastard had said it wasn't Will.

The reverend read, "Then Jesus went with them to a place called Gethsemane." Will knew the story, knew the ending, and it troubled him. "Then he came to the disciples and said to them, 'Are you still sleeping and taking your rest? Behold, the hour is at hand, and the son of man is betrayed into the hands of sinners. Rise, let us be going; see, my betrayer is at hand.' And he came up to Jesus at once and said, 'Hail, Master!' And he kissed him."

The minister's words pulsed through Will's head.

"Jesus said to him, 'Friend, why are you here?' Then they came up and laid hands on Jesus and seized Him. And behold, one of those who were with Jesus stretched out his hand and drew his sword, and struck the slave of the high priest, and cut off his ear."

Will squirmed in his pew.

"Then Jesus said to him, 'Put your sword back into its place; for all who take the sword will perish by the sword.'"

"Who showed strength?" Reverend Rosner said. "Simon Peter who cut off the slave's ear or Jesus who stilled the sword? Who shows strength, the man who calms the bully or the man who knocks him down?"

Will thought about Jesse, his poor, maimed brother he hadn't seen in over ten years. He thought about the day he knocked Jesse down. He thought about Grandfather slamming Jesse to the floor.

"President Roosevelt said 'carry a big stick,'" Reverend Rosner said. "Your father taught you to defend yourself. Your coach told you to hit first and hit hard. But Jesus said to turn the other cheek. Jesus tells us that a strong man shows mercy. Violence is naught but cowardice hiding behind a sword."

Will drove home in silence. The day had turned dark, the sun shrouded by clouds. He thought about the time he'd almost drowned his brother when he held him at the bottom of the water tank. How Jesse's eyes pleaded for mercy and how he mouthed unintelligible words that floated upward as bubbles. At that moment, Will hadn't thought about murder. Anger had boiled up inside when Jesse slandered his new bride. He'd hated Jesse for ruining the cake, for ruining his wedding. And afterward, he'd hated himself for his violent response. He'd vowed to never let that happen again. Reverend Rosner was right about cowardice behind a sword.

"Did Reverend Rosner upset you, Will?"

"What is strength?" he caressed Mary's hand. "Who is the strong man? It seems I've struggled with that all my life."

"Reverend Rosner said the strong man shows mercy."

"Grandpa didn't think so."

"Your Grandpa wasn't always right."

And that was the truth. He'd argued with Grandpa all his young life. He certainly didn't think his grandpa was right when he went against custom and willed his farm to Will's younger brother. Frank was so much like Grandpa, and, like Grandpa, Frank could be a bastard, too. The reverend's comments about strength hung heavy on his mind.

5

Will rose earlier than usual to prepare for the day's work. While he dressed he noticed the contrast of his deeply tanned arms against his white body. His skin felt taut and his muscles firm under his shirt. A couple weeks of hard work under the hot spring sun was beginning to shape him into the farmer he'd wanted to be. And it felt good. His excitement grew as he planned to prepare the ground for spring planting. He could see that the field had been plowed last fall and then disc-harrowed to fill the furrows and break up the clods.

Unfortunately, when Barnes put his disc harrow away, he'd stored it in front of the spike harrow that Will wanted to use today. It would have saved a lot of time if Barnes had positioned the spike harrow for spring planting. Will anticipated preparing a seed bed by raking out the new, small weeds and loosening the topsoil so water could soak into the sub-soil.

Will was glad that no one was around to hear the cuss words he uttered as he positioned the heavy disc harrow so that his big horses could back into the hitch and pull it out. He growled in frustration over having to do the same with the spike harrow in back. He couldn't be too critical of old Mr. Barnes. More than once, when he was just too tired to do the work, Will had ignored the adage that he'd preached to his daughters: don't put off for tomorrow what you can do today. And he supposed that last fall, knowing he was about to lose the farm, was a hellish time for Barnes. Will wondered how hard he would have worked if everything he owned was about to be taken away.

After he moved the spike harrow from the tool shed, Will headed for morning milking. He was about halfway through when he heard Ruby and Catherine engaged in what sounded like an intense discussion. Will didn't like to intrude on his daughters' conversations, but when he heard

Ruby say "Gusta," that grabbed his attention. He knew that Mary had just gotten a letter from Aunt Allie, but he thought she was keeping that to herself.

Mary's brother Nick had been gone for more than ten years now. He died far too young, wasted away from some debilitating disease, probably from the cyanide that he used to separate gold from rock during the mining process. And Allie was having trouble handling their only child, Gusta. She must be sixteen years old now. Mary had said that Gusta was being sent here because she had stabbed a too-ardent, rich man's son in the arm with her penknife. Gusta's mother wondered what she might have done to lead the boy on. Will knew that's why Mary had kept the letter from his girls.

"Cathy, you'll never guess what I heard Mom tell Dad," Ruby said. "Aunt Allie's sending Gusta to live with us. She wants Mom to teach Gusta discipline. She's getting to be a… a vamp."

"I thought vamps lived in Chicago," Catherine said.

"Silly, vamps wear naughty clothes."

Will was used to his daughters passing secrets as if they were alone in the barn. He wasn't sure whether the girls talked openly because they trusted him or because they forgot he was there. And he knew they didn't like milking, so he supposed the conversations speeded the chore along. Either that or sing. They sang a lot, too, and he loved listening to his girls' voices.

"Gusta has naughty clothes," Ruby said. "In her last letter, she said she has a dress that you can see right through." Ruby flicked her braid over a shoulder and smirked. "I'd wear it, even if you could see my bloomers."

"Mom better not see them."

Will laughed to himself. He knew that Catherine was right on that one.

"Mom's tough, but it'll be a challenge." Ruby tossed her hips. "Gusta's strong-willed. I like her."

Although he found little time for it, tonight Will was intent on catching up on his last two issues of *Hoard's Dairyman*. And it was a good time because Mary was leaving for church choir practice. So after the evening milking he changed into clean clothes, replaced his barn boots with slippers, and headed for his big, horsehair easy chair in the parlor. Catherine worked on her poetry anthology at the living room writing desk, while Sharon, sitting on the parlor sofa, waited to teach Ruby how to knit. Will knew that neither Sharon nor Ruby were eager to proceed, but Mary had insisted that Ruby and Catherine must learn a few womanly tasks, and tonight was Ruby's turn.

Sharon was so different from her younger sisters. Will doubted that she could tempt a single drop of milk from his most cooperative cow, nor would she even try. Her interest was housework. And Mary was delighted by that. Will supposed it began when she was young, when she had two little sisters to help care for. Or maybe she was just inclined toward domestic tasks.

Sharon had taken two balls of yarn and two sets of knitting needles from Mary's sewing basket, and she sat waiting for her sister, who, after milking, had stopped at the little house out back. Sharon sat patiently for a while, but then she began to fidget. She picked up a needle, fished the yarn end from the ball, and, absentmindedly, began looping and straightening the yarn. Five minutes passed, then ten. Will saw Sharon slip the loop onto the needle, peel it off, slip it on again, frowned while she looked toward the kitchen door, paused, then she pulled another loop over the needle. She repeated this a few times while her foot began tapping in rhythm to her finger movements. Finally, she threw the yarn and needles down, stood up, and mumbled, "Where is that girl? I'm losing patience."

Will knew that Ruby could anger even her patient, older sister when she chose to be obstinate. So to keep the peace, he laid his magazine down and headed for the kitchen door. Five minutes later, Ruby, looking as if she'd rather be shoveling fresh cow manure, followed him into the parlor.

"Well, it's about time," Sharon said. "Don't think that I want to do this, either. I could have had a scarf knitted and a matching mitten started while waiting for you."

At first Ruby stood with her hands on her hips and stared sullenly at her sister, but when Mary stuck her head through the doorway and glared in her direction, she flopped down beside Sharon and said, "Okay, okay, I'm here. Let's get this started."

Will heard car brakes outside.

Mary called, "Marge Roberts is here. I'm leaving now."

Sharon frowned at Ruby. "Do what I do." Sharon thrust a ball of yarn and two needles at Ruby, and then she made a loop in her yarn, with the end that was attached to the ball looped over the top.

Ruby copied Sharon as she made a knot in the loop and tightened it around a needle. Then Sharon added more stitches to the needle. "This is called casting on," she said.

Ruby dutifully did her casting, but by the look on her face, Will could see that she would rather be back in the smelly outhouse.

Sharon draped the strand of hanging yarn behind her left hand and brought it across her palm, and then she looped it around the knitting needle.

When Ruby did it all wrong, Sharon said, "I'm only the number two student in my class, and I don't have any trouble."

Will knew that Sharon had always been a bit jealous of Ruby's and Catherine's top standing in their classes.

Ruby looked more closely at Sharon's work and copied it perfectly, while she commented, "I bet you can't dissect a toad."

Will smiled to himself at Ruby's response. Sharon had an irrational fear of toads, but he doubted that his oldest daughter would willingly dissect anything. He also knew the dissections they did in Ruby's biology class were on worms, mice, and crayfish, maybe on frogs—but not toads.

"I'll make this a pre-primer lesson, just for you, Ruby. We'll only do the simplest of stitches."

Then she went through the next few steps so rapidly that Will's eyes couldn't follow.

Ruby threw her needles and yarn on the floor, surged off the sofa, and shouted, "I'm going to bed."

As Ruby raced up the stairs, Sharon smiled toward her sister's backside but continued her lesson on speed knitting. Will knew the scarf would be well along by the time his oldest daughter retired to her bedroom. And despite Mary's insistence, Will knew that his middle daughter wasn't cut out for domestic life.

❧

Mary O'Shaughnessy didn't mention the letter until two nights later when the family gathered for supper. "Girls, I received a letter from Aunt Allie saying that Gusta's coming to stay with us this summer, and next school year, too."

"Mom!" Sharon screamed.

"Shush, Sharon. I'll tell you the truth. Aunt Allie says Gusta's high spirited and that she needs discipline."

"Mom'll teach her discipline," Catherine said.

"We don't have room for anyone else," Sharon said. "She can't sleep in my bedroom. It's too small, and there's no space in my closet. Besides, I've never liked her ways. She's too much like a… a… floozy. She'll embarrass us."

Mary glared at Sharon. "It'll work because we'll make it work. There's always a place here for family. This is a Christian home, and you'll live up to His teachings. Must I remind you of the prodigal son?"

"She's not your daughter," Sharon cried.

"She's my dead brother's daughter," Mary said. "And that's close enough. I won't hear another complaint."

"Where will she sleep?" Ruby said. "Will you clean out an upstairs storeroom?"

"I'm not ready to get rid of our extra furniture," Mary said. "Dad'll pull a cot into your and Catherine's room." She turned to Will. "You can pull that old cot down from the attic."

Mary eyed Sharon. "And to show that her heart's in the right place, Sharon will clean up the cot."

Sharon glared.

Will could see that Sharon's heart wasn't where Mary wanted it to be—not in the least.

"Sharon, I can't make you like it, but you will do it. Do you hear me?"

"Yes, Mother."

Mary turned toward her other two daughters. "You'll need to make space for her clothes in your closet. Now, go do your school work. It's getting late."

Given what he'd heard about Gusta's wardrobe, Will thought that closet space could be a problem. But he could see that Mary was determined to weave her wayward niece into the fabric of their happy home. He knew it would be a challenge.

❄

Today they'd meet Gusta at the station. Packed into the buggy, they headed for town and arrived at the depot with time to spare. The train was later than usual, but Will soon felt the tracks vibrate, and before he heard the whistle in the distance, he saw puffs of smoke over the bluff where they'd picked blackberries in summer.

Catherine watched intently as the train pulled into the station—whistle blowing, drive wheels screeching, bell clanging. "Why can't the train

32

stop and let Gusta out at our farm?" she said. "The track runs within fifty yards of our house."

"The train would never be on time if it stopped at every farmhouse," Will said.

Mr. Franklin, the stationmaster, waited with a cart while the engine pulled up to the platform. He always seemed to know when it was about to arrive. Will supposed he had received a telegraph message, but maybe he just knew.

Will scanned the passenger cars, but before the train stopped, Ruby shouted, "There she is," and pointed toward the engine.

All eyes turned upward, and the waiting crowd emitted an audible gasp when they saw a young lady perched atop the coal tender. Gusta wore a fringed buckskin skirt and a red chenille shirt with a white floral pattern, white fringed trim, and a black yoke and collar. She sported a red Stetson and red boots and twirled a lariat while she sang, "Buffalo gals won't you come out tonight, come out tonight, come out tonight! Buffalo gals won't you come out tonight and dance by the light of the moon!"

"Oh, good Lord," Ruby said.

"The hussy," Sharon said.

Catherine stared, mouth open.

Mary ran toward the engine. "Get down from there this instant," she called. Then she turned to the engineer. "What did you do to my niece? She could have been killed. I'll have your job for this."

"Lady, I was too busy reining this beast in to babysit your kin. She crawled up there on her own."

Gusta climbed down and hugged her aunt as if she never planned to let go. "Aunt Mary, I was so excited to see you that I just couldn't help myself. Back home, I'd have saluted you from atop a saddle, but I didn't have a horse, only this iron one. Please, don't be angry, Aunt Mary."

Mary O'Shaughnessy melted.

Sharon didn't. She spun away and strode back to the buggy.

Will stepped forward and took Gusta's soft hand between his two burly ones. "Welcome to Wisconsin, my little Texas cowgirl."

"Uncle Will. It's been so long. I can't wait to hear your latest story."

"Did you hear about the Irishman who visited Texas?"

Ruby frowned. "Dad!"

"Yes, my dear," Will said. "Gusta, is your suitcase in the passenger car?"

"Uncle Will, I brought two trunks and four suitcases. They're all in the baggage car."

Will gasped. "We don't have room, not in the buggy or the house."

Mary stepped forward. "We'll make room. There's space in the attic."

Will talked to Mr. Franklin, and with his help, he began to slide the luggage onto the platform. "I'll send my girls back for this in the morning."

While they walked to the buggy, Will heard Ruby say to Catherine, "Something's fishy here, sister."

"What do you mean?"

"How'd Gusta get on top that coal tender? It's fifteen miles back to the Spring Green station. Surely she didn't climb up there and ride the whole way."

Will had wondered about that, too.

"Ask her," Catherine said.

"I will."

When Ruby and Catherine caught up with everyone at the buggy, Ruby asked Gusta, "Surely you didn't ride in that smelly coal all the way from Spring Green?"

"Well, cousin, you're right. I didn't ride the tender from Spring Green. I rode the engine."

"The engine?" Ruby said. "I've heard that it's against rules for passengers to ride the engine."

Gusta lowered her voice. Will leaned in to hear this answer. "Ruby, you don't know men. Why, I just smiled real pretty and batted my lashes, and that engineer didn't mind one little bit. I crawled atop the tender when he was busy stopping the train."

Catherine stood slack-jawed.

Will could see that Mary was about to get all she could handle. He had confidence, though. His Mary was a resolute woman.

"Uncle Will, can we get two suitcases in the buggy? I must bring two today."

"I'd planned to take one home today and come back tomorrow for the rest. I don't think there's room enough in the buggy."

"But, Uncle Will, I must take two. I have my . . . well . . . my unmentionables in one, and I just must bring the other. It has the presents I brought for everyone. I've worried the whole trip that I selected properly. I won't sleep tonight if I don't know how y'all like my gifts."

Sharon insisted upon sitting in front with Mary and Will, while her cousin and sisters hid in back under Gusta's two suitcases.

That night the family gathered to watch Gusta remove each gift from her suitcase and present it to its recipient. Will had never seen gifts so beautifully wrapped. Perfectly proportioned folds created the impression of seamless blue paper that was adorned with red and blue ribbons that coiled into rose petals at the bow. Gusta gave each of the girls a western blouse—Ruby's with a floral print embroidered on the yoke and light blue cotton cuffs; Catherine's a yellow denim with a beaded rose pattern on front and back yokes; and Sharon's a black gabardine with embroidered red and yellow tulips across the front. She also gave each a turquoise and silver pendant and a turquoise row bracelet.

Gusta gave Mary a Spanish piano shawl made of black silk covered with rose, blue, and white silk embroidered flowers. An eighteen-inch, black silk fringe surrounded the entire shawl. "Aunt Mary, I had Mom's seamstress make this to your size. Mom wrote to Grandma Tregonning to get your measurements. I have one for her, too."

Gusta even remembered Sharon's new beau, Ed Meadows. She handed Sharon a turquoise cluster belt buckle with seventeen gems set in silver and a calfskin ranger belt. Its buckle and the first two loops were set with turquoise gems. They admired their gifts while Gusta presented the last package to Will. When he opened it, Mary cried out, "That's Nick's meerschaum pipe. He wrote that he bought it during his last trip to Europe. But he fell ill soon after he returned and his lungs were so bad that his doctors insisted he shouldn't use any tobacco."

"Uncle Will, Mother said that Daddy would have liked for you to have this. She's wanted to send it ever since he died, but she just couldn't give it up. She said that now I'm visiting, it's time you got it."

Will handled the pipe like a mother might touch her first born.

"Most of the gemstones are turquoise that Daddy dug from the prairie when he was superintendent of the Gold Road's Mine at Kingman. I found an old Navajo craftsman who cut, polished, and set each stone in silver. I do hope y'all like these little things."

Mary dabbed at her tear-stained face.

"I'm sorry that I made you carry all this stuff home, Uncle Will, but I couldn't wait one more day before giving you these gifts. I picked them out and wrapped them myself. I was so excited for you to get them."

"How could you have known about Ed?" Sharon said. "We only began dating last fall?"

"I read Aunt Mary's letters. I do hope he likes them. I so want for us all to be happy together, to be family."

Sharon pulled Gusta forward and hugged her. "I'm sorry for not being friendly, Gusta. I'm not used to, well, you know, not used to someone so flamboyant. Welcome to our home."

Mary walked to the organ. "Gusta, we don't have the money to buy nice presents, but we'd like to welcome you to our home with an evening songfest. Before I begin, let Ruby tell you what we've planned for an official welcome. This was the girls' idea."

"A week from Saturday," Ruby said, "we're going to hold a dance right here in your honor. We want you to meet our neighbors and friends. We want them to become your friends, too."

"Whoopee," Gusta shouted. "There's nothing I like better than a dance. I'll teach y'all the Texas two-step."

As Mary played "The Eyes of Texas are Upon You," Will was glad that Gusta seemed enthused about her exile to the Northland, but he worried that she might turn their happy little family's harmony topsy-turvy.

The day of the village picnic began peaceful enough.

Mary O'Shaughnessy dug deep into her closet. "Will, I can't find that flowered dress your mother gave me for my birthday. We wouldn't have left it behind, would we have?"

"That house was bare as a newborn's hinder," Will said. He looked through her closet. "It must be here someplace." But he couldn't find it either.

Mary sat on their bed. "It'd be perfect for so bright a summer day. Whatever could I have done with it?"

Will pulled his old suit out and fished along the back wall for a vest he hadn't worn since they moved into the house. When he saw a flash of yellow and pink, he pulled his clothes aside. "Mary, guess what I found back here. It looks like a dress fit for the prettiest lass in Iowa County."

"How'd it get in there, Will? You weren't planning on wearing it to one of your lodge gatherings, now were you? I always wondered what you men did at those meetings."

"I s'pose you might as well take it back." Will handed her the dress. "I'm too busy to join the Willow Lodge."

"It probably got there in our hurry to unpack. I'll let you off the hook this time, my dear."

Fully dressed, they stood before each other. Attired for the day's outing, Mary looked exceptionally beautiful. She must have spent an hour on her hair. Not a strand was out of place. Will was sure that his wife kept the local hairpin business flourishing. And he'd noticed that even when she came home after a late evening church meeting, her hair always looked combed and pinned, as beautiful as it had been on their wedding day. "I'll never know how a beautiful lass like you could have fallen for an old hayseed like me. Miracles never cease, now do they?"

Mary approached Will and put her arms around him, and with her head on his shoulder, she whispered in his ear, "You don't know how sexy you looked in that suit when you were young and perky. Why, my heart did flip flops."

Will pulled her tight against him, savored her every curve. "Wanta see how much perk I've got left?"

"Later, my dear." Mary stepped away. "I've got a dress to show off."

The sky was bright and cloudless, and a slight breeze cooled Will's face. Wisconsin didn't have many clear days, so Will took noticed when it happened. He hoped it signified a good day ahead.

Will didn't push Fanny Too as he drove the eight miles to Willow. He didn't want her lathered, because he'd not have the time, and the stable may not have the curry tools to properly rub her down. When, forty-five minutes later, they moseyed down Main Street, Will noticed the Midtown Waterin' Hole. He quickly looked away and directed his attention to the boxes of food that rested alongside them in the buggy. "I wonder how many of our neighbors will have eaten Cornish food? Not many Cousin Jacks in Willow." He stepped off the buggy, reached back for a box, and handed it to Mary. "You take the plums, scald cream, and saffron bread." He lifted another box off the buggy floor. "I'll carry the pasties. They'll eat Cornish fare today, and they'll love it, now won't they?"

The grassy mall's perimeter was lined with russet, dark brown, and gray colored tents. Women and a few men scurried about arranging utensils and laying out food on the tables inside each enclosure. Mary and Will approached a lady who seemed to be directing the traffic.

"Where would you like us to set up?" Mary asked.

The woman paused for a moment, scanned the tables, and, with a swooping motion that pointed nowhere, said, "Take any open spot." Then she was on her way.

Will headed for a gray tent whose peak almost touched the branches of the oak tree above. "This looks as good as any."

He took the pasties, which were wrapped in wax paper, from the box and placed them on a platter. Then he helped Mary set out a platter of saffron bread, the bowl of plums, and a pitcher of scald cream.

Mary busied herself talking to a lady who'd just placed her food at the far end of their table. With nothing more to do, Will told Mary that he'd be back for lunch and headed up the street. He nodded to a few people. He'd been so busy getting the farm started that the only neighbors he knew were the farmers he saw when he took his milk to the factory. If he wanted to meet his neighbors, he'd have to visit their trough. And by the sound of voices, he could tell that it was the Waterin' Hole. Will stepped inside and sidled up to the bar. "A small beer, please."

"A Mineral Springs do?"

"Unless you'll sell your Jameson for a nickel."

The bartender smiled. "You're new in town, that's for sure. Name's Reilly, Colin Reilly." He handed Will the beer.

Will dropped a nickel on the bar and offered his hand. "Will O'Shaughnessy."

He stood with his back to the bar and inspected the room while he sipped at his brew. Four men argued at a table, their words heated at times. Will looked down the bar and saw a man slumped over his drink. He must have begun early.

One of the four men from the table ambled toward Will. "O'Shaughnessy, isn't it? I've seen you at the cheese factory." The man reached his hand forward. "I'm James Henning."

Will had to crane his head upward to see a deeply tanned man with fetching blue eyes and straw-colored hair that sprouted from under an old gray cap. He took Henning's hand. "Will O'Shaughnessy. Glad to meet you, Mr. Henning."

Henning pointed to the table where the three men continued their heated discussion. "Will you join me and my friends?"

"Looks a bit violent. Is it safe?"

"They're civilized men." Henning waved his hand through the air. "They just get excited when government issues come up."

Will sat down, his glass in hand. "Hello, gentlemen. I'm Will O'Shaughnessy. Up the river, on the Barnes farm."

Henning motioned toward each in turn. "Saul McPherson, George Snell, Arnie Johnson. We all farm in Willow Township. Saul's our town chairman."

Saul was a plump, little man with a border of snow white hair and wire rimmed glasses that hooked his ears just in time to hang on his nose. He reminded Will of pictures he'd seen of one of his favorite patriots, John Adams. George Snell was tall and muscled, with a long brow and squared jaw. He looked rather dour to Will. Johnson looked as if he could use a few good meals, but his broad smile was so compelling that it drew Will's attention away from a top so bald that it reflected light off his hatless head.

Will sipped his beer. "Mr. Henning tells me you've got government issues."

"I heard about a new government program that I might try," Arnie Johnson said. "Low interest. They don't call the mortgage until crop's in. And they'll loan as much as I need."

"If you meet their conditions," Will said.

"What do you mean?" Snell said.

"Government money never comes cheap, not if you value your independence."

"I need the money," Johnson said. "It's tough these days."

"There may be a better way," Will said.

"What's that?" McPherson said.

"Cooperatives. They're a way we can buy for less, sell for more, and get the money we need as well."

"What do you know about cooperatives, O'Shaughnessy?" McPherson said.

"I've studied them a quite a bit. By working together we can avoid problems. There's one thing I've learned over the years, fellas. You save lots of grief when you learn to plow 'round the stumps."

"You got that right," Henning said. "Here, I'll buy another drink." Henning grabbed Will's glass. "Whatta you drinkin'?"

"Take it easy, friend. I'm here with my wife."

"Just one more, neighbor. Bartender, over here. Fill 'em up again."

⊷⊱⊰⊶

Two hours later, Will and his friends stumbled into the food tent. He knew that Mary wouldn't be happy. There was no way around it, so he approached her directly. "Mary, meet our nagbors—Shak Hennig, Shawl Mcferoon, Yorge Schnell, and… Johnson. What's yir frist name, Johnson?"

"Will, I'm ashamed of you. And gentlemen, although I have my doubts, I'd like to meet you but some other time."

Mary turned and hurried back to the food table.

"I said she'd not be happsy."

"That's why I leave my wife at home," McPherson said.

"Thatch why I don't have a vife," Henning said.

"Letch go back to the bar. More friendsly there," Johnson said.

Will decided that black coffee should be his drink now, so he bid his new friends goodbye. He stopped at Jordy's Ice Cream Parlor to buy a large cup of brew, and then he sat alone on a park bench, sipped at his coffee, and watched the people walk by. He continued to be surprised by how a small community could overflow when the farmers came to town. Will watched boys play kitten ball on the village green, and when he saw them erupt into a heated argument, he headed in their direction. "Boys, boys, what's the problem here?"

A boy pointed at a bigger kid. "He hit my ball so hard that the stuffin's coming out. "We can't play with it anymore, not until my dad tapes it."

"He's just a spoil sport," the bigger boy said. "That ol' ball'll take a lot more beatin'."

"Hold on, boys," Will said. "I think I can help."

He pulled a roll of electrical tape from his inside pocket. "I keep this for emergencies, yes I do. I'll fix the ball, but on one condition."

A tall, older boy stared Will in the eye and then spat toward his feet. "Yeah?"

"If I fix your ball, you'll let me play? I used to be a pretty good hitter. And I can pitch, too."

"You play?" the tall boy said. "Didn't I see you stagger out of Midtown awhile back? You're just an old souse."

Will offered his hand. "What's your name, son?"

The boy refused to take it.

"Jack Hornking," another said. "He's our umpire."

"Well, Jack, I'm Will O'Shaughnessy."

"O'Shaughnessy? Ruby's dad?"

"That's right. Sharon, Ruby, and Catherine are my daughters."

"She said you might have a job."

"I'll be needing help, but I can't afford it now. Come see me next spring. I can use some help with my crops."

"I s'pose you can play."

Will wound the last strip of electrical tape around the ball. "There, that oughta hold it."

He tossed the ball to Jack who rolled it between his fingers. "Kinda sticky, but guess it'll do." He threw the black laced orb to the mound. "Play ball."

Will was assigned to the scrub team, the younger kids who didn't play so well.

"Mr. O'Shaughnessy, I'm Billy O'Dell." Billy reached out his hand. "I'm captain of this team. Will you pitch for us? Junior can't get them out."

"Why sure, Billy. I've pitched a bit over the years."

"Scrubs, you're at bat," Hornking shouted. "Top of the order."

Will gathered his team. "The third baseman's playing too far back. Bunt the ball toward him until he moves in."

Will's strategy worked. The scrubs' first three batters got on base, and Billy had designated Will as their clean-up hitter. He hoped that he could still hit a baseball like he could when he was younger.

"Strike one," Jack called out.

The pitcher then threw two balls, just missed with the second pitch.

"That was a strike," the pitcher shouted. "You just want a job."

"Shut up and pitch," Jack called back.

The pitcher wound up and threw a hard, fast one right down the middle of the plate. Will made solid contact, and by the time the ball bounced off a post and rolled away from the outfielder, Will was around second base. His third base coach shouted, "Go home. Go home."

Will, now running low on fuel, should have known better, but his memory of better years outvoted his weary legs. So he rounded third toward home. With each step, his pace slowed, and when he looked up, the catcher stood tall, a grin on his face, the ball in his mitt. That's when Will's remembrance coaxed him into his second mistake. He'd slid under tags when he was young, so he hit the dirt, but before he stopped short of the plate, he heard an ominous ripping sound.

Billy O'Dell screamed, "He tore his trousers!"

Jack Hornking shouted, "You're out."

Will's pitching kept his scrubs close. He threw fast balls that the older kids had difficulty hitting, and when they began to center on his pitch, he delivered a ball that was so slow, they almost hit it with their backswing.

"Wow," Billy said, "it sure does fool them. Where'd you learn that?"

"Oh, that's a pitch that Satchel Paige showed me."

"Satchel Paige. Who's he?" a short, fat boy said.

Another said, "Does he play for the Yankees?"

"No," Will said. "He plays in the Negro leagues. He may be the best pitcher ever. He has so many pitches that he gives them all names—bat dodger, hurry-up ball, nothin' ball, four day creeper. Other names, too."

"Just an old nigger," a thin, muscular boy said. "Can't be as good as Lefty Grove."

"Now just a minute, boy," Will said as he sat down at the mound. "Negro players don't get the chance to show it, but some may be as good, maybe better than, our major leaguers. Someday they'll get that chance. Then we'll see."

"Just dumb niggers," the thin boy persisted.

"Boys, I've studied farming all my life. I went to the University of Wisconsin and studied under Professor Babcock. You've heard of him." Will pushed himself off the ground. "But I learned the most from Dr. Carver. When I was young, he was at Iowa State College of Agriculture, and later, I went south to meet him and learn about crops. A brilliant man." Will tossed the ball to Jack. "And he's a Negro. George Washington Carver. A scientist down in Alabama now. A place called Tuskegee Institute. You don't want to be judging him by his color. It's a small mind that's weighed down by prejudices."

"A black man scientist!" Billy exclaimed.

Before he left, Will called Jack Hornking over. "Jack, stop around. Maybe I can find some work for you."

"Will you, Mr. O'Shaughnessy? I sure do need the money."

When Will got back to the food tent, he couldn't find Mary. He asked the few ladies who were still around, but at first no one could help him. He worried that something might have happened to her and was about to panic when someone grabbed his arm from behind. He whipped around and was greeted by a dour-faced old lady. "Are you Will O'Shaughnessy?"

"Well, yes, that's me."

"Your wife said to tell you that she went home."

He looked down the street towards the livery where he had tethered Fanny Too earlier that day, but he didn't see his buggy or any sign of Mary.

"And I must tell you, sir, she was none too happy."

"She doesn't drive the rig." Will felt a bit sheepish. "Left without me?"

"Sure did. Didn't have much trouble either. She got the stableman to hitch her horse, climbed in the buggy, and that old horse took off might smartly. I don't think that horse wanted to rile her either."

"But... it's eight miles home. I'll have to walk."

"Kinda looks that way, doesn't it? You better get started if you want to get there before dark."

Will stumbled along, his knees and back sorer by the minute. This was not like Mary. She must be awfully riled up. He kicked dust with every step, and it didn't flow away like the ribbon of powder behind his buggy. It billowed around him and before long he felt the grit in his shoes and the filth creep upward under his pant legs. He felt as if he'd spent the day plowing ground in a dry field. Will pulled his hanky and mopped filth and sweat from his face. His mouth was dry as the Sahara and his body felt drained long before he turned into his driveway.

When he stumbled into the yard, nearly three hours later, Fanny Too stood in front of the house, still hitched to the buggy.

Will dropped the rigging, grabbed the lead, and walked Fanny Too toward the barn. He opened the gate and guided her into her stall. "I suppose Mary thinks this day was a complete disaster." He guided her to the feed bin and poured a scoop of oats. "It wasn't good, that's for sure, but it wasn't a complete disaster, was it, old girl? I think those boys learned something today." He looked down at his dusty shoes and torn trousers. "I don't suppose I look very sexy right now, so I don't guess I'll be showing any perk tonight."

7

Will heard Mary talking on the phone again. They had only been in the township a few months when neighbor women began calling with their problems: sick children, husband disputes, and cooking tips. Will hoped that the regard she was garnering among their neighbors would rub off on him, and help him gain support for the co-op he wanted.

He sipped at his coffee. "Mary, you make the best coffee in Iowa County. Is it the raw egg?"

"Get on with your blarney. Sometimes I'd swear you've visited the old country and kissed that famous stone."

"Everyone agrees with me, yes they do, Mary. They don't understand how you do it, you being English and all."

"Cornish, Will. You should know by now there's a difference."

"You wouldn't have a little sugar hidden someplace, now would you?"

"Don't tell the girls." Mary opened the cupboard and fished a sugar dish from behind the flour canister. "I just talked to Lydia Snell. She's worried about her husband."

"Oh, how's that?"

"George Snell's blood pressure is high. He gets so worked up over Franklin."

"Why so?"

"He doesn't come home until the middle of the night. George can't get him up for milking in the morning."

"Out howlin' at the moon, huh?" Will shook his head and smiled. He knew that farmers fought a perpetual battle with sons who couldn't balance their milking responsibilities with their social lives. He patted Mary on the bottom. "He'll outgrow it—when he finds a good woman."

"Will! This is serious. Lydia's worried about George's heart." Mary refilled Will's empty cup. "He gets so worked up trying to get Franklin out every morning."

Will savored the hot liquid, smacked his lips, and dipped his cup toward Mary. "Best coffee in Iowa County, and that's no lie."

"She says he's beside himself, hollering and screaming up the stairs. He's threatened to kick Franklin out of the house."

"He won't do that. He can't get by without his help, not with harvesting and all."

"Well, I've been thinking about it, and I have an idea."

"Oh?"

"First, you go over and talk with George. He respects you. Maybe he'll listen."

"I don't know what I can do. What do you have in mind?"

"I need to think on it awhile."

Two mornings later, Ruby and Catherine joined Will and Mary for coffee. Ruby poured herself a cup. "Catherine, get me the cream."

"Who's your servant when I'm not around? Get your own cream."

"Girls, it's too early to squabble." Mary handed the cream pitcher to Ruby. "Here."

Catherine banged against the table as she flopped into the chair. "I don't even like the stuff," she said.

"My, my," Mary said, "who got up on the wrong side of the bed this morning?"

Catherine poured herself a glass of milk. "I'm tired of Ruby bossing me around."

"You're just mad because I said we had to leave 4-H early last night. You were all gaga over Franklin Snell."

"Not so. He's far too old, even for you."

"Well, he did make eyes at you." Ruby winked at her father. "She got red as a beet."

"You're just jealous because no one paid attention to you."

"I get all the attention I want. Besides, Dad said we had to be home by ten o'clock, didn't you, Dad?"

"The Snell boy was there?"

"He left when we left," Ruby said. "He and his friends headed toward the Midtown Waterin' Hole."

"Did you talk to George yet?" Mary said.

"I saw him at the mill. I told him to stay calm, not to holler and scream over Franklin, not to get his blood pressure up."

"What did he say?"

"He didn't—just nodded his head. Maybe he'll think about it."

"I'd better talk to Lydia."

Two busy days followed. The downed hay dried, so Will and the girls didn't stop for coffee but went straight to milking. Hay must be harvested while the sun shined; so they had no time to waste. George Snell's problem was the farthest thing from Will's mind. They ate supper late after the milking that night, but the hay was in the barn, and Will was glad for that. He couldn't have done it if not for his two daughters helping. Mary had wanted her daughters to learn housework, like other sensible young ladies, but Ruby and Catherine insisted they wanted to be outdoors with the animals. After many discussions, Mary finally relented. And he'd wanted boys. Just no telling what the Lord has in mind.

"I'm bushed," Catherine said. "I'm too tired to lift a crumb to my mouth."

"I'm not hungry either," Ruby said. "I drank so much water that there's no room for food. You'd think my body would beg for fuel after all the energy it used, but it just doesn't care."

"Girls, eat a little, and then go up to bed," Mary said. "You'll need nourishment. I'll have bacon and eggs ready in the morning. Cold fries, too."

Mary boiled a few extra potatoes each night so that she could slice the cold leftovers and fry them for the next day's breakfast. Will thought those cold leftover potatoes, when they were fried, tasted better than freshly sliced new ones.

Before the girls came down for breakfast the next morning, Will asked about George and Lydia. "Did you talk to Lydia? Did you tell her your idea?"

"I rang her on the phone. She liked my idea, but she wasn't sure George would cooperate. She said he's completely irrational when it comes to Franklin. He's getting desperate."

"You're a clever woman. Tell me your plan."

"Not yet. I wanta see if it'll work."

The girls bounced down the stairs and dived into plates filled with two eggs easy over, bacon piled high, and hot and crispy cold fries hanging off the edge. "I'm famished," Ruby said. "I feel like I haven't eaten for a week."

Catherine stuffed her mouth with fries.

Oh, to be young again, Will thought. If only a night's rest restored his energy so quickly.

"Girls, you worked hard yesterday. After milking, you can go visit your friends. Take a break from the work. You'd like that, wouldn't you?"

"Do we have to wait until after milking?" Catherine said. "Can't we go now?"

"Oh, my dear daughter, I do wish that I could release you from that awful chore, but the milking pays the bills, now doesn't it?"

"I know, Daddy. I was just joshin'."

Mary flinched when the telephone rang. "Who'd be calling so early in the morning?" She took the receiver off the hook.

"Hello? He won't do it? You want Will to talk with him again? Okay, I'll try. We'll find a way, Lydia. I know you're worried, but have faith. . . . Yes." Mary hung up the phone. "Girls, you go do your chores. I want to talk with your dad."

"What did Lydia say?" Will said. "It sounded like George's being stubborn."

"Lydia said he tried, but when Franklin didn't respond, he got so worked up he didn't think. He just screamed and ranted, then went out and started the milking alone. It's not good for his blood pressure."

"And I thought I wanted boys," Will said.

"Adults holler far too much," Mary said. "It's not necessary. I learned that teaching those big farm boys. Some of them were in their twenties, and I was only eighteen."

"You scared the bejeebers out of them, didn't you?"

"You think so? They'd have laughed if I got worked up. They already got too much of that from their fathers. I couldn't possibly measure up. Strategic action worked far better. Now, if Lydia can just convince George."

W ill was so busy preparing for Gusta's dance that he forgot about George's problems. He contacted Hank Swenson and Cloony McBride, two musicians that James Henning had recommended, to ask if they'd help him with the music. Mary gave him the responsibility of inviting the neighbors so she'd have time to pretty-up three old dresses for her girls to wear. She said she wasn't worried about Gusta's dress, other than it might put her daughter's clothes to shame.

Will hoped he hadn't forgotten anything.

Will herded his girls into the living room to help move the furniture, clearing a space for the dancers who would fill the room that evening.

Before he got them organized, Ruby grabbed his arm. "Where's Gusta? I thought she'd be down by now."

"I said she could nap in my room," Sharon said, "so you wouldn't wake her when you dressed."

"You sure did a turnaround since she arrived," Ruby said.

"I was a little hard on her. I misjudged her. She's got a big heart."

"I think it's her big purse that you like," Ruby said.

"She was considerate. I didn't expect her to think of Ed."

"I think she's smart," Catherine said. "But I don't know how she can nap every afternoon. And she doesn't get out of bed until we're done with milking."

"That's Southern style," Ruby said. "She told me all about it."

"She works hard, once she gets going," Sharon said. "She's been a help in the house."

"It's no wonder she sleeps in the day," Ruby said. "She said that at home she's out late every night. I think she was trying to impress me."

"We better get moving, girls," Will said. "The living room and parlor have to be emptied before dinner."

Will, Sharon, and Ruby lifted the horsehair chair and carried it toward the back porch. Catherine followed with the footstool.

"Let's get this done," Will said. "I've gotta warm up my fiddle."

Will pushed the pocket doors into the side walls and set three chairs inside the back parlor. He plucked on his fiddle strings to make sure they were in tune while Hank Swenson and Clooney McBride brought a mandolin and banjo from their rigs.

"Been a little nippy at night," Clooney said. He pulled a flagon from his pocket. "Good thing I brought this flask along."

"Didn't I see that flask at Cornwell's auction?" Hank said. "And it was over ninety degrees."

"For Will." Clooney nodded toward Will who had started to play a few chords of "Old Dan Tucker." "Wouldn't want his throat to go dry. Then who'd call the squares?" Clooney turned toward the parlor, away from the people who streamed into the living room. "Here, Will, have a swig. It'll lighten your vocals and lubricate your tonsils."

"I better not. Mary won't like it."

"Mary's in the kitchen. I'd give one to Hank, but he's dry as the Sahara. Only drinks milk? Ugh!"

"Don't knock the milk drinkers," Will said. "That's our livelihood." He reached for the flask. "Just one. Don't let Mary see or we'll both be sent packing."

Will took a swig and the three men got ready to play. "Ready? A one, a two, a three."

The three instruments filled the room with "Old Dan Tucker" as guests grabbed a partner and paraded onto the floor. Will called out, "Honor your partner, honor your corner!"

Each time a guest arrived, Catherine, Ruby, or Sharon headed toward the back bedroom to stack a coat, hat, or sleeping child on their parents' bed. The older children stayed in the living room and danced until their legs became weary and their eyelids became heavy, and then they joined their younger brothers and sisters on the coat pile.

After twenty minutes, Will called a break. "Ladies and gentlemen, you'll find refreshments on the dining room table."

"Did you see Phil Withers come in, Dad?" Catherine said. "I think he's got eyes for Ruby." She poked Sharon. "Where's Ed? I thought he was coming tonight."

"He'll be here soon. He said he'd pick up the Sanders on the way. They lost their driving horse last week. I can count on Ed. He's as faithful as, well, you know, that geyser in Yellowstone. What do they call it?"

"Old Faithful, Sharon, that's what it's called," Ruby said. "Yeah, I guess he is an OLD faithful. Wouldn't you agree, Dad?"

Will knew better then to get drawn into his daughters' squabbles. Besides, it was time to begin the second set.

"He's not old," Sharon said. "He's... mature. You'd not know about mature, given the little boys that interest you, now would you, Ruby?"

"Come on, Ruby, let's go dance," Catherine called as she started toward the floor. "Where's Gusta?"

Will finished the call:

The squirrels they love a hickory tree
The clover loves the bumblebee
The flies they love molasses and
The ladies love a ladies man

Will lowered his fiddle. "Take a break, ladies and gentlemen," he called to the dancers.

Ruby started toward the stairs to find her wayward cousin, but before she got to the bottom step, Phil Withers handed her a bouquet of flowers. "Why, Phil, you're so thoughtful. I'll get a vase to put them in."

Catherine curtsied and, in her best imitation of Ruby's voice, said, "Why, Phil, you're so thoughtful."

Will laughed at his daughter's shenanigans. He saw Sharon look around the room and heard her sigh before she turned toward the kitchen. Will knew she was anxious about Ed's late arrival—or maybe it was Gusta that worried her.

"Have you seen Gusta?" Mary said to Will.

"Ruby said she's still upstairs. Isn't that right?" Will said to Catherine, who wandered aimlessly now that Ruby was occupied with Phil.

"I told her the dance is in her honor," Mary said. "When she comes down, introduce her around, will you, Catherine? I'd not want her to feel unwelcome."

Will noticed Catherine stare toward the stairs as he readied for the next set. Gusta was nowhere in sight.

"I don't think that'll be a problem, Mom," Catherine said.

Will, Hank, and Clooney began to play.

"Form your squares," Will called out.

I've got a cow I call Old Blue
But all that crazy cow can do
Is shake her horns and beller and moo
So promenade boys two by two

When a collective gasp emerged from the crowd, Will, Clooney, and Hank stopped playing, and all eyes turned upward. The vase that Ruby carried from the kitchen dropped from her hands and crashed to the floor.

"Oh, good Lord, it's Jean Harlow," Ruby said.

"The hussy," someone said.

Gusta slinked down the stairs, one step at a time. She wore a black and silver knit gown that was covered in sequins and had a red and black fringe that bottomed out way too far above the black jacquard evening pumps. The neckline plunged toward her breasts, which were adorned by beaded appliqué. A red feathered boa hung from her shoulder, and a red sequined headband encircled her head.

"Mama, it's indecent," Sharon said. "We'll never be able to face our friends again."

Ed, who just entered the room, didn't seem to mind though. He stood slack-jawed, joined by the other boys who shared his admiration. Although most of the ladies averted their eyes, Ruby ignored the broken glass at her feet and stared right along with the boys. Sharon grabbed Ed's arm. "Ed! Help Ruby pick up the pieces." Then she turned to her mother. "Mom, do something."

Mary hesitated for a moment, and then she slowly walked to the stairway. She turned to face her neighbors, most of who were frozen in place. "Friends, I want you to meet my dead brother's only child, Gusta. She's visiting from Texas and will go to Willow High School this fall. As you can see, Texas is a bit more stylish than we are here in Willow. Because this dance is in her honor, I hope you'll introduce yourselves and welcome her."

Sharon looked at Ed, at her mother. "Mom, you can't."

The boys rushed forward—to be neighborly, Will thought wryly.

Will plucked his fiddle strings. Hank fingered his mandolin. Clooney took a swig from his flask. At Will's signal, they began to play.

Oats all heated, spuds all froze
Wheat crops busted, wind still blows
Looks some gloomy, I'll admit
Get up Dobbin – we ain't through yit

So engulfed by admiring neighbor youth—Ed among them—Gusta hadn't made it off the stairs. Will smiled and assumed that Gusta didn't notice the women's reaction to her grand entrance. While Sharon ran to the kitchen, the ladies who weren't dancing clustered, tongues wagging.

The wise old owl he lived in oak
The more he heard the less he spoke
The less he spoke the more he heard
Why aren't you like that old bird?

Will saw Gusta turn to Ed. "You're Ed Meadows, aren't you? Ed, do you suppose that Uncle Will can play 'Tea for Two?' I'd like to dance a Texas two-step. Can you do the two-step, Ed? Will you do it with me?"

"I don't think anyone here can dance a Texas two-step, Miss Gusta, but I bet Will can play 'Tea for Two.' That's an old song we all kinda know. Can you play it, Will?"

Will nodded, but he wondered if this might turn out bad.

"Well, I can't dance alone," Gusta said. "I'll teach you, and you can dance it with me. We'll cut the rug so that no one will forget tonight."

"I don't know, Gusta. Sharon wouldn't—"

"Oh, come on, Ed. Sharon's too busy in the kitchen to notice. Let's go to the back porch and practice." She took Ed's hand.

"I'll tell Sharon—" He tried to pull away, but Gusta's grip was firm.

"Ed, do you think I'm going to undress you? You're not scared of a lil old Texas girl, now, are you? I thought you were a ladies man."

Will heard her suggestions and saw Gusta lead Ed to the back porch— and he worried, but he didn't want to stop the music and make a scene. He felt a bit better when he saw Catherine follow them. She'd alert him if there were any shenanigans going on.

I love wine and Jeanne loves silk
The little pigs love buttermilk
And ever since the world began
The ladies love a ladies man

Will finished calling another set before Ed reappeared with Catherine a few steps behind him. Will noticed that Catherine seemed to be a bit flushed.

Just then, Sharon walked from the kitchen.

"Dad, where's Ed?" Sharon said. "I've looked all over for him."

"Why, there he is now, with Catherine. It looks like they're coming from the back porch."

"What would he be doing on the back porch?" Sharon said to her father before she rushed across the room toward Ed, who slid behind Catherine as she approached. "What were you doing in the back room?"

Catherine stepped toward her sister. "Ed and Gusta were dancing, Sharon."

"On the back porch? Why not out here in the living room? That's where the music is."

"Don't be angry, Sharon," Ed said. "I was learning the Texas two-step, that's all. Miss Gusta needed a—"

"Gusta needed? Gusta doesn't need much of anything. It seems she gets whatever she wants. Two-step?" Sharon glared at Ed. "Two-timer is more like it. You can dance with Gusta the rest of tonight, if that's what you like. You'll not dance with me."

Sharon raced toward the kitchen. "Mama!"

It was a shame that on such a gala night his oldest daughter was so upset. Will had worried that Gusta might upset his family's harmony, but there was little he could do right now that Mary wouldn't take care of.

A call came from the couples who'd arranged themselves into squares on the dance floor. "Will, we're waiting. Are you going to play or not?"

Will shouldered his fiddle. "A one, a two," and the room filled with music.

If I had a girl who wouldn't dance
I'll tell you what I would do
I'd put that gal in an old row boat
And paddle my own canoe

Will didn't see Gusta go up the stairs, but he saw her come down with a ukulele. Gusta came over to Will. He paused and listened, and then he stopped the music and motioned toward Gusta.

When everyone was quiet, Gusta said, "I want to thank y'all for this evening, especially Aunt Mary and Uncle Will who were gracious to host it. I know that my clothes may have shocked y'all, but I'd saved them for a special occasion, and I couldn't think of anything more special than this dance you threw for me tonight. I do hope y'all forgive me."

All nodded affirmative, even the old ladies, but none so energetically as the young fellows who had welcomed her earlier. Will thought their heads would topple off.

"Now, I'd like to offer my thanks in two ways. First, I'll sing you a song, and then I'd like to show you a Texas dance that I do hope y'll all like. I can't do the dance alone, so I enlisted Ed's help. With cousin Sharon's blessing I'll ask Ed to join me after we've sung one of your favorite songs. Is that okay, cousin Sharon?"

Without much enthusiasm, Sharon nodded her agreement.

Gusta picked up her ukulele and began to strum. "Now y'all join me as soon's you're ready."

On, Wisconsin! On, Wisconsin!
Grand old badger state!
We, thy loyal sons and daughters,
Hail thee, good and great.

Soon everyone was singing so loud that the doors rattled in their casings. Until the screams began they forgot that little children were sleeping in the back bedroom. After a few women rushed toward the back to still the tears, everything quieted and Will took the fiddle again, this time with a less familiar song, "Tea for Two." Gusta explained the Texas two-step and then invited Ed onto the floor. Ed looked at Sharon who nodded her consent. At first Ed was awkward, but Gusta guided him into the rhythm and steps of the dance, and Ed did himself proud, Will thought. Soon, everyone clapped their hands to the beat, none more enthusiastically than Sharon.

Applause erupted at the dance's end, and Gusta walked to Sharon and said, "I'll ask Uncle Will to play it one more time while I show you the steps. Then, you and Ed can dance it together."

Sharon took Gusta's hand, and with a smile as wide as the living room, she walked onto the dance floor.

All we need to make us happy
Is two little boys to call me pappy
One named Paul and the other named Davey
One loves ham and the other loves gravy

Will stopped playing and waved his fiddle at the dancers. "It's been a fun night. I don't know what I'd do without friends like you and nights like this. It keeps us sane in this sometimes insane world. I hate to end it, but Mary tells me it's time. We all have work to do in a morning that's not very far off. One more set, and then we'll call it a night. Everyone to your squares."

Allemande right and allemande left
All hands round
Ladies in the swill barrel
Upside down

The next week, Catherine commented after an evening 4-H meeting, "Franklin Snell wasn't at the meeting tonight. His sister says they're milking late now."

After the girls retired, Mary said to Will, "Sounds as if George's getting some sense. Maybe my plan'll work after all."

"Milking late? That doesn't sound good. Is that your plan, Mary?"

"I'll tell you in due time. I'll know that I'm successful when they get back to early milking again.

And when, after their next 4-H meeting, Ruby said that Franklin had told her they were back on their old schedule, Will knew that his wife's advice had helped George avoid a heart attack.

"It looks like you've done it." Will patted Mary on the backside. "A clever woman, you are."

Ruby frowned.

"Ruby, you've got the smartest mother in Willow, maybe in Wisconsin. Now get up to bed."

Mary sat next to Will on the parlor settee. She reached for his arm. "Will, you helped, too. Every youngster needs to learn they'll reap what they sow. Maybe Franklin's learned that lesson."

"I hope so, Mary."

Will had never doubted that Mary would think up a successful plan to get Franklin into the barn on time. He wasn't so certain they could convince George to do his part, but it seems that he did.

"Mary, how'd you ever do it?"

"I told Lydia that if George would just sit and wait, that it'd all work out. And most important, he shouldn't start the milking until Franklin came down to help." Mary picked up her knitting needles. "Even Franklin knows that cows must be milked every twelve hours. If they didn't start their morning milking until he got out of bed at eight, they couldn't start until eight that night either." Mary began to cast yarn onto a needle. "It looks as if an eight o'clock milking start cut into Franklin's night life."

"You're a smart woman, Mary. I don't know how I'd ever get along without you."

Will knew that was the truest statement he'd ever made. He hoped that she fully understood just how he appreciated her. His heart beat a little faster when she was near, and when she smiled that ever so sweet smile and touched his arm, he still felt a shiver down his spine. He wasn't sure where he'd find the money, but he knew he must save enough to buy her a new dress. It had been a long time since she had anything new. And he worried about that. She deserved better.

10

Will had done the plowing alone, but he was having difficulty getting his fields planted in time to stay within the limits of Wisconsin's short growing season. So after a discussion with Mary, they decided to hire a worker to help with the cultivating and upcoming harvests. Will remembered his conversation with Jack Hornking and brought him onboard.

Two weeks after the dance's merriment, Will had more serious things on his mind. He pondered his future over a plate of fried potatoes and eggs. "I think it's time to buy a good bull."

Mary continued to clear the table.

At first, Will didn't think that she'd heard him. "Mary, I… "

"I heard you." She stopped and faced him. "We don't have the money, Will."

"George Tyler said he'd loan it, but I don't want more debt. I planted the north ten acres in corn and when it matures this fall, I'll sell it and use that money." Will drained his coffee cup. "A good bull's worth his weight in gold, and this one has stellar bloodlines. He costs more, but in a couple years we'll have some of the best heifers around."

"We don't have enough heifers now?"

"I want to add quality."

Will knew they were getting by with what they had, but barely. If they wanted to send their girls to college, and if he wanted to buy that new dress for Mary, he'd have to improve the quality and increase the size of his herd.

Mary filled the sink with water she'd heated on the cook stove, but Will didn't leave for milking. He circled his spoon through his coffee.

"Something wrong, Will?"

"It's Jack. I don't know what to do. I probably shouldn't have hired him. He needs the money, and I need the help, but his heart's not in it. I don't think he wants to farm."

"He won't work?"

"When I'm there to prod him. But I can't trust him. He doesn't do what I tell him."

"Have you talked to him?"

"I told him about the time I came home without the groceries, and my dad made me walk all the way back to town. The story whizzed past his head and never mussed a hair. He didn't have a clue."

"Your stories aren't enough. You've got to be direct."

"I suppose so. You heard what happened when Pastor Jorgenson wasn't direct."

"Pastor Jorgenson?"

"Reverend Jorgenson. Up river a ways."

"I don't know him."

"Well, his sign read, 'You've come to the end of the road. Turn yourself around.' After old Mr. Franks drove into the river and drowned his wife, Deacon Jones said they probably should have written, 'Bridge out ahead.'"

"You and your tall tales."

"I swear on St. Patrick it's the truth. But Jack's got to get serious, or I'll have to let him go."

"And that's why you need to be direct."

Will did as Mary said. "Jack, I want you to cultivate the north cornfield. Harness Ned and Ted and walk them down there. The cultivator's inside the fence. When you're done, take Gusta to town to pick up a trunk at the depot." That should be clear enough. "Get back in time to help Ruby and Catherine milk, because I'll get home late tonight. And Jack, don't forget to latch the gate when you leave the cornfield. Do you understand?"

"Sure, Mr. O'Shaughnessy. Cultivate the field, take Gusta to town, and get back for milking."

"And latch the gate." Mary would be proud of him.

Will's thoughts turned to that night's meeting. He was glad that his neighbors were interested in a cooperative, but were they ready? They weren't well informed. During his years in town, he'd studied cooperatives and thought about their potential, and he was certain they were the farmer's best chance to make a profit.

Jack waved as he, Ned, and Ted headed toward the north cornfield. Will smiled. Maybe he'll be a farmer yet. Now, where's that whetstone? He would sharpen his sickle before lunch, and if there was time, he'd shell some corn, too.

When the sun reached its peak, Will supposed that Mary'd have dinner on the table, so he stowed his Little Speedy corn sheller and walked toward the house. Sixteen cows were fresh now, and he was quite satisfied with their production. He wanted to get up to twenty, maybe twenty-one or twenty-two, but milking that many would be a challenge. He hoped that Jack would pan out, that he'd earn the right to stay on.

Will sat down at the table. "Mary, I did like you said. I told Jack exactly what I wanted him to do. I left nothing to chance. He's out on that north ten acres cultivating corn now. And I told him to get back to drive you to town, Gusta."

Gusta jerked her head up, dropped her spoon, and peas rolled across her plate. "I don't need help. I've driven more teams in a week than Jack's driven since he's been here."

"It's good for him to get the practice," Mary said. "You can help if needed, but don't embarrass him. He needs to build confidence."

"I'm not sure what Mother's sending." Gusta buttered a slice of bread. "Do you have any Swiss cheese, Aunt Mary? I sure love your Wisconsin cheese."

"I'm going to the woodland pasture to fence," Will said as he left the table. "I'll have the buggy hitched and ready by four." He grabbed one more cookie before he left the table. "You sure know how to make a good cookie, Mary. I think it's the raisins. Are you taking these to the meeting?" He didn't wait for a response but rushed toward the door. "We can't be late. The picnic supper was my idea, you know."

Will heard a meadow lark sing its lilting call as he walked into the pasture. That small bird had a better voice than some people he knew. The sun burned the back of his neck, so he stayed under the trees as he walked the fence line toward the downed posts. A slight breeze kicked up and rustled the leaves overhead and cooled his brow. Nothing felt as good as a small breeze or a cold drink of water when the body was hot and fatigued. And they didn't cost a red cent.

How'd his sheep always find the fence's weak spot? If Catherine hadn't seen them grazing in his bean field, he'd have lost his entire crop. He inspected the posts and found where the staples were pulled out. Rotten wood. No telling how many had shed their nails. He walked the fence line, Teddy racing ahead as if he wanted to help. Will tugged the wire at the posts. A bit spongy, but most would last awhile longer. He'd only have to replace half a dozen.

Will was thankful for the leaf canopy overhead. He worried about the boy working in the sun but supposed he should be done by now. When he returned to the house, Jack and Gusta had already left. "Were there any problems, Mary?"

"I don't think so. He tended the horses and off they went."

Maybe firmness worked after all. He was a lucky man to have a woman like Mary. And she could cook, too. Will snatched two cookies.

"Will! I'll have to stop baking. You're eating too many sweets."

"I eat a balanced diet. Didn't you notice? I took one for each hand."

She swiped at him with the dish towel. "Get on with you."

⊱⋅⊰

That night they gathered at the township hall. Now that the front lawn picnic was over, the business meeting was ready to begin. "Will, your idea to serve supper sure did the trick," James Henning said. "We've never had so many here before."

"A little food draws the ants. And people, too, it seems," Will said. "Let's go inside."

McPherson opened the meeting with a brief account of his past efforts to get people interested in a co-op. "Tonight, we have good attendance. It's probably the food." He looked at Will. "Maybe it's the government. They've gotten mighty intrusive. Will O'Shaughnessy said there might be a better way. Okay, Will, tell us."

Will stood and looked around. He knew only a few of the men. "First, let's thank the ladies for their contribution tonight. Ladies, come in here, will you?"

Applause erupted as the women entered from the kitchen and stood in back of the room. Will invited them to stay, but most begged off, saying they had kitchen work to do.

"Well, O'Shaughnessy, you were right about government snooping," George Snell said. "They even wanted to know how many kids I planned to have."

"Did they ask you how you do it, George?" someone shouted.

62

Another shouted, "Just like the rest of us, I suppose, but the government hasn't figured that out either."

After the laughter subsided, Will continued. "I've given lots of thought to the cooperative idea and studied it a bit, too. It has possibilities."

"The government offered possibilities, too," Henning said.

"This is different, James. We can ride the free enterprise system. Do it as a group. Use our ingenuity."

"We do that now," Arnie Johnson said, "and we don't have to answer to anyone. Don't have to get permission either."

"Arnie, maybe you should practice getting permission," someone shouted from the back. "When you havin' that first kid?"

McPherson pounded on the table to quiet the laughter. "This is serious, folks. Tell us more, Will."

"If we organize, we can buy in volume. We can sell in volume. We'd get better prices. Instead of buying fifty gallons of gasoline or kerosene, we could buy hundreds of gallons."

"Can't hear you, Will."

Jackson McGried slid a chair toward Will, who stepped up. "If we organize, the wholesalers would want our business. They'd give us better prices. Then we could pass those lower prices to our members. We'd all benefit."

"Why'd you want gasoline, Will? You don't own a tractor."

"There'd be something for us all. No, I wouldn't buy gasoline, but I'd buy seed, and grease, and cattle feed. And we could sell through the co-op, too. We'd get better milk prices that way."

Will built his case for the advantages of a co-op, told how they'd prospered elsewhere. McPherson and Henning were inclined to give it a try, but others argued against it. They discussed pros and cons for another half an hour, and then some members lost interest and drifted away.

McPherson pounded his gavel and called out, "Give it some thought. We'll get back together after the summer harvest."

On the way home, Mary said, "Do you think you convinced them?"

"There's interest, but I think they need time to think about it. Farmers don't change fast. I wish McPherson would have set a date for the next meeting. We need to keep this moving."

When they got within sight of the farm, Will was surprised to see activity at the barn. Milking should have been finished an hour ago. He dropped Mary at the house. "I'll bed Fanny Too and check the girls. They should be done by now."

He left Fanny Too standing in her hitch outside the barn. Catherine poured her pail of frothy milk into the eight gallon can as he approached. She was so intent on her work that she didn't notice. "Catherine, you're awfully late with the milking. Are there problems?"

Catherine recoiled and looked up. "Oh, it's you, Dad. We got a late start. Jack and Gusta didn't get back from town until an hour ago. Ruby's fit to be tied."

Will looked across the barn at Ruby who bent under a cow and stripped the last milk from her teat. She slammed the stanchion open and released the animal. After a slap on its backside, it slipped in the gutter, almost went down, but regained its balance and hustled out the door.

"I'd better change into my coveralls," Will said to Catherine as he turned towards the house.

It was almost midnight by the time they finished, and Will was too tired to begin an inquisition.

The next morning, Will told Jack and Gusta to meet him after milking.

"Jack, I told you to get home for milking. And I didn't mean midnight. I can't keep you if you disregard my orders."

Jack hung his head.

"It was my fault," Gusta said. "I talked Jack into taking me to visit Sheri. He told me he was supposed to help with milking. I shouldn't have begged him. I'm sorry, Uncle Will. I won't do it again."

"No you won't. That's the last time I'll send Jack on your errands. I'm disappointed in you, young lady. You didn't consider the work you put on your cousins. You owe them an apology." He pointed toward the door. "You can go now."

"But Uncle—"

"Please leave, Gusta. I wanta talk with Jack."

After Gusta left the room, Will turned to Jack. "I told you to get back for milking, didn't I?"

"Yes, Mr. O'Shaughnessy."

"I know that Gusta can be persuasive, and I'm sure you wanted to impress her. But you'll only get in trouble trying to impress the ladies. Why, I knew a lad who bragged to a lady friend that he'd soon be a millionaire. He said that his mother was dead and his father was sickly. But his boasting was a big mistake. The next month that lady friend became his stepmother."

"I don't think Gusta'd want my dad."

Will sighed. "No, but this isn't the first time you've disobeyed me. It's gotten to be a habit with you, and I can't put up with it. If Gusta wasn't involved, I'd let you go right now. Do you understand? But—go clean the gutters."

Will found Mary making their bed. "It's more of the same with Jack. I should have fired him, but I know how persuasive Gusta can be. And how a boy can be influenced by an attractive woman. I remember the first time I was alone with you. Do you remember, Mary?"

"Will! We were completely proper."

"You couldn't read my thoughts."

Mary grinned and slapped him on the rear.

"I should have known better than to send him alone with a female from your family, now shouldn't I? What'll I do?"

⚜

Will had finished cleaning the calf pen and was on the way to the house for lunch when Fanny Too raced up the lane toward him. He had told the girls not to gallop Fanny Too in the heat. She wasn't so young anymore.

"Daddy, Daddy," Ruby screamed. "The cows are in the cornfield and they've trampled lots of it down. Someone left the gate open."

Will raced into the house. "Mary, come help. The cows are in the cornfield. Jack left the gate open."

Will called for Teddy while he untied Fanny Too from the post where Ruby had snubbed her.

"Ruby, I'll take Fanny Too and Teddy. Get Catherine and saddle Lyda and Mabel, then come help."

He quickly mounted Fanny Too and, with Teddy racing along behind, headed towards the downed corn. He knew that he had no choice now. He'd have to let Jack go. He hoped that he could salvage some of the crop, that the damage wasn't as complete as Ruby said.

When he got there he saw that Ruby hadn't exaggerated. The corn in the small field had mostly been eaten or trampled.

With Teddy's help, Will shooed the cows from the field and Ruby and Catherine headed them down the lane toward the barnyard. Then he raced to find Jack who was pitching hay down the chute into the lower barn.

"Jack, I told you to close that gate when you left the field."

65

"I—"

"The cows got in and destroyed all the corn. I can't keep you anymore. Get your belongings. I'll have Ruby take you to town."

"I closed the gate."

Jack looked so distressed that, for a moment, Will felt sorry.

"I jumped off the cultivator and tied Ned and Ted to the fence post before I closed the gate. I remember doing it."

"I'm sorry, Jack. You've had your chances. I can't afford to keep you around."

Jack raised his pitchfork, and, for an instant Will expected to be skewered. But Jack turned, threw the fork into a hay pile, and, as he ran from the loft, he shouted back, "You're an SOB O'Shaughnessy! I'll get you someday!"

Will wasn't too worried, but he knew that he'd made an enemy. At times like this, he hated being the boss.

That night at dinner, Mary asked, "Oh, Will, what'll we do? That's the money you were going to spend on the bull."

"I'll have to see George." Will was glad that he'd maintained contact with his Ashley Springs banker. "I hadn't wanted to borrow, but I have no choice now. Not if I want quality heifers."

11

Rain delayed second crop hay for a week. Will was anxious to get into the field, but they couldn't, not yet anyhow. Downed wet hay could mildew where it lay. And damp hay in the barn could cause more serious problems. If it molded, they'd have to use it for bedding, or worse yet, piled deep in the loft, it could heat and smolder until it spontaneously erupted. While he waited for sunshine, Will put Ruby and Catherine to work cutting thistles in the pasture.

Will knew that his nearest neighbor, Earl Roberts, wouldn't be in the fields, either. He and Mary discussed it and decided now would be a good time to meet their neighbor in a more relaxed setting, so they invited Earl and Marge over for an early afternoon tea.

That morning Mary had picked some of the biggest and reddest strawberries that she'd ever grown, and when she handed one to Will and asked his opinion, he bit into a berry that was manna straight from heaven.

"There's no doubt about it, these sweet nubbins would be wasted on anything less than your strawberry shortcake."

But Mary didn't make her strawberry delight with a shortcake. Instead, she made a sponge cake, which was sweeter and drew the juices of her freshly crushed strawberries into its core. It was cloaked in cream that was skimmed from the top of the morning's milk and then whipped into a frothy cap that was stiff enough to stand under a noonday sun. Will thought Mary's strawberry delight was far too beautiful to eat. But when she served it to him, he closed his eyes and devoured this creation from the gods, one delicious bite at a time, and with a clear conscience.

"I can't imagine a better way to win over a recalcitrant neighbor. Earl didn't say anything at our co-op meeting, but by the frown on his face when I explained the advantages of uniting, I fear that he wasn't convinced. Maybe you've provided the yeast here." Will savored another mouthful of Mary's sweet dessert and mumbled, "This will surely raise his enthusiasm."

Earl and Marge arrived at two p.m., just in time to appreciate the sweet aroma which infused the kitchen, given off by a pot of freshly brewed coffee. Mary handed a cup of her brew to Marge and guided her toward the living room while Will pulled two chairs to the kitchen table and set a full cup in front of Earl. "You do drink coffee, don't you, Earl?"

"I've not yet turned down a good cup."

"I think you'll find that Mary's coffee fits that bill."

Will knew that many claimed her coffee the best they'd ever tasted. She'd say that it was the egg in the bottom of the large pot that filtered out any nasty flavors. Will wasn't sure about that, but he never complained about the result. He took a sip, and then he set his cup down. "It's a bit hot." He held up a finger. "I think I've got what's needed to tame it a bit."

He pushed his chair from the table and moved to a large pottery jar on the counter. "Have you ever eaten Cornish tea biscuits, Earl?"

"Can't say that I have."

Will hoisted the jar toward his neighbor. "Try one. There's nothing better with a good brew."

Earl fished a large cream-colored biscuit through the jar's wide mouth.

"I hope you like raisins," Will said. "They're full of raisins."

Earl took a small bite, smiled, then he took a mouthful of the biscuit, but he chewed for a while before drowning it in coffee. "They're okay." He finished the tea biscuit before drinking more coffee. Then he eagerly pulled another biscuit from the jar when Will pushed it toward him. Will could see that Mary's biscuits were a successful prelude to the strawberry delight that was soon to come.

"This weather has me stymied," Earl said. "I haven't been able to get into my fields for a week."

"It'll be a bumper crop," Will said. "If it grows any higher, I'm afraid my horses won't make their way through it."

"My Farmall won't have trouble getting through."

"See, new ways do help you prosper."

"New-fangled ideas don't always work. My tractor's lugs cut up a muddy field. You'll be in your fields while I'm still waiting for mine to dry out."

New-fangled ideas? Will supposed that Earl had the co-op in mind. "Would you swap your tractor for a horse or two?" Will knew the answer.

"No one would do that."

"There's been lots of progress toward producing milk," Will said, "but more milk's giving us a headache when it comes to selling. There aren't many of us who milk grade A in this township, but the few of us who do have the same problem: unsold milk spoils. We need to find faster ways to distribute it, and new and bigger markets. We can't hold our fluid milk like those turning it to butter and cheese."

"And you think cooperatives are the answer?"

"They are, Earl. Several horses pulling the wagon will get your load to the barn faster than the best horse pulling alone."

"If you want to send neighbors over to help me pull wagons, I'm all for it. I know you're trying to help, Will, and I appreciate that. But I've got no mind to let others make my decisions for me. I'll decide when and who I'll sell my milk to."

Will was glad when Mary interrupted. "It's time for the dessert," she said.

After another hour of light conversation, Earl's last words as he and Marge headed for the door were, "That's the best shortcake I've ever tasted."

Will smiled and said, "That's because my wife's doesn't make shortcake the old-fashioned way."

Earl scowled at Will for a moment before he grasped the doorknob.

Every day, after morning milking, Will drove his full cans to the River Valley cheese factory. Like most Iowa County cheese factories, the building's lower level extended into the hillside for storage of the cheese and butter. The cool ground that surrounded the back of the building provided refrigeration. The farmer would drive his truck or wagon to an unloading platform at the front and dump his milk into a small tank that was positioned on a scale for weighing each deposit. After weighing, the grade B milk was moved into a large vat where the cheesemaker performed his magic. He rarely shared the secret of his distinctive mixture and process. Liquid milk was held in a refrigeration unit until it was picked up for distribution. Bob McGuire, River Valley's cheesemaker, lived above the factory.

James Henning was busy filling his empty cans with whey drawn from the large wooden tank at the corner of the building, when he called Will to his truck. Will was dismayed but not surprised when James told him the rumor he'd heard. James cautioned that maybe there was nothing to it, but Will knew that he must confront Gusta. If James was right,

Gusta's need to be disciplined was greater than he realized. If James was right, Mary had good reason to worry. And if Mary found out, Will knew there'd be little tolerance this time.

Later that day Will caught Gusta when she came alone to the barn for the house milk.

"Gusta, I heard that you've been playing cards lately."

Gusta blushed. "Aunt Mary wouldn't like that, I know." She cozied up to Will. "You'll not tell her, Uncle Will? I don't want to cause her worry."

Will stepped away. "This isn't just about a deck of cards, Gusta. I hear you were playing strip poker with Pete Simmons, Adam Baxter, and Henry Laurie. Is that so?"

Gusta pulled back and looked shaken. "Uncle Will, on my honor, I didn't do anything that you wouldn't approve of. I promise."

"Strip poker?"

"I played cards with those boys and I taught them a lesson, but I never undressed any more than I am right now." She reached her soft feminine fingers toward Will's burly hand. "I'll swear on a Bible that I never did anything that would make you ashamed."

"Your Aunt Mary?"

Gusta emitted a strained laugh. "Aunt Mary doesn't like cards."

Will wasn't entirely convinced, but he thought it best to not press further. Gusta had never lied to him—at least not that he knew—and there was no use upsetting Mary over a rumor. He remembered the penknife incident in Texas and was afraid that would color Mary's response if she heard this rumor. He decided it was best to wait and watch.

⦿⦿⦿

The rainy weather broke. Will cut hay, dried it two days under the hot sun, and spent a day behind Ted and Ned raking it. His recently purchased side delivery rake was a huge improvement over his old, multi-tined dump rake that required him to raise and lower the tines, first to gather, then to dump his loads.

The days were long and the work had always been hard, but he loved his time alone in the fields. He loved working with uninterrupted moments to think about the joys of living—to appreciate his wife, his children, and the farming life that he loved. He took a deep breath and savored the sweet aroma of newly cut alfalfa and clover. And then he

70

exhaled when he could hold it no longer. He was a lucky man.

The chain-driven reel on his new rake, mounted at a forty-five degree angle, gathered and pushed the hay to the side, forming a long windrow. His old dump rake had required him to move back and forth across the field, picking and then dumping his hay into a long pile. Then he'd have to pick up a new load and drop it at the end of the first pile, and continue doing so to create the windrow. Without the repeated gathering and dumping, his new rake left a continuous ribbon of hay that his hay loader could lift off the field and load into the wagon.

While his hay finished curing in the field, Will greased the equipment and checked ropes and pulleys to be sure they operated safely.

Catherine and Ruby continued to clear thistles until the hay was ready. They complained, but Teddy seemed to enjoy his time in the fields. He sniffed the ground and chased along hot trails, intent on ridding the field of dangerous varmints that might harm his young charges.

While the girls grumbled over their drudgery, Will and his horses pulled the loader, and their day worker, Spike Willis, forked hay inside the wagon that bounced along behind; then they brought it to the barn.

After positioning the loaded wagon below the hay door, Will stood on the wagon's platform and thrust a huge fork into the pile of hay. Then he jumped up and down on the fork's crossbar to drive it deep into the loose pile. Spike waited in the haymow for the first load to arrive.

From back to front, a track traversed the barn under the ridge of the roof and protruded out the hay door. After Will buried the steel tongs into the hay, he shouted to Ruby who stood alongside the barn where she could see Will on the wagon at one end, Catherine on Fanny Too behind him, and if she positioned herself just right, she could see Spike at work in the loft. When Will signaled, Ruby shouted Catherine forward and Fanny Too pulled the rope that lifted a mountain of hay upward to where the large fork snapped into the track's carriage. Will pulled the carriage rope, sliding the hay along the track until the mountain poised above Spike. Ruby then shouted for Will to pull the trip rope and hoped that Spike was agile enough to avoid the falling stack. While Spike spread the hay, Catherine backed Fanny Too to their starting point. Will pulled the hayfork back through the hay door and down to the wagon. Then the process repeated—all day long.

When the day was over the girls said they were too tired to eat dinner, but Will urged them to take a few bites and then to go to bed early. "I'll walk down and pick up the mail," he said. "The *Ashley Springs Democrat* should be here."

Will pulled the newspaper from the box and tucked it under his arm. He felt good about the day's work. They might have been held up for a while, but a few more days like this and he'd be back on schedule. When he opened the newspaper at the door, he was shocked by the headline. He raced into the house. "Mary! Mary! They've shot George Tyler!"

He held up the front page and pointed to the heading.

"GEORGE TYLER SHOT AND KILLED IN BANK HOLDUP."

Mary gasped. "What's this world coming to?"

"I gotta get up there."

12

After milking the next morning Will hitched Fanny Too to the buggy. The night before, while he pulled his suit from the closet and hung it from the door to stretch out the wrinkles, Mary told him that her mother had called and asked to see the girls.

"Gusta hasn't seen her grandma since she was a baby. Could you go through Hinton on your way to Ashley Springs?"

And he had agreed. "They've worked hard. They deserve a break. Have them ready first thing after morning milking."

When he saw Ruby, Catherine, and Gusta waiting in the buggy, Will grabbed his coat and hustled toward the door; but first he stopped and embraced his wife.

"I wish you could go along."

"Sharon's way behind on her vegetable display for the county fair. I promised I'd help."

"And I know you have the girls' clothes to alter for school next week. I hate to leave right now, but I feel I must go. That little community's suffered through terrible times, such a loss these last years. I've gotta see his wife, do what I can to help."

Mary reached up and kissed him. "Pass on my condolences." Then she pushed him toward the door.

<hr>

Will returned from Ashley Springs late in the afternoon the next day. "Mary, I haven't seen such malaise since Tommy Burns's death. The mayor and now their banker. It's a lot for that community to bear." Will laid his suit coat over a chair.

Mary handed him a plate of ham and baked beans. "I'm afraid it's cold."

"It'll do," Will said as he picked at a bean. "After the funeral, I stopped at the bank, asked about the loan."

"For the bull?"

"They didn't have any record of our agreement. I guess George didn't write it down."

"Will they do the loan?"

"They said they can't do anything until they get a new manager." Will cut a sliver from his ham but didn't raise it to his mouth. "Right now, they're not making loans outside the township. Money's tight."

"What'll you do?"

Will pushed back his chair and eased away from the table. "I'm plumb tuckered out, Mary. I'm going to get out of this monkey suit and rest for a while."

Mary took his arm. "Will, you've hardly touched your dinner."

Will pulled away. "Got no appetite. Call me at chore time."

"Will, take… "

Will turned and shuffled toward the back bedroom.

13

Will had pressed to get his neighbors together for a second meeting, but McPherson said that he couldn't generate enough interest to attract a quorum. Will was getting antsy, so he continued to push McPherson. He knew that if he didn't press the issue, they weren't likely to ever have a meeting.

The crops were in the barn and Gusta and his girls were back in school. All reports indicated that Gusta was a bright, astute student. And she hadn't caused any ruckus—not yet, anyhow.

One day in January, after completing her Saturday chores and home-work, Gusta visited her friend Alice Derryberry. The temperature had dropped to below freezing, and Gusta wasn't back yet. That worried Will. Gusta didn't understand that temperatures in Wisconsin could drop so quickly.

Will had finished forking hay down the manger and was calling the cows in to the barn when Catherine shouted, "Gusta's coming. I'm going to tell Mom. She'll be relieved."

Will hustled the cows down the walkway and fastened each stanchion after the cow poked her head into the fresh hay. He always worried until his girls came home, especially if one was out alone.

He had settled under a cow they called Mazy when Catherine raced into the barn. "Dad, something's wrong. Lyda's back and Gusta's not on her. Maybe she's down and hurt."

Mary O'Shaughnessy raced from the house with blankets while Will hooked Fanny Too to the cutter. "I can't imagine Gusta losing her mount. It's no night to be afoot," he said to Catherine and Ruby. "I'll finish the milking. Retrace the path to the Derryberry's. Take Teddy. Hurry."

Will had milked the last cow, and still, no girls. He opened the barn door to turn his herd out when he heard the cutter's schuss in the distance. He heard Fanny Too's wheezing and the girls' loud calls. He couldn't make out the words until he raced around the barn and started down the lane. "Dad, Mom, Gusta's hurt!" he heard Catherine shout. "Get hot water and blankets!"

Will saw Ruby rubbing Gusta's legs. "What happened?"

"Gusta went into the river," Catherine said, "but she got up on an ice flow and Ruby pulled her out."

Will rushed to his older daughter's side and vigorously massaged Gusta's arms while Ruby continued to rub her legs.

"Press lightly, Dad," Ruby said. "I've read that you can damage the skin if you rub too hard."

Gusta moaned but said nothing. "Catherine, run to the house and tell Mom to get Dr. Snyder out here quick," Will said. "Let's take her inside and get her warmed." Will jumped off the cutter and turned to Ruby. "Help me get her down."

They carried Gusta to the living room sofa and worked over her until the blue in her limbs turned a pale shade of pink and she began to stir and muttered somewhat coherently, "Ouch, that hurts."

"Ruby, heap the blankets on, and Catherine, stoke the stove and heat some water."

Catherine told how, after a frantic search as nighttime neared, they finally found Gusta; how Ruby stripped her own clothes and went into the water to pull to shore the small ice mass that Gusta lay on; how Catherine wrapped them both in blankets while Ruby removed Gusta's ice-encrusted clothing and massaged life back into her limbs.

Will supposed that because she was in the water for only a short time, Gusta's tight snow suit and balky Mackinaw had kept the frigid water from her body. His daughters had laughed at the expensive clothing that Gusta had brought to keep warm, but her fear of cold weather had probably saved her life this time.

When Dr. Snyder arrived, he shooed Will from the room while he examined Gusta. After fifteen minutes of stewing in the kitchen, Will heard Dr. Snyder call, "You can come back in, Will. I think this young lady will be okay. She's had a scare, that's for sure." He placed his stethoscope back in his bag and snapped it shut. "You can leave some of these blankets off, but keep the room warm. Call me if she takes a turn."

Mary spooned a dollop of butter onto the baked potato. "I hate to leave Gusta, Will. Maybe you can get some food into her. She's lost her appetite. I can't get her to eat a thing." Mary handed Will the plate. "Hurry up, girls. I don't want to be late for the service."

Will carried the food to Gusta's bedside. "You gotta eat, girl, gotta get your strength back."

"I'm not hungry, Uncle Will."

He felt her forehead. "Do you have a fever, my dear?"

"I'm okay—but I've been doing lots of thinking." Tears ran down Gusta's face. "I miss home. I miss my horse, Travis. I miss Mother and the ranch. I miss Texas."

"You've been through an ordeal, my child."

"Not just that." She grimaced as she looked up at her uncle. "It sure did put a scare into me. But I've been thinking about Texas since the days turned cold."

"There's no place like home, is there? But we've tried to—"

"You, Aunt Mary, and the girls have been wonderful to me—even when I didn't deserve it. I like the farm, but I miss the ranch. I miss the open spaces, the all-day outings across the prairie where you can ride for hours and never see a fence. I miss the round-ups, the rodeos, and the cowboys. I could never live in town."

"No, I don't think you could, my little Texas wildflower."

"Why'd you ever leave for town, Uncle Will?"

"I hadn't wanted to either. I had no choice."

"Couldn't you have stayed on the farm?"

"I was getting married, and I had to make my way. I'd expected to take over Grandpa Duffy's farm. Then he yanked it out from under me."

"Why?"

"The farm usually goes to the oldest son, but Grandpa didn't have any sons, just my mother. And Dad already had his hands full. Grandpa decided to turn the farm over to Frank."

"How could he do that?"

"He was getting old, Gusta. I sometimes wonder if he knew how that decision would tear the family apart. Jesse never forgave Grandpa or Frank, but he came to detest me as well. I'll never understand why. And Frank doesn't give a hoot about any of us."

"Do you think your grandpa wanted it that way?"

"Maybe it wouldn't've made any difference to him. Grandpa never liked me."

"How could he not have liked you?" She placed her hand on his arm. "You're the nicest man I know."

"He felt the same, I suppose. He didn't think I was tough-minded enough to farm."

Until he was faced with building his own farm, Will hadn't considered how Grandpa's decision had set him back, how many years he'd lost. He was beginning to appreciate that Grandpa had been right about farming's difficulties. And that made Will resent him all the more. But he'd be damned if he'd let Grandpa's words hold him back. He felt sure that his ideas would help his neighbors prosper, but he wasn't doing a very good job of convincing them—not yet, anyhow. And most of them had far more farming experience than he did.

"Why, Uncle Will?"

"It probably started when I was nine years old. He wanted me to hold the baby pigs while he cut away their manhood. I couldn't do it. I couldn't take their squeals and the blood. He called me a coward and never asked me to help again."

"When Chester and the boys did that, Mom wouldn't let me outside."

"Ruby'd want to help."

"Nothing scares Ruby. I bet Catherine stays away."

"Catherine's like me, a bit weak in the knees."

"How could your grandpa be so mean?"

Will thought about the day Grandma had died. Grandpa had thrown Jessie into a heap on the floor. "He was a hard man."

"You were only nine years old."

"Oh, there were lots of things. Once, I wouldn't shoot the neighbor dogs that chased his sheep. Maybe the final straw came the day he wanted me to take back the cow."

"A cow?"

"Old Mr. Jacobson bought a milk cow from Grandpa, but he didn't have the money, so Grandpa said he could pay installments." Will handed Gusta a slice of buttered bread. "Just take a bite? You need something in your stomach."

"What happened to the cow, Uncle Will?"

"After Jacobson missed several payments, Grandpa said business is business and ordered me to get the cow." He looked toward Gusta's hand. "I can see that moment as clear as I see the bread you hold."

Gusta nibbled at a slice of cheddar. "I sure do like your cheese."

"I remember that Grandpa bit a plug of Red Man and chewed a spell before spitting into a cow pie, right on center. Grandpa always hit his target. 'Did you get the cow?' he said."

"At first, I didn't answer."

"'Well?' Grandpa said."

"'I couldn't do it.'"

"'What do you mean, couldn't do it? By rights, that's our cow.'"

"'Why, the old man is almost blind.' We had an awful row over that."

"That's the Uncle I know and love," Gusta said.

"Funny thing, if they'd not had that agreement, Grandpa'd probably have given him the cow. But it was business. And to his thinking, that's not the way you do business. That's probably the day I lost the farm."

"Well, Uncle Will, you've got a better farm now. All's well that ends well. That's what Mother says."

"Yes, Gusta. All's well that ends well."

Will had his doubts.

✦

Gusta recovered rapidly and Will's attention was drawn to other problems. He had pressed for a co-op meeting all winter, so he was happy when McPherson called the township farmers to a second meeting on the third Monday in April, 1937. The meeting started well with another dinner and acknowledgement of their wives' contributions. But when McPherson pressed for a motion to form a committee to explore incorporation, Roberts and the other fluid milk producers argued that they already sold their grade A milk for more than those who sold grade B milk for cheese, but that was fair because the government set higher quality and cleanliness standards for the grade A producers.

Will argued that a good co-op manager could find new markets and acquire higher prices for all the township's milk producers. Although they couldn't agree to establish a committee, they did agree to reconvene in two weeks.

The discussion continued each morning when farmers met at their local cheese factories. It soon became clear to Will that the main stumbling block was the pricing of grade A versus grade B milk. Grade A was sold for immediate consumption and demanded a premium price, but cost more to produce. Grade B was made into cheese and butter, products that could be stored until prices improved. Most Willow Township farmers produced grade B, so they were the ones he had to convince, but he didn't want to lose the A producers either. How could he get an agreement?

Although physically recovered from her ordeal, Gusta didn't resume her carefree ways. After the last day of school, she announced, "I'm going back to Texas, back to the safety of snakes, scorpions, and lizards. But before I go, I'm going to throw a party, a real Texas hootenanny, and I want everyone in town there."

Mary told Will that she was disappointed but not surprised that Gusta decided to go home. "When Gusta talked to me about it, she said, 'I just don't understand you Yankees. You're as cold as your weather.' She hastened to add that she didn't mean us. I suppose it's hard to behave like a Yankee when you're a born rebel. She misses her sunshine and cactus plants. It seems that our Eden is her wasteland."

"She loves you," Will said. "I know that."

"I've tried my best, and I hope I didn't fail my brother, but she's old enough to know her mind. She'll be seventeen before she leaves for home. She means well, even if her ways aren't ours."

Gusta announced that she would hold her party on the Fourth of July. "A good day for a celebration," she said.

Will knew that Gusta was writing letters south since the day school ended, and that she had made arrangements for food and entertainment to be shipped north from Chicago and Texas, but she didn't reveal the details.

Will expected the party to be special, but he had no idea how spectacular it might be until Justin Jasperson told him that Gusta rented four rooms in his father's boarding house for two nights before and one night after the Fourth. Then Esther Bohanning said that Gusta bought enough space in her father's ice locker to stash a whole steer. What could that girl have in mind?

Summer days were busy days for everyone. They worked the fields during the heat of day and milked cows each morning and night. There was little time to talk with Gusta during the day, and Will was too tired at night.

Early on the first of July, Gusta said she'd spend the day in town, that she'd made arrangements for a livery driver to pick her up, and that she'd not get home until the next morning. Mary took the news so calmly that Will supposed she must know something the others didn't. Whatever could his imaginative, dramatic, and exotic niece have in mind?

The next morning, Gusta and three men rode into the yard. Three strangers were reason enough for excitement—but black men? When Will greeted the men, he could see that his girls were flabbergasted. They'd never seen a black man before.

Catherine stood slack-jawed when Gusta said, "Please meet Mr. Allen, our pitman, and Jasper and Jacob, his helpers."

Jasper and Jacob looked so much alike that Will knew they must be twin brothers.

"What's a pitman?" Ruby said.

"He's a master cook," Gusta said. "Just you wait and see. You'll never have tasted anything so good."

Mr. Allen set his men to digging, and within two hours they had dug a pit three feet deep, three feet wide, and twenty feet long. Will couldn't believe how fast they worked.

"Easy diggin'," Jacob said—or maybe it was Jasper.

"Not like Texas hardscrabble," the other said.

Before noon a second wagon arrived loaded with sacks of wood chips which the men unloaded into a crib-high pile and immediately set fire to it. "Why are they burning it?" Ruby said. "Why'd they bring the chips this far just to burn them?"

"You'll see," Gusta said. "Those aren't any old wood chips. They're mesquite chips. The best there is for cooking a Texas barbecue. You'll be eating beef, cowboy style. You've never had anything so good. You'll see."

The chips flared and then smoldered until the next morning, when Jasper and Jacob shoveled the embers into the pit. Within an hour, a third wagon pulled into the O'Shaughnessy yard, this one loaded with the most beautiful beef briskets that Will had ever seen. More than a hundred pounds of brisket were laid on racks across the pit, about two feet above the hot coals.

"Where'd you get those?" Ruby said. "Did you bring them up from Texas?"

"Not Texas, Chicago," Gusta said. "From the Chicago stock yards. The best I could buy."

"They'll burn to a crisp," Catherine said. "We don't eat until tomorrow."

Gusta laughed. "Not when they're cooked this way," she said. "We call this hot smoking, just smoke and low heat for hours and hours. They'll be tender as a baby's hinder and sweeter'n sugared ham by noon tomorrow. Just you wait'n' see."

◦》》》◦◦◦◦◦

People began arriving mid-morning on the Fourth. The first carriage carried a bunch of exuberant men, and the second, right behind, was filled with musical instruments. Gusta called the family over. "This is Bob Wills and his orchestra, friends of mine, straight from Texas. You'll love his music. He calls it Western Swing. I'll teach y'all a new dance. He's the best musician in Texas. Just you wait; y'all hear his name up here soon."

Will listened with admiration. The music didn't sound like what he played. When Wills played his fiddle, the melodies flew from his bow.

The party was like none that Will had seen. The barbecue was everything that Gusta promised, and the potato salad, mustard coleslaw, spicy pinto beans, peach cobbler, and sweet potato pie more than satisfied the three hundred townsfolk who had gathered. Will knew only a few of them. His girls had told their classmates to bring their families, and, before summer break, Gusta had announced in school that everyone was welcome. The lively music entertained the throng throughout the day, and those who left for milking returned for a late night encore. The young people, and many of the old as well, spent the day swaying their hips and tapping their feet to Bob Will's Western Swing.

When the crowd was the largest, Wills stopped in the middle of a set. "Miss Gusta has something to say. We'll continue the music after she's made her announcement."

Gusta strode forward looking as proud as a debutante at her coming-out ball. "Ladies and gentlemen. As y'all know, I'll be returning to Texas soon, but I wanted to do something that you'd remember me by."

Will saw Sharon elbow Catherine in the side and heard her say, "As if anyone could forget cousin Gusta. You'd forget her like you'd forget a twister that flattened your living room."

83

Gusta continued. "Mostly, this is for Aunt Mary, Uncle Will, Sharon, Ruby, and Catherine. I knew there was nothing I could do that would mean so much as entertaining their friends and neighbors. Thank you, Aunt Mary, Uncle Will, and my cousins. I love y'all."

Sharon hung her head while Ruby and Catherine rushed to hug Gusta.

"Just one more thing," Gusta said. "Aunt Mary's teaching me to be a lady. Notice that today has been uneventful." She demurely curtsied to the crowd.

Will shifted uncomfortably, but smiled a bit, too. He remembered the day Gusta gave his mother a pitcher of fermented cherry juice to help calm her headache. It was probably the first time Gertrude ever tasted an alcoholic drink—and she thought it was wonderful until the next morning when her head felt like a busted melon. And then there was that night that Gusta returned home two hours after Mary's designated curfew. Will smiled to himself. This day wasn't over yet.

Everyone applauded. "A toast to Aunt Mary," someone shouted. All raised their glasses and proclaimed, "Hail, Mary O'Shaughnessy. Hail to a lady."

Pete Simmons and Adam Baxter exploded firecrackers all afternoon, but after Will cautioned them, they stayed at the crowd's fringe. Still, Will kept an eye on them, and Catherine followed them around as they blew cans into the air and threw explosives onto the road. As the music drew attention away from them, the boys moved toward the barn. Will heard Adam say, "Let's make some real excitement."

"Yeah, what you thinkin', Adam?" Pete said with a smirk.

Adam strolled toward the loft. "Have you ever seen how fast a cat moves when he's got one of these sizzlers sparkin' outta his butt? I think I spotted a kitten near the barn earlier."

Will knew that Catherine heard them, too. She turned and raced toward Ruby, and he heard her shout, "Ruby, Pete and Adam are after our cats." She explained what she heard the boys say, but before she finished, Ruby, fists clenched, raced toward the barn.

Gusta was performing rope tricks to the tune of "Ida Red" when a crimson-faced Ruby raced after Catherine. Will thought the boys may have bitten off more than they could chew when Gusta coiled her rope and raced after them. Ruby and Gusta were a force to behold. They wouldn't shy from trouble.

Will followed behind Catherine and Ruby when they ran up the ramp to the loft, but he stayed back a bit.

Pete and Adam grabbed a cornered cat. "What do you have in mind, boys?" Ruby shouted at them.

They turned toward Ruby. Pete held the cat by the scruff of its neck but tried to conceal it behind his leg. "Nothing, nothing at all, Ruby," Adam said as he edged away from Pete. "We just like cats," he said with a strained laugh that faded into a wan smile.

"Yeah," Pete agreed as he took the cat into his arms and patted at it. "We sure do like little kittens. I've got a bunch at home."

Ruby edged toward Pete as Gusta approached, rope in hand. "What's going on?" Gusta said.

"I think these boys have mischief in mind," Ruby said. "Tell her what you heard, Catherine."

Catherine began her story, but when she got to the sizzling part, Pete tossed the kitten to Adam who started toward the open door. As he raised his leg for a second step, a rope coiled around his foot, and with a quick jerk, Gusta tipped him forward and into the air. "Just like roping calves, boys."

Before she got the words out, Adam, cat, and rope disappeared, as if an invisible hand had snatched them from the loft.

"She's a sorcerer," Pete squeaked.

Will knew immediately what happened, and he might have panicked if he hadn't remembered that he'd left his morning chores unfinished.

"You tripped him down the chute!" Catherine screamed. "You killed him, Gusta!"

Gusta turned pale.

"Quick, let's get down there," Ruby shouted over her shoulder as she ran past Will and around the corner of the building. She was gone before the others moved.

Catherine split away from Gusta and Pete when they turned toward the milk barn below. "I'll get Dr. Snyder," she called.

Will knew she wasn't keen to see a bloodied Adam.

When Dr. Snyder entered the barn, Will saw Catherine hang back, but her curiosity overcame her fear of blood, and she peeked around the corner. Adam sat upright on a pile of hay, but he was as pale as the white-washed walls and as quiet as a kitten stalking a mouse.

"Take deep breaths," Dr. Snyder said as he checked his ribs.

Although he appeared to be okay, Will could see that the fall had scared the bejeebers out of the boy. Will looked up through the chute and could see that hay surrounded the opening, having hid it from their view in the loft. Will was glad that he had been called away before he'd leveled the hay that Adam sat on. Without that big cushion, the outcome might have been quite different.

By now, half the revelers had gathered at the barn, but when they heard the story, they agreed that Adam had gotten his dues. As they walked back to the yard, Bob Wills and his orchestra played Dixieland music, and Will heard Mr. Allen comment to no one in particular, "This time, the reb' won."

Gusta didn't look like a victorious soldier. Head down, she sidled over to her aunt. "I'm sorry, Aunt Mary. I so wanted to have one doin's where I didn't embarrass y'all."

When Mary Pulled Gusta close and hugged her, Will knew that his wife wasn't upset by the girls' routing Pete and Adam. She'd complained earlier about the boys' rowdy behavior.

Will felt a tug on his trousers. Catherine slipped her small hand into his big burly one and looked up at him. "I'm glad Gusta roped him. I think Adam got exactly what he deserved."

Yes, Will thought. Catherine's rebel cousin wasn't about to leave without one last hurrah.

15

When they reconvened for the third meeting, Will noticed that the B producers congregated near the front of the room, shunning Roberts and the other liquid milk producers, who were pressed to the room's outer edge. A bad omen.

Although Roberts had agreed to join with his neighbors, Will knew that his participation was tenuous. The cold shoulder now might be all he needed to change his mind.

Jackson McGried argued that the many grade B producers could do okay without a co-op, because unlike the A producers, they could hold their cheese until prices improved. As Will listened to Roberts and the A producers argue their need for higher prices, Will knew they were right, but he knew that his wish for a farmer cooperative was doomed unless he could convince the many grade B producers that they could gain, too.

He'd thought a long time about a co-op's advantages, and he wasn't ready to give up. He stood up and argued that co-ops had already proven their value throughout Wisconsin, and even more so in Illinois and Minnesota. The Illinois Farm Supply Company, and the Midland Cooperative Wholesale and the Land O'Lakes Creamery in Minnesota were making millions of dollars. "We can be successful, too," he said. "I know we can."

They continued to disagree about the money distribution. Will knew that he had to move the discussion along, so he proposed a new idea: blended pricing. He suggested that they pool all their proceeds and give a higher than normal proportion to the B producers as an incentive for them to join the new organization. But, he argued, the A producers would still come out ahead because of the co-op's ability to bring more revenues than each individual could earn on his own.

Earl Roberts shouted, "I'll not work harder and sell for less just to buy a pig in a poke."

McPherson called for them to reconvene on the third Monday in August.

The next morning at breakfast, Will lamented the inaction. "I so want to get this co-op started. I just don't understand why my neighbors won't support it."

"Will, did you ever consider that they might think your resistance to modern machinery is a bit peculiar, too."

"That's different, Mary. These Southwest Wisconsin hillsides aren't suited to tractors and large machines."

"I think you're not wanting to lose your horses. Change is difficult for everyone. Stay patient, Will. Every road has its potholes."

Will met Earl Roberts and Arnie Johnson at the cheese factory the next morning. "Look, you only have seven cans of milk each today, half as many as you had last spring when the price was low. Now the price is up, but you don't have the milk to sell, do you?"

"It's always been that way," Roberts said.

"It doesn't have to be, Earl. A good manager can find ways of selling in places where there's more demand and the price is higher. Certainly Milwaukee, maybe Chicago and Minneapolis."

"We sell to Madison now," Roberts said. "Do you really think we need those other cities?"

"Madison's a drop in the milk pail," Will said. "Why, Chicago or Minneapolis would quadruple our demand. Can you imagine the milk they drink in those cities? Big demand means big prices. We'd never have to sell our milk for cheese."

"Do you think so, Will?" Arnie said.

"I'm not so sure," Roberts said as he swung around and strode to his truck.

Arnie stared after Roberts for a moment, and then he turned to Will and said, "I'm not sure that you'll ever convince Earl. I'm afraid that we'll lose him."

"He's a hard one to crack, that's for sure, but I'm not giving up yet. I'll find some way to keep him with us. Just you wait and see."

But at the moment, Will had no good ideas to back up his words.

16

Another winter passed, and now, in 1938, Will was preparing for his third spring planting. He hired a new farmhand, Petr Rucinski, who immigrated to the United States to escape the many regional conflicts his country endured following World War I. Will felt certain that Europe was on the verge of chaos, and although he hated to admit it, that gave him hope for the American farmer. If he could just find a way to buy that bull.

Thunder cracked, and lightning flashes lit up the calf pen. A good day to work in the barn. He threw a forkful of soiled straw into the spreader while Teddy sniffed around the cows' empty stanchions. Will could see that his dog preferred to stay inside, too.

The girls' voices coming from the loft above were a comfort. He was confident the lightning rods would protect his family and barn, but he winced when he thought about his cows out in the weather. He had never lost a cow to lightning, but that was little comfort. He had never seen a tornado either, but Will knew that, too, was just a matter of being in the wrong place at the wrong time.

Whenever a summer storm approached, Will kept his herd inside, but this one caught him unawares. And he wasn't about to send his girls after the cows now. He had considered keeping his herd inside during the storm season, but it wasn't humane or practical to hold them in an overheated barn when lush pastures beckoned down the lane.

Will continued to pitch wet straw until the rumbles subsided and the light bursts moved upriver. He breathed deep and inhaled the fresh ozone filled air. And when he looked out the window and saw a rainbow, his spirits lifted. A summer storm wasn't all bad. Will could hear his herd, their bags full of milk, complain as they approached the barn. When he opened the door to let them in, two cows were missing.

Will shouted up the chute toward the loft. "Ruby, Catherine, come on down. The storm's moved away, so we can start milking. All the cows are up except Mazy and Betsy. We're half an hour late already, so you better take the horses and go look."

He heard footsteps bounce across the loft floor on the way to the ladder.

"They're probably under the sugar maples at the end of the lane," Will called, "but if they're not there, check along the slough. Maybe they got bogged down in high water."

Will commenced milking but he continued to worry. He wasn't surprised that Betsy lagged behind. She was often late. But Mazy was his bell cow. She usually led the herd, and they were all at the barn. He stripped the last drops of milk and emptied his first pail into the eight-gallon can. He was satisfied with his milk output, but Mazy and Betsy were the beginnings of the higher producing herd that he envisioned. Without a prized bull, that future was at risk, too.

Will had finished three more cows when he heard hoof beats and shouts in the distance. He dropped his pail and raced from the barn.

"Dad," Ruby shouted, "Mazy and Betsy were struck by lightning. They're lying dead under the big sugar maple in the north forty."

It was too late to help now, so Will finished milking before he went to the house to tell Mary.

"What'll we do, Will?" Mary said. "Mazy and Betsy produced almost fifteen percent of our milk. That's our profit. We'll have to sell our heifers."

"No, Mary. Those heifers will keep us going, even if I can't afford a bull to sire better ones. They'll replace Betsy and Mazy's production, but we'll have to tighten our belts for a while."

"Tighten our belts? I'm afraid there's no slack left." Mary placed a hand on her husband's shoulder. "We'll find a way. God won't give us more than we can handle."

"Maybe so, my dear, but sometimes I wish He'd not trust me so much. Those heifers will freshen in the spring. If we can just make it till then, if I can convince my neighbors to get this co-op going, then with stronger sales, we'll have a chance to pull out of this. But if we want to improve our herd, I've got to find a way to buy that bull."

17

oday they milked early because Will wanted to get on the road. It was his dad's seventy-first birthday, and his mother planned a surprise dinner. Will didn't like adding an hour between morning and night milking. It wasn't good for the cows' health and comfort, but once shouldn't do much damage. Will wondered if Frank would be there. He usually didn't stop work for so frivolous a thing as a party, even a family birthday.

Catherine poured her last pail of milk into the eight-gallon can. She started to turn her cow out of the barn, but Will tapped her on the arm. "You and Ruby go to the house and get prettied up. Your mother wants to fit the new blouses she sewed for you." He reached inside the door and grabbed a shovel from the milk house. "I'll finish up here."

Will hitched Mabel to the buggy. He preferred Fanny Too, but she'd thrown a shoe the day before and he didn't have a spare one.

The fall foliage on the drive to Ashley Springs was more beautiful than Will had remembered. The red maples were brilliant scarlet, the sugar maples even more impressive in their orange and red cloaks. On some of the high ridges, the maples' bright red and orange colors intermingled with the golden yellow of the poplars and birch, and with the browns, russets, and subdued burgundy of the oaks. Occasionally a purplish red dogwood fought its way through the myriad of brighter colors. Red sumac leaves, boasting a deeper, more modest color than the flamboyant red bush alongside his house, sprinkled the fence lines along the way.

Before they got to Ashley Springs, Mary said, "Can we drive past our home on the way to your dad's?" Mary turned away from Will. "So many memories."

"Let's stop," Sharon called from the back seat. "Maybe they'll show us inside."

"We won't have time," Will said. "Mother'll be fit to be tied if we're late."

"I'm not sure I want to see how our drunken tenant keeps it," Mary said.

"I suppose his wife keeps it," Will said. "You can't find fault with her, now can you?"

"Marie's an angel to put up with that old sot."

"They pay their rent every month."

"It's been a godsend. I'll admit that. And it's a bit late to protest, I suppose, but I'm still uncomfortable renting to a drunkard."

Although Will believed Mary was way too critical, he felt nervous, too. She was seldom wrong about people.

Will hadn't expected that Mabel could hold her pace, but she hustled right along, getting them into Ashley Springs half an hour early. Their house towered over its neighbors. And it had style, too. The roof flowed in all directions, valleys and copper eaves troughs everywhere. Elaborate decorative trim intersected tassels and brackets that supported the eaves and anchored porch posts to the roof. Visitors were greeted by side-by-side entry doors under a large fan window sporting an elaborate semicircular sunburst overhead.

A pang of guilt flooded Will's consciousness. It was an awful thing he had done, taking Mary away from this home, a home that put their farm dwelling to shame. But she never complained. The house was far too nice for a rental, but during these bleak years, Will thanked God for the extra income.

Will hauled on the reins. "Whoa, Mabel. Let's rest a bit."

Mary clasped her hands and gasped. "I almost forgot how beautiful it was."

Will slumped in the seat.

"Do you think we can go in?" Sharon said. "Do you think they'd show us through?"

"That wouldn't be proper," Mary said. "We didn't call ahead."

"Oh, Mama," Sharon said, "let me ask. Just a peek inside." She jumped to the ground. "We do own the house, now don't we?"

"Me, too," Ruby said as she jumped down.

Catherine followed close behind.

"It looks like I'm outvoted again," Mary said. "I'm not sure that I'm ready for this."

Sharon beckoned from the doorway. "Mrs. Swartz says to come in."

"Will, we shouldn't."

"We can't stay for long, but I am kinda curious." He stepped off the buggy, circled round, lifted Mary down, and then led her toward the house.

She followed, but Will understood her hesitancy. A town girl, Mary liked things proper. She's no country hick like him. Or maybe she feared what she might find inside. When he walked through the entry and peeked into the living room, the house looked as if they'd never left. He was sure that Mary must be pleased.

"Oh, Mrs. Swartz, I'm so embarrassed barging in like this," Mary said. "I hadn't planned—"

"That's all right. I just love your house, never expected to have one so nice. You're not thinking about moving back, are you?"

"Oh, no,—"

"Mother." Ruby grabbed Mary's arm. "Look what they've done to the entryway. Why, it's beautiful."

A veritable garden under a roof, the entryway presented the family's fall food-stock displayed like a work of art. Gourds, pumpkins, squash, and zucchini dotted the perimeter. Bunched corn stalks interspersed with full-blossomed sun flowers leaned against the wall. Pole beans, looped around wooden standards, looked as if they had spent the summer inching toward an appointment with the ceiling. All thrived inside this well-lighted enclosure. Wall space was filled with racks of vegetables and fruits from the summer's garden. Multicolored ribbons accented the fall's harvest. And the harvest bounty framed a large newspaper print of Christ on the cross under cutout paper letters that proclaimed, *We Give Thanks*. The entryway shouted the family's gratitude.

Will saw Mary smile, but no one said a word as they scanned the walls, absorbing the colors and fragrance.

"We have much to be thankful for," Mrs. Swartz said. She smoothed her apron. "My daughter Margie prepared it as a church project."

"It's beautiful," Mary said, "and a fine tribute to our Lord. Is Margie here? I'd like to thank her."

Marie disappeared through the doorway and called, "Margie, come on down. We have company."

After a minute, a short, plump girl with carrot-red hair tied back in a braid bounded through the doorway. Blue eyes and a face full of freckles complemented her rosy cheeks.

Will supposed she was a newly christened teenager. An ebullient smile raced up her cheeks and flowed through her eyes and reminded him of his youthful anticipation of a world to overcome, but that was so long ago. Just like his daughters, she undoubtedly believed that only thornless paths lay ahead.

"Yes, Mama?"

"This is Mr. and Mrs. O'Shaughnessy, our landlords."

Margie, awkward and unpracticed, like a young stork that hadn't mastered its legs, curtsied and almost tipped tail over teakettle into Will, but no one laughed. Mary stepped forward, steadied her, and then she grasped her hand.

"My dear, this is the loveliest I've ever seen this entryway. Is it you I thank?"

With Mary's assistance, Margie regained her balance, reddened, and blurted out, "I'm sorry." Without looking to see if there was a vegetable underneath, she continued, "I must have tripped over a gourd."

Will peered down, but he didn't see any obstacles.

"I'm glad you like it," Margie said. She smiled at the girls.

Mary pointed to each in turn. "Sharon, Ruby, and Catherine. These are my daughters."

"You've made it beautiful," Sharon said as she sniffed the air. "And it smells like a hundred harvests all bundled into one."

Will inhaled the earthy aromas—the pungent odor of the pumpkins, squash, and gourds, the sweetness of the corn and melons, and the sharpness of the onions and garlic. It did smell like a hundred harvests.

"I wish I'd thought of it," Sharon said, "but I don't have a creative idea in my head."

Will knew better. He remembered the Christmas decorations that Sharon made for their tree and hung throughout the house last December.

"Tell them why you did this," Marie said.

"Oh, Mama. They don't want to know."

"We certainly do want to know," Mary said.

Sharon and Ruby nodded.

"Oh, we do," Catherine said.

"It was my confirmation project," Margie said. "Father McCrery told us that confirmation is a sacrament of commitment, and I wanted to do something special."

"And you have, my dear," Mary said. "This is very special indeed. It not only honors our Lord, it honors this house as well."

"Won't you come in?" Marie said. "I don't have much prepared but—"

"Oh, no," Mary said. "We can't intrude further. We must get along. We have a birthday party." She hugged Marie Swartz before she shooed her family out.

As Will helped her into the buggy, she whispered, "I feel so ashamed."

"And you should," Will said, thinking about Mary's comment questioning how their drunken tenant might keep the house. Mary had always been too critical of Paul Swartz. The splendid condition of the house made Will feel justified for having rented to the man over Mary's objections. He didn't mention that he'd heard noises in the kitchen and had seen cigarette smoke curl through the door.

"Giddyap, Mabel," Will shouted forward. "We can't be late."

Will wanted to see his Ford dealership once more, so he drove the long way through Ashley Springs. Brock McDougal had proclaimed that Ford dealerships would prosper again, and he'd put his money where his mouth was. The remodeled building sported an expanded showroom, an enlarged bay window, and Will saw three shiny Model As inside. McDougal had the money, that's for sure. Will felt a twinge of jealousy, and he wasn't sure why. Hadn't he gotten his farm, achieved his life-long dream? But he wasn't as confident about his future as he thought he'd be. At first, he'd thought only about the things he would do to become a successful farmer, but he was finding it more difficult than he had expected.

"Daddy, can I stop at Samuels' department store and buy a new slate for school?" Catherine said. "I can't find one anywhere in Willow."

Will stopped in front of Samuels' and handed his daughter a quarter. "Hurry up, now. We're already runnin' a bit late."

The noon whistle drowned Will's "Whoa, Mabel," but a tug on the reins stopped her just the same. His father's house atop the hill stood as a testament to Thomas's engineering ability. Resistant to western blizzards that swept the ridge each winter, the house stood tall and stolid on its native limestone foundation. The ravaging wind's only influence was a slight, eastward list. Will remembered that cloudy fall day when five horse teams pulled the massive building up the hill. He laughed when he remembered his father perched on top of the huge oak skids while he shouted his orders to the workers below. Thomas had reminded Will of Napoleon directing his men, but Will didn't remember Napoleon with a flask in his hand.

Will hadn't expected to see Frank's Chevrolet parked in front of the house, but there it was. And half a dozen Fords as well. All Model Ts—Will's old customers, most likely. He never understood why Frank wouldn't do business with him.

Gertrude ran out the door before Will stepped off the buggy. "Will, everyone's at the table. I thought you weren't going to make it." She grabbed Catherine's arm and almost pulled her into the back wheel when a startled Mabel lurched forward at the sound of Gertrude's sharp voice. "Hurry now, get in the house."

"Grandma!"

"Git, girl."

Gertrude slapped her granddaughter on the behind and Catherine moved, but not without a sour glance backward.

Thomas O'Shaughnessy sat at the head of the table. Charlie Nesbitt was there. Silas and Matilda Murrish, Bert and Agnes Whitford, too. To Will's surprise, Maud Burns sat alongside Charlie.

While his family took the chairs that Gertrude pushed at them, Will rushed to Maud and took her hand. "Maud, I've felt so guilty all these years. Just when you needed us most, we left town. And I'd promised to look after little Opal."

"We couldn't have gotten by without Mary's help, without the money she sent now and then."

Will looked at Mary and saw her redden, but she didn't waver. She held his gaze with a triumphant expression in her eyes. She'd never said anything about sending money to Maud. He smiled and shook his head.

"Haven't you heard? Charlie and I are to wed."

Charlie Nesbitt? Why, he must be at least twenty years older. Robbin' the cradle. Charlie looked pleased as a rooster who'd just had his way with the spring chickens. "Charlie, congratulations. I'm—"

"Will, sit down," Gertrude intruded. "You haven't even said hello to your father. You'd think you were raised in the barn."

Will supposed he was.

"Let's get on with the meal," Frank chimed in from the far side of the table.

Will clutched his father's hand. "Happy birthday, Dad."

Then he turned back to his friend as his mother dragged him toward the last empty chair. "Later, Charlie. I'm so happy."

And he was.

Charlie and Esther Nesbitt were family friends for as long as Will could remember. That was an awful week, the week Esther died in the accident. And Will still felt a bit responsible.

After the meal, all gathered in the large living room. Mary helped Gertrude serve the dessert, a moist banana cake with thick, brown sugar frosting that was topped with embedded black walnut halves. Thomas's favorite. Will heard some people complain that black walnuts weren't as good as their English cousins out in California, but Southwest Wisconsin nuts were all he had ever known, and they suited him fine. True, not as tasty as the hickory nuts he liked, but a whole lot easier to shuck and pick—if you didn't mind your hands turning black for a week or two.

Will noticed that Frank choose a chair across the room. It had been a long time since he sat in the same room with his brother; he hadn't seen him since they moved this house off St. Mary's parish grounds. Will sat next to Charlie and Maud who snuggled on the divan as if they were alone in the room. He supposed that love was blind no matter what one's age is. He looked toward Mary but she didn't notice, so intent was she with her chat with Agnes Whitford. Will turned back to Charlie and Maud.

"Maud, how is little Opal? I've felt guilty about leaving after I promised Frankie to be like a godfather to her."

"She's not so little anymore," Maud said. "Why, she's a proper young lady."

"You should see her," Charlie said. "She looks just like Tommy, freckles and carrot top. Got his sense of humor, too." He pulled his bride-to-be close. "I do love these girls—my Opal and Maud. They make me feel young again."

Charlie leaned toward Will. "You don't think Esther'll mind, do you? That worries me a mite."

"I think she's looking down on you with the love she always had for her husband." Will squeezed Charlie's hand. "I'm sure she's pleased that you're happy again. And I couldn't be more delighted."

Will was just about to gather his family to leave when Frank called across the room. "Will, did you hear that Jesse's back in the area?"

"You've seen him?"

"Not me, but Silas here says he heard that someone saw a strange looking man 'round Barreltown. Said he was badly disfigured. Ain't that right, Silas?"

"That's what the man said. We wondered if it might be Jesse. Didn't he stay at Barreltown one time?"

"Sure did," Frank said.

"Not likely," Will said. "No one's seen Jesse in years. He's probably dead."

97

Will hoped he was wrong about Jesse. As he said his good-byes and ushered his family toward the door, Gertrude handed him a letter.

"It came from the bank. For you, Will."

Will helped his family into the buggy before he opened the envelope. He saw that it was signed by the new bank president, Raymond A. Fellows, a name he didn't know. Will supposed they brought him from out of town. "He must not have my new address," he said to Mary.

Will read the letter.

"What does it say?" Mary asked.

"It says they won't loan money outside Ashley Springs. I guess we'll not get that bull after all."

"We'll find a way. Have faith, my dear."

Will believed that faith worked best when he used his God-given wits. But his mind was as blank as the new slate he'd just purchased for his daughter.

—18—

When he stepped through the front door of the township hall, Will was delighted to see his neighbors intermingling. The discussions parroted those of past meetings, but until Earl Roberts protested, they were without the temper. Still, when men repeatedly turned to him with questions, Will felt that he'd earned their trust. Then Earl suddenly turned on him. "I've liked you, Will, but I won't subject my livelihood to the folly of an outsider. We got by before you came, and we'll get by after you go. I don't know why the rest of you would listen to this false prophet in our midst."

Will had thought that Earl was a friend. Although they'd disagreed about the co-op all along, Earl had never attacked him so directly before. But Will knew a person could change when his income was threatened.

Roberts grabbed his hat and raced from the room.

Will was a bit shaken, but he felt pleased as he rode home. It seemed he'd earned their trust after all. They selected a group to explore incorporation, and they elected him temporary chairman. He wasn't sure about that. It wouldn't help pull Roberts back into the fold. Will wanted it unanimous, to have all his neighbors benefit from their united action. He did seem to be ahead of the others in his thinking about cooperatives, so he supposed he should take the lead.

Will was surprised to see all the rooms lit so late in the evening. He hadn't finished unhitching Fanny Too when Ruby rushed into the barn, her face stained with tears. "Daddy, something awful's happened. Mom got a phone call from Ashley Springs. Our house burned down tonight. Mr. Swartz and Margie died in the fire."

Will ran to Mary while Ruby cared for Fanny Too. "Mary, what happened?"

Mary took his hand. "They said she died in the fire. That lovely young girl died because of her drunken father."

"God be with them."

"Gertrude heard that a cigarette might have started it. That drunk probably smoked in bed."

"You don't know that." Will knew that his compassionate Mary was less tolerant when alcohol was a problem. Will thought about the smoke he saw float through the hallway door. But it wasn't unusual for people to smoke in their homes, and few burned down. "The poor girl," Will said.

"It's a blessing she received the Holy Spirit. Now she's with our Lord."

Why do the young have to go? Will thought about his son, Michael. So young, so vibrant, so innocent? "It's hard to understand God's purpose."

"We must accept His will," Mary said. "Thank heavens you had the foresight to buy insurance when everyone thought it a waste of money. We'll rebuild."

Will turned pale and sat down. "We dropped the insurance on the house, don't you remember? We couldn't afford both the house and the business."

"Didn't you reinstate after you sold the business?"

"No, Mary. I needed the money. We got by so long, I thought a little longer wouldn't matter."

"What will we ever do?" Mary said.

Will knew he'd made a terrible mistake, and now he'd run out of options. He couldn't afford a bull, and without the rent money, he'd have to sell his heifers. His future didn't look bright. Grandpa had been right all along. Damn him.

19

The call came at eight in the morning, just after Will entered the house and pulled a chair to the breakfast table.

"Who was that?" Mary said.

"The fire chief wants me to come to Ashley Springs. He wants information."

"It was that drunk smoking in bed."

"Chief Pederson's not so sure. He thinks it might be arson."

"Who'd do such a thing? Mark my word, Will, it's that drunken sot we rented to."

"This isn't like you, Mary. You know better than to jump to conclusions."

"You'll see. You'll find that I'm right."

Will drove past the burnt house on the way into Ashley Springs. He was glad that Mary refused to come along. He thought of the smoke that he had seen coming from the kitchen. If he hadn't rented to him, maybe Swartz and his daughter would still be alive and he'd still have his house. Insurance had never been popular, but he had spent hours trying to convince his neighbors to buy policies on their homes and farms, and now, he was caught without.

After leaving the remains of his once grand home, Will guided Mabel toward his father's house. Before going to the door, Will stood for a while and looked across the yard to the north side where he thought that he spotted a loose rock in the foundation. When he looked closer he could see that it was as newly tuck pointed and solid as the day they'd moved that house a quarter mile up the slope. Will looked down the hill where he could see the steeple on St. Mary's Catholic Church.

He smiled when he thought about that day. He'd not seen his father so energized since before he'd lost the farm. Buying that old schoolhouse

from the parish, two days moving it up the hill, and six months of resto-
ration work had given Thomas a new lease on life. Before this house, the
only thing that fueled his days was the alcohol. A person had to have a
reason to get out of bed each day. Will had seen many a man wither away
with nothing to do. He wondered how he'd handle the loss of everything
he owned.

Thomas stepped out the door before Will made his way back to the
sidewalk. "I saw you inspecting my tuck pointing. Not so bad for an old
man, now is it? I figured that I'd better git it tight for the winter. I just
finished last week." Thomas fished a plug of tobacco from his pocket and
bit off a chew. "It's surprising how busy a big, old house can keep a man.
It beats me how I ever managed a farm."

Will knew that after he and his brothers left the home farm, his father
hadn't managed very well.

"Losing your house's a terrible thing." Thomas placed his hand on
Will's shoulder. "I suppose you're here to see about that. Have they found
how the fire started?"

"I'm on the way now to see the fire chief. Maybe he'll have some ideas."

"I almost forgot to tell you," Thomas mumbled as he spit out the tobacco plug. "Jesse stopped here."

"The day of the fire?"

"No, it was about a week before."

"Are you sure?"

"He said that he planned to hop a freight train west. I asked around
but no one has seen him since, so I figured he's long gone."

"Was he okay? What'd he want?"

"Money. I gave him the little that I had saved, but that won't take him
far. I tried to talk him into staying, but he was adamant."

"How'd he look?"

Thomas frowned and Will supposed that it was a dumb question.
How would anyone look with half of their face blown away? "I mean,
was he thin? Did he look like he's been eating?"

"He's always been wiry. I don't think he looked much different. I said
that if he'd stay, we'd furnish him three square meals a day, but he wasn't
interested."

"His life must be terribly hard."

"He said that he couldn't stand the pitying looks that he got from those
in town who'd known him before the war."

Will remembered how his youngest brother was always said to be the handsomest lad in the family—and now… he felt nauseous just thinking about it. He supposed that strangers' reactions were more subdued when they saw his maimed brother. They'd never known him any other way.

"I've got to get to the courthouse," Will said.

As he flicked the reins across Mabel's back, he waved at his father who stood hunched over on his doorstep. Life hadn't been easy for Thomas.

Ashley Springs wasn't the same anymore. Tommy and Bernie Burns were gone, so too his good friends David Tate and George Tyler. And the happiest couple that Will had known, Charlie and Esther Nesbit, destroyed by Esther's tragic death. All victims of this terrible depression. He was glad that Charlie had found a new love.

He reined Mabel into the courthouse turnabout and tied her to the hitching post. Fords, Oldsmobiles, and Chevrolets lined the drive, but his was the only horse and buggy. Things had changed since his youth, and he'd helped start it all with his Ford dealership. He should be grateful, he supposed. It had given them a running start, but he didn't miss it. Too many bad things had happened after that terrible day in 1929.

Will had served on the volunteer fire brigade when he lived in town. Mrs. Clark, their telephone operator, would ring the siren when an alarm was phoned in, and every member who heard it came running. Fire chief Connie Pederson moved to town after Will left Ashley Springs, so he never knew the man.

Pederson lowered the telephone receiver and nodded toward Will.

"Mr. Pederson," Will said. "I'm Will O'Shaughnessy. You wanted to see me?"

"Just a minute, O'Shaughnessy, I'll be with you as soon as I finish this call. So you can't get down before next week?… That's the soonest?… I know, I know, you're a busy man…. Next week then."

He slammed the receiver down.

"The state inspector can't get here until next week."

"For my house?"

"The evidence is muddled. Can't make head or tails. It might be a murder case."

"Murder? What makes you think that?"

"Do you carry insurance? Half the fires I see these days are for the insurance."

"You think I burned my own house?"

"Well?"

"What?"

"Do you carry insurance?"

"Not anymore."

"You did?"

"It lapsed years ago."

"We can check the records, you know."

"You think I did it?"

"I don't think you did it. But I've gotta check all leads."

"There must be something that makes you suspicious."

"It's a strange one. The fire looks like it started in two spots. Not likely. Not 'less someone set it."

"I think Swartz smoked. Maybe he fell asleep."

"Could be. One of the fires started in his bedroom. Why the other one? It doesn't make sense."

"You said murder? You think someone killed Swartz?"

"I can't rule anything out. Those two flare points, and… "

"There's more?"

"It smelled like kerosene, and the smoke was black at first. Archie Drake called it in. Wood burns gray or brown."

"I don't know him."

"He's new to town. But two flare points, kerosene smell, and something else."

"What's that?"

"The back entry window was broken. Glass all over the place. That's where one fire started, inside the entry wall. Beats me how it started on the second story, too."

"What did Mrs. Swartz say?"

"I haven't talked to her. She's still in the hospital. Only a few burns but she's in shock. The kids were visiting their aunt, all 'cept Margie. Such a sweet girl."

Will stopped at Bennie's Bar before turning toward home. He was glad that no one else was there. "Bennie, pour me a Mineral Springs, will ya?"

"Sorry to hear about your house. Does Pederson know what happened?"

"It could be smoking in bed, but he thinks it's arson. He suspects me. Why'd I burn my own house?"

"Easy money, especially if you're behind in payments."

"I paid it off before the crash."

"I suppose he has to ask."

"S'pose so."

"Did you hear? Rich Turner saw Jesse the day before the fire."

"Are you sure it was Jesse?"

"Can't mistake a face like that."

Will didn't buy a second drink, but hustled Mabel toward home. Jesse was still around when the fire broke out? He remembered his horse barn fire, remembered that Jesse had wished his brothers would burn in Hell. Could it be Jesse? Louise and Mildred, the conjoined sisters, wouldn't think so.

At dinner Mary said, "Well, what'd you find out? Was it a cigarette?"

"Pederson doesn't know. He thinks it might be arson."

"Who'd want to burn our house down?"

"The state fire inspector'll come next week."

"Mark my word, it's that drunken Swartz. Liquor and cigarettes don't mix."

"Maybe so, Mary. Maybe so."

Will didn't say that Jesse was back in town. And he didn't tell her the fire chief suspected him.

"We can get by for a while, but those heifers were our future," Will said. "I always had hope, but now, I'm at the end of my rope."

"You're not at the end of any rope, my dear. We've got each other, and that's a tie that will never break. Not until the good Lord decides otherwise." She pulled him close. "We'll make it, Will. God has a plan. He'll never leave us."

He forced a smile. The feel of her body against him lifted his spirits. "Nothing else really matters, does it?"

Mary removed Will's plate from the table. She returned, placed her arms around him, then lifted his head and kissed him. "We'll work our way through this. We always have, and we will now."

20

Will's spirits rose when his efforts to get the cooperative off the ground moved forward with little resistance. Roberts had cooled down and was back, but Will knew that he was still an unenthusiastic participant.

The members unanimously elected a permanent board to guide their business, elected Will their president, and selected McPherson as second in command. Will knew he could work with McPherson and was pleased when the newly elected board granted his request to have their attorney file incorporation papers.

Then the process bogged down. The members couldn't agree on a compensation formula. The grade A producers agreed, in principle, to a blended reimbursement that overpaid the B producers, but they couldn't decide the blend. The A producers argued that their production expenses were higher because the government demanded more exacting standards for liquid milk than what they required for cheese or butter production. "We do more work, but they get more money," Roberts said. "How's that fair?"

Jackson McGried, the most obstinate of the B producers, said, "Then go to the government and get your money."

His grade B colleagues argued that the A producers had the best of it. They could sell milk for the table or sell it for butter and cheese. Earl Roberts was about to pull out again. What a headache, Will thought. Was it really worth the bother?

Finally the B producers agreed to a modest excess over the usual blended price, and a temporary peace was established. Will felt they were on track again when the board agreed to hire a manager.

Will chose carefully. Jacob Swinstein had been a bank president and had owned his own farm before the crash, and like so many others, he had been wiped out, but his good reputation survived the fate of his money. Will heard about him through Ron Tyler, the Willow bank president. Jacob knew farming and he knew management, but he hadn't made the necessary market contacts, so Will sent him to Milwaukee, Chicago, and Minneapolis to meet the buyers and wholesalers.

When the board set the entrance fee for each farmer, turmoil ruled once more. After many compromise attempts, Swinstein proposed a fee that pleased no one but was eventually agreed to—although not without an appropriate level of complaint. Running his own business was easier, Will thought.

Swinstein's wisdom served the small cooperative well, and they were soon selling their milk, cheese, and butter to the larger cities.

Then all hell broke loose. When in February 1939 the federal courts overturned the New Deal regulatory pricing system, the price of milk dropped and a summer drought in upstate New York devastated its farmers. These farmers from the northern counties called for a strike and were soon joined by others across the state. And this led to sympathy strikes and milk holidays throughout the Midwest. Milk haulers came under fire from union organizers, who didn't want milk delivered to non-unionized dairies in the big cities, and milk trucks were attacked and their milk dumped or contaminated. If the truckers persisted, they were assaulted. Milk and milk product movement plummeted, and local farmers found themselves with excess production. The grade A producers suffered the most, their milk spoiling in the barns. Will, like Roberts, Johnson, and the other liquid milk producers, saw his income diminish to a trickle. Once again, Roberts threatened to leave the co-op, and some of the members seemed to sympathize with him, but Will and others argued against it.

McPherson called a meeting to convince members to stay with the co-op. "We can't let these bad times break us apart," he said. "They won't last forever."

After a heated discussion, Roberts walked out the door, and others expressed doubts about the co-op's value in these difficult times. McPherson terminated their meeting with no agreement on how to move forward.

Will knew that he couldn't last much longer, not with such little income. The others increased their pig and sheep production, and turned their souring milk toward hog food. Will bought more chickens.

Roberts terminated his co-op membership and withdrew his money, and then he found independent distributors who'd buy grade A milk for more than the co-op's blended price. Will's argument—that if he would just stay with the co-op he'd eventually get a better price—hadn't persuaded Roberts, who said he had to feed his family now.

Roberts's withdrawal from the co-op angered some members who, at a hastily called meeting, voiced their displeasure. "If we let him go scot-free, it'll damage our ability to recover," McGried argued. "And if that little weasel goes, others will follow. We've gotta do something."

"What do you have in mind?" McPherson said.

"The same as the rest of the country. Make him pay for undercutting us."

"Are you suggesting a strong-arm approach?" Will said.

"You'd better believe it. And if the rest of you lily-livered ladies won't join me, I'll do it myself."

"We can't do this," Will said. "We can't resort to violence."

Will thought about his wedding day and his knees almost buckled. He could see Jesse under the water, like an inner tube with a pinhole that was slowly releasing its air, bubbles floating upward from his lips.

"You can't, I can," McGried said as he raced from the room.

McPherson stared after him. "I don't think he'll do anything rash," he said. "Not without the rest of us."

"Maybe McGried's right," George Snell said. "Maybe we should protect our interests."

Two weeks passed, and Will didn't hear from McPherson. Then the news flew through Willow Township like a prairie wildfire. The prior morning, Earl Roberts was bloodied and his milk was dumped.

Will demanded an immediate meeting. McPherson was hesitant but agreed when Will said he'd act on his own.

Will insisted that McGried be expelled from the association.

"We don't even know he did it," Henning said.

"Who else would have done it?" Will said. "He's the one who threatened violence."

"We don't know," Henning said.

"James, I thought you were my staunch supporter here," Will said.

"Will, I've always been behind you, but this is different. How can we expel a member for actions against a non-member? Roberts left the co-op. He's no longer our problem. This is the sheriff's job."

Will demanded an expulsion vote, but when it was held, McGried retained his membership.

"I can't remain in an organization that condones violence," Will said.

"Calm down, Will," McPherson said. "We don't want violence either, do we men?"

A murmur of agreement ran through the group.

"Do you pledge to keep this civil then?" Will said. "No more violence."

Once more, concurrence echoed through the room.

Will wasn't pleased, but he didn't know what more he could do. For all he knew some of these men participated in the assault on Roberts.

That night, Will visited his maimed neighbor. "I don't know who it was, Will. They were masked, but it's your fault, you know. You were so blamed certain this co-op could succeed. Are you still so cocksure?"

"I think so. I just don't know. I'm sorry, Earl."

He left the house and walked home leading Fanny Too. "How'd we get in such a mess anyhow, old girl?"

Fanny Too nickered softly.

"You understand, don't you, old girl?"

Will spent half an hour bedding and feeding his horses before he went into the house. He wanted to sneak off to his bedroom, but Mary met him at the door. Hair strands hung lose on her forehead and red moist eyes conveyed her distress. Will thought she was about to cry.

"I'm so ashamed," she said. "I blamed the poor man, and now he's dead."

"What? Who's dead?"

"Swartz. I was wrong about him."

"How's that?"

"It wasn't him after all." She pressed herself into Will's arms and leaned against him. "A rat did it."

Will pulled his wife close. They both needed the comfort, it seemed.

"Chief Pederson called and said the state inspector ruled that a rat started the fire," Mary said. "It wasn't a cigarette after all."

"It started in two places."

"It appears that a rat got into the house wall through a hole alongside the milk box that Swartz had started to replace. They found remains of the rat's nest near the entryway light switch. They figured that he gnawed the wiring, caused a short, and caught fire. Then he tried to get away by running up the side of a stud through the wall cavity, and attic debris above Swartz's bedroom caught on fire."

"What about the black smoke and broken window?"

"Pederson talked to Marie. She told him her husband came home late a week earlier and broke the entryway window to get in. That's probably where the rat got into the entry room."

"The kerosene smell?"

"Swartz stored kerosene on the back porch. He used it to burn leaves."

"You were wrong, my dear." He pulled her closer. "But I still love you."

"I wasn't all wrong. He was drinking when he broke that window."

"I stop for a drink now and then."

"I'd not rent to you either."

"Would you bed me?"

When Mary didn't object, Will took her in his arms and ushered her up the stairs.

⁂

During the next month, Arnie Johnson and two more grade A producers left the co-op. Will knew that some members thought his soft stance on Roberts had led to the others leaving. He worried about that, too, but he couldn't condone violence.

McGried tried to get him stripped of the presidency, but the effort failed.

Will couldn't understand why McGried and other B producers were against him. He remained a staunch co-op advocate even though he suffered more than most.

Will finished the night's milking later than usual because Ruby and Catherine were practicing for the community musical. Both had leading roles, and both were singing solos. Will was proud of his daughters, proud of their abilities, but he knew, because of milking, he'd not be able to attend their performance. Still, he smiled every time he heard them singing their songs while they worked around the barn. Although he loved music and played a little fiddle, he wondered where they'd gotten their fine voices. It must have been from Mary's family.

Mary went to bed, but Will waited for his girls to come home. He supposed it was his lot to be the family worrier. The clock struck ten. They were always home by ten. Will went to the window and looked through the moonlit yard and down the road. He paced the floor. After another fifteen minutes, Will went to the hall closet and took his jacket off the hook. He opened the door and was about to step onto the porch when he heard hooves in the distance, moving fast, too fast for Fanny Too. But as the sound got closer, he saw that it was Fanny Too.

Ruby jumped from the buggy before Fanny Too stopped. "Daddy, the fence is down. Our cows are on the tracks. We tried to herd them back, but we couldn't do it, not without help."

Will called for Teddy and grabbed the reins as he jumped into the buggy. "Get in, Ruby. Hurry."

"Daddy, I don't think the cows pushed the fence down," Catherine said. "It didn't look right."

"We didn't have time to look carefully," Ruby said, "but it looked like posts were pulled from the ground."

When Mary stuck her head out the door, Will shouted, "Get Petr. The cows are on the tracks. Send him down to the cow pasture as fast as he can get there."

Will urged Fanny Too on. He was glad to have the light of a full moon. They found the herd strung a quarter mile down the track, grazing as if grass along the tracks was their usual supper table. They didn't worry about trains, didn't worry about anything but sweet, green grass. If only life were so carefree and easy.

A train whistle screamed from behind the bluff.

"We've got to get behind them," Will said. "Catherine, take Teddy and go around to the left. Push those outliers towards the center so we can get them moving as a group. Ruby, come with me." He motioned ahead. "Hurry. The train will be here in a couple minutes."

The cows ignored them until Teddy nipped at their heels and Will and the girls shooed them back toward the pasture. And even then, the animals resisted leaving their newly discovered feast. They would hustle a few yards ahead of the pressure, then stop and eat from their bountiful banquet table.

When Petr arrived, Will waved him in Catherine's direction.

Catherine sent Teddy to round up a stray while she urged three other outliers toward the slow moving herd.

Ruby shouted and whooped at the cows as the train bore down from behind.

Will raced back to help Teddy herd the cow that lagged behind. "Get those cows off the track," he screamed toward Petr, Catherine, and Ruby. "Hurry, they'll not make the pasture in time."

The girls pushed the herd away from the rails, but Will hadn't yet reached the confused stray. He waved his hands as he ran down the track and shouted for the train to stop.

The engineer saw him. The whistle shrieked, black smoke poured from the funnel, and the rails screamed their protest at the drive wheels sliding along their shinning surface.

The cow panicked and lost ground with every step as she ran back and forth in front of the surging train. Teddy lunged at the last moment, then cow and dog disappeared behind the iron beast.

Will ignored the cursing engineer and raced around the engine toward where he last saw his dog. The cow, broken and bloody, lay dead on the ground. At first, Will didn't see Teddy, but he heard a weak whimper and saw a black and white tail protruding from under the cow's tangled legs. Will called Petr, who rushed to the dead cow, and together they grabbed her legs and pulled them off his dog. Teddy crawled from underneath, his tail between his legs.

"Come here, boy," Will said. "You needn't feel guilty." He reached to him and stroked his neck. "You did your best to save her."

Catherine and Ruby raced to their dog and engulfed him in their arms.

After another half an hour of herding, the cattle resumed grazing inside their pasture as if no grass could be better. Although Will was tired and distressed by the loss, he was glad that his cows were dedicated to their life's work, and happier still that Teddy wasn't hurt. He'd lose production, but he was lucky to have suffered just one casualty.

"Now, let's look at that fence," he said to no one in particular.

Will walked along the downed wire. Suddenly he bent to pick a post off the ground. "Ruby, Catherine, come here."

Will swung the butt-end toward Ruby. "This isn't broken. It was pulled out, now wasn't it?"

"I thought so," Ruby said. "Who would have done it?"

They walked to the next downed post, which wasn't broken either. Ruby said, "Why?"

Why indeed? Will thought. Who could hate him so?

He heard the train whistle in the distance.

Will's stomach churned at the thought that someone wanted to destroy his farm, destroy his family's future, but he didn't plan to report the incident to the sheriff or to anyone else. Maybe he should. Maybe it was cowardice to show restraint. He thought about Jesse. Had guilt over that terrible incident sapped his manhood? Couldn't he even defend his family? Grandpa would have grabbed his shotgun and gone looking for someone to shoot at. But too much hostility already existed within the co-op, and he didn't want it torn asunder. He was glad for the full moon while he spent the night repairing his fence.

❦

Then on September 1st, 1939, twelve days before Catherine's thirteenth birthday, a momentous event gripped the attention of every Iowa County resident. Sunday evening, Will heard the staccato beat of telegraph keys pulsing from his Crosley, and he knew it was Winchell time.

"Good evening Mr. and Mrs. America from border to border and coast to coast and all the ships at sea. Let's go to press. There's grave news in the world tonight. Hitler has invaded Poland, and the free world stands by unwilling or unable to defend this country that's been in turmoil since the end of the Great War."

Will understood that his co-op's little conflict was inconsequential when compared to the brewing cauldron of European antagonisms. He also knew that world conflict would benefit American farmers, just as it had during the last European war. Europe would no longer be able to produce its own food. All the more reason to hold his fledgling co-op together.

21

Mary paced the floor. "What did he say, Will. Can you get the money?"

Will had spent the morning at the Willow Community Bank. "Ron said that he'll give me money for a bull, but not enough to buy a registered one."

"Does it have to be registered?"

"That's the only way I'll know its bloodlines, know its breeding history. It's the only way I can be sure of improving my herd."

"How much more money do you need?"

"Another hundred. It might as well be a thousand though."

"I've got a little put away, but not that much."

"Maybe Finian can help."

"I never liked that man."

"You didn't like Swartz either."

Mary turned away.

Will called McCarthy that morning and was pleased when Finian responded, "Might be able to help. I know a registered bull for sale at your price. Just one problem."

"Oh?"

"He's a bit skittish, but he's got great bloodlines."

"Skittish?"

"Knocked a man down. Almost killed him."

Will knew that he couldn't be choosy—not if he wanted to improve his herd.

Sharon had graduated from high school the prior June, and now, in September 1940, she was going to school to become a teacher. Mary's insistence that her girls prepare themselves for careers was beginning to reap benefits. Sharon had graduated number two in her class and Ruby and Catherine were at the heads of theirs. And that high standing brought Sharon financial rewards. She had received a Ladies Auxiliary scholarship, an Elks Club scholarship, and the local 4-H club gave her money, too. But those awards wouldn't pay her full bill, so she searched for a job, and the baking skills that she'd learned from her mother produced results. The local bakery offered her the opportunity to come in after hours and help bake the next morning's pastries.

Will noticed that Catherine became more distressed as summer days passed and Sharon's departure was at hand.

Ruby discussed her career preferences with her older sister and was adamant. "I don't plan to be a teacher. I couldn't tolerate being around those little brats all day long." Will wondered if his middle daughter would ever want children of her own. Ruby said she'd rather be a doctor, or a nurse if they wouldn't let her in medical school. Sharon countered that she'd not want to be around sick people all day long. As far as Will could see, Ruby's only regret about Sharon leaving was the end of their lively conversations.

Sharon had continued to date Ed Meadows, and when he came to drive her away to school, Catherine grabbed her hand and clung to it all the way to the car. "I feel like a family member has died," she proclaimed as tears rolled down her cheeks.

"Don't be silly," Ruby said as she waved goodbye.

That just brought more tears, so Sharon opened her door, beckoned to Catherine, and hugged her one last time. "I'll come back home for vacations, and I'll bet Mom will let you come visit me during your school breaks. Why, Thanksgiving is only a couple months away."

As Ed turned the car and slowly drove down the driveway, Catherine looked so sad that Will began to feel despondent as well.

❖

Will slept little at night, arose before sunlight, and didn't get much work done. He had no gumption any more. It seemed that his get up and go had got up and went. Whenever he had a problem, he had the urge to go fishing. He believed he thought better with a fish pole in his hand. And lately, he'd spent lots of time at the water.

He walked through the field's stubble as he headed to his favorite spot on the river bank. The alfalfa and beans had produced better than Will expected these last three years, but what good was that if he had to spend his meager earnings replacing cows and fences? He didn't understand the unfairness of it all. Sure, everyone wanted to make the most money possible, but to resort to violence against him? Violence, to Will's way of thinking, should be avoided. It usually just created more problems. It seemed that men turned to violence when they weren't wise enough to find a better way. Maybe he was wrong. Maybe some men were just inclined to violence.

Will unhooked the gate's chain, but before he entered, he scanned the pasture to make sure his bull was nowhere near. There were plenty of cows to keep that bull busy, but this one had a reputation. He seemed calm enough, but bulls could be unpredictable. Will wasn't sure whether they thought someone who entered their territory was competition, or whether they became just plain ornery, but he wasn't about to take chances. When he saw his herd grazing at the far fence line, he entered the pasture and walked toward the river.

Will dug into the soft, cool soil until he found a fat, white grub that should look pretty appetizing to a big walleye. How an over inflated lump of flesh with minuscule legs could look appealing to any living creature was beyond Will's comprehension, but he learned long before to not guess about a fish's taste. For Will it was a matter of fishing with whatever bait he could find, and today, he'd see what grubs could do.

He got not a strike, not even a nibble. After he waited longer than his usual fifteen minutes, he moved downstream, and he kept moving, but without better results. He hadn't noticed how far he'd walked, but he didn't want to go home empty handed, so kept tossing his bait. He was maneuvering his line around a low hanging branch when he heard a noise behind him and a shout, "O'Shaughnessy, get your fat co-op busting ass offa my property."

He jerked his head around and saw Jackson McGried staring at him. "McGried!"

Will thought about his cow under the train's wheels. For a moment rage surged through him. He wanted to knock the stuffing out of this bastard. He whipped toward McGried, but then the vision of Jesse deep under the water flashed through his mind. "I was just thinking about the cowards we have in our association. How they strike at night and they stay hidden. I'd never have believed a farmer had it in him, but I guess every tree has some rotten apples." Will extracted his bait from between some branches and turned to McGried. "So you want me outta here, do you? This river bank's not your land anymore than my shoreline's mine. Anyone can fish these waters." He turned toward the river. "But I'll tell you what. I'll sit a spell and wait for my water to makes its way down. Does that suit you?"

Will sat on a fallen tree that jutted into the river and concentrated on his bobber.

"Strike at night? Have you lost all your marbles, O'Shaughnessy?" McGried took a step forward but retreated when Will popped back up. "Do your fishing, but stay away from the co-op. You've done enough harm already. Roberts was right about one thing. We don't need an outsider's advice." He turned and darted back toward his farmstead.

Now both sides hated him.

After another half hour, Will decided there was no sport in tossing his bait at the water, so he wrapped the line around his pole, picked up his gear, and strolled toward home. It was too early to milk, and his field work was finished. No sense rushing back to draw others into his funk, so he sat on a stump and pulled out his Meerschaum. He enjoyed the purity of the tobacco taste. No residue from past smokes or flavors from the bowl with a Meerschaum, but only a cool, dry smoke. Everyone should puff on a Meerschaum before they die. One never knew how many days are left.

Feeling better after finishing his pipe, Will returned to the pasture and checked his herd. Done feeding, they rested under the far maple, undoubtedly chewing their cuds and relaxing before another round of grazing.

Will strolled toward the lane. As he approached the gate, he noticed it had swung partly open. Could he have left it unfastened when he entered the pasture? Maybe one of the girls or Petr came through and forgot to close it. He looked around but saw nothing out of place, so he hooked the gate and strolled toward the barnyard. Behind the milk house he saw an animal's tail pop out to flick marauding flies. Petr must have let Annie out. She showed a slight limp that morning, so they held her back to keep an eye on her. She wasn't much of a producer, but he could ill afford to lose more cows.

He walked to the haymow. "Petr," he called but received no answer. He called again but still no response. He should be pitching hay down the chute about now. Maybe he was at the outhouse.

As Will walked toward the buildings, he thought he heard a stomping sound. The horses? Then he heard it again, this time a bit louder. It sounded as if it came from behind the barn, not the horse stalls. He walked toward the sound, but when he saw a pitchfork lying tines up, he turned away and bent to grab the fork. He had just begun to straighten when he heard a bellow and rushing hooves behind him. Will twisted and instinctively thrust the fork outward. Then he was hit by a charging mass of fury that left him sprawled on the ground.

The animal raced past him, turned, and assessed the damage from the far end of the barn yard. Will twisted toward his adversary. Stunned, he shook his head to clear the cobwebs, blinked his eyes fast a couple of times to remain conscious, but gasped when he took a deep breath. His chest hurt something awful. He thought he heard barking, but it seemed far away. He shook his head vigorously and tried to lift himself off the ground, but each time he moved his chest felt as if a sharp knife had been shoved between his ribs.

Will heard the bull's rage. It pawed the ground and bellowed, and he expected to be overrun again. He was afraid to move, but knew he must get to the gate, get out of the barnyard. Will lifted his head to look. A bloodied, enraged bull with a pitchfork hanging from his shoulder faced him. Teddy was there, too, standing between Will and his attacker. Feet spread, head low, his eyes demanded the larger animal's attention. A snarling Teddy was ready to act if the bull moved toward his master. The bull snorted once, twice. He circled, pawed the ground, and made a trial charge before retreating a few steps. Then he lowered his head and rushed at Will.

Teddy changed tactics. He sidestepped the surging animal and flew at the bull's hindquarters. He bit the animal's tail and swung like a pendulum when the three-quarter-ton bull whipped back and forth, trying to dislodge the one hundred pound dog. When the bull twirled, Teddy flew through space, lost his grip, and tumbled onto the muddy ground. Before the bull could react, Teddy, dirty and ruffled, returned to the attack, and once more, he leapt for the bull's tail.

Will heard the gate's hinges and the voice of his hired man. He looked up to see Petr and Catherine just outside the fence. "Don't come in," Will called. "I'll try to crawl toward you."

He started to move but recoiled from the pain. He caught his breath and whispered toward those outside, "I don't know if I can make it."

Petr unhooked the gate. "I'm going after him," he said to Catherine. "Keep the gate open so I can get through quickly, but if that bull heads this way, close it. Fast!"

Catherine nodded and opened the gate wider.

Then Will saw Ruby push Catherine aside and grab the gate. "Sis, run and tell Mom to call Dr. Snyder. I'll hold the gate."

Petr eased toward Will, but his movement caught the bull's attention. Ignoring Teddy, the bull started toward them. Teddy was ready. He raced to the front of the bull and leaped at his face, grabbed the ring in the bull's nose, and swung, his weight pulling the bull's head to the ground.

Petr grabbed Will's arms, and while Ruby opened the gate wide, he dragged Will through the opening into the yard. The grass felt good on his face. Ruby shouted, "Teddy, come here." Then the gate slammed and Will felt his dog's tongue on his cheek. He'd never appreciated Teddy's attention so much. As he slipped in and out of consciousness, he felt as if he he'd been run over by a steam roller.

22

Mary covered Will with blankets while Ruby swabbed the blood away and bandaged the cuts. Catherine sank to the ground. Better to sit down than fall down, Will supposed. They didn't need another casualty. He tried to push himself up.

"Stay there, Dad," Ruby said. "We're going to keep you here until Dr. Snyder examines you. We'll not take any chances."

Half an hour later, Will heard a car in the distance and knew it must be the doctor.

After checking Will carefully, Dr. Snyder moved him to his bedroom and proclaimed him fit to fish another day. "Plenty of cuts and bruises and a couple broken ribs, I think," Dr. Snyder said. "You'll be sore for a while, but I can't do much for those ribs other than to bind them tight."

Dr. Snyder turned to Will's middle daughter. "You did the right thing, Ruby, not moving him. He won't get around for a few days. Make him stay in bed and keep an eye on him. He may have a concussion. If he has severe headaches, vomiting, or seems incoherent, call me fast."

Dr. Snyder started toward the bedroom door, and then he turned back. "Oh, if I were you, I'd give that dog the biggest bone you can find. Maybe it's time to butcher that bull and give your dog his share."

"No chance of that," Will murmured. "I've got too much money in him. That bull's my future."

But today, that bull was almost his past. Keeping it was a big risk.

◆◆◆◆◆◆◆◆◆

The next morning Will heard car engines and looked through his bedroom window.

"Who'd be coming so early?" he said to Mary.

"I think that's Henning's car. And others, too."

But Henning didn't come to see him. Instead, he entered the milk house door. Three other cars stopped behind, and Will heard someone shout, "Can you use some help, girls?"

Will, propped up by a large down-filled pillow, lay in his bed. His body ached, even when lying still. And whenever he moved, his chest felt like he'd been skewered and roasted over a hot coal fire. Finian had warned him about that bull. He probably shouldn't have taken the chance with him. He repeated his old mantra, "It's no sin to be poor, just damn inconvenient." And dangerous, too.

He looked around the small bedroom. There was room enough for their double bed, a small chest, dresser, night stand, and chamber pot. And not much space between each, either. A month before, he'd struggled to move the new feather tick past the furniture to the bed. Will was glad that Mary had insisted they stay downstairs. He'd not have made the stairs today, not unless they'd carried him.

A few minutes later, Mary, Catherine, and Ruby entered his room. "Dad," Catherine said, "Mr. Henning, Mr. Roberts, and the others are doing our milking so that Ruby and I can get to school."

Will was surprised to hear that Roberts had come to help.

"I was afraid I'd miss my literature class," Catherine said.

"I wanted to miss old Gurdle's civics class," Ruby said. "Darn it. We'd have had a good enough excuse."

"Oh, Ruby, you just don't like Mrs. McGurdle."

"I don't like civics. Now, if it was biology, and we were dissecting a pig, I'd be there early."

"Ugh, I'd rather sit through Gurdle's class."

"Some of the men said they'd stop up as soon as they have a free minute," Catherine said. She turned to her mother. "And they said you're not to bring any food to the barn. You've got enough work with Dad down."

Will pulled a second pillow behind his back and groaned as he pushed himself to a sitting position. He took a few shallow breaths before speaking. "I grew up on the farm, and I never knew a farmer who'd not help his neighbor, but it's been so long that I'd almost forgotten." He winced and repositioned himself. "It's something we shouldn't forget, girls."

After school, Catherine and Ruby rushed into Will's room.

"McGurdle gave Ruby detention for being late to class," Catherine said.

"Catherine, you snitch, you weren't supposed to tell."

"How could you be so careless? You knew we had to get home to help with chores."

"I was only five minutes late."

"You know McGurdle. Five seconds and you catch—well, you know what."

"Yeah, you miss the bell, you catch hell."

"Ruby!" Catherine said.

"I talked her into letting me do the time after Dad gets back on his feet."

"How'd you do that? Nobody cons McGurdle."

"Daddy needs the help, don't you Dad?"

"Yes, but—"

Mary called up the stairs. "Girls, Mr. Henning is here. He wants to know how much ground feed you give each cow."

"We'd better get down there," Catherine called as she ran from the room.

⬥⬥⬥

Will settled into his down pillows and read the *Farm Journal*. He seldom had time to read anymore, so he'd make use of this opportunity. He'd learned more about farming when he lived in town, when it was easier to find time to read. After reading about a new hybrid blight-resistant corn, he dropped the journal and dozed for a while. He awoke when he heard laughter in the hallway, and before he could find a pillow to prop his head higher, Ruby and Catherine raced into his room.

"Daddy, you've never seen the likes," Catherine said. "Mr. Henning, Mr. Johnson, and Mr. Snell know their business, but you should have seen Mr. Tyler. It's good that Petr was there to help."

"Our banker is here?"

"What a hoot," Ruby said. "I've never laughed so hard as when I saw him pushing cows up the lane. He stumbled from fence line to fence line. Starting, stopping, and hopping to avoid the fresh cow pies. You'd have thought he was doing a new dance, and not very graceful either. If Petr hadn't shooed them along, I don't think we'd ever have got them in for milking."

"I bet Mr. Tyler won't help with the milking," Catherine said. "He's probably afraid to get under a cow."

"Daddy," Ruby said, "Jake McGried said his dad would come to help."

"Jackson? That'd be a surprise. He's not been too happy with me, you know—nor I with him."

"Do you think he pulled our fence over?" Catherine said.

"It's this co-op business." He adjusted his pillow. "People get riled when it affects their livelihood. They act different."

"He's just an old hypocrite," Ruby said. "That's what I think."

"That's not very nice," Catherine said.

"He'll hit you when you're down," Ruby said.

"You don't know," Catherine said.

"He did it. And Jake probably helped."

"Times are hard," Will said. "He's not a bad man, you know."

"Tell that to Earl Roberts," Ruby said.

"Girls, you'd better get to the chores. You can't let our neighbors do all the work."

Will thought about how his daughters were so different, how Ruby was quick to judge but Catherine not so ready to take offense. He knew that men weren't saints, but he'd give any man the benefit of doubt. At least until he was proven wrong. He preferred Catherine's way.

After milking, the girls reentered Will's room.

"Daddy, Mr. Tyler did help with the milking," Catherine said.

"Just protecting his investment," Ruby said.

"Don't be cynical," Will said. "Even bankers can be good guys. And I think Ron is."

"They don't have many friends these days," Ruby said.

"I suppose not," Will said.

"You should have seen him trying to get milk from a stubborn teat," Catherine said. "His thumb and forefinger weren't strong enough to stop the milk from pushing back into the udder, so every time he squeezed down, only a few drops trickled into the pail."

"And George Snell wasn't much better," Ruby chimed in. "Seems he's lost his touch now he has machines. Why, Mr. Henning milked a cow and started another before Mr. Tyler balanced his stool."

"Did you see Mr. Tyler take a lick from that cow?" Catherine said to Ruby. "I heard a crash and saw a stool fly into the gutter. I saw Mr. Tyler sprawled between two kicking cows, and then, with a loud clang, his pail flew across the aisle and into the calf pens. He cussed and said, 'These danged one-legged stools.' Except, he didn't say 'danged.' Then he gingerly lifted the manure-covered stool from the gutter and muttered, 'How can anyone balance on these?'"

Will suspected that tonight's work gave Mr. Tyler new respect for the farmers who did this twice each day. A new respect for the work his money supported.

━━━◆◆◆━━━

The next morning before milking, Jackson McGried slipped into Will's room.

"Will, I don't want you to think I've gone soft, but I wanted to help. We're still neighbors."

"Jackson, I appreciate your coming. I didn't expect it."

"Don't misunderstand. I still think you're a soft-headed old fool. This co-op business was your idea, and when we needed you to stand up for it, you folded like a paper bag in a rainstorm."

"If you feel that way, why'd you come?"

"I can't let a neighbor down. I think you'd do the same."

"I would." But Will wasn't so sure.

"That doesn't mean I agree with what you've said or done. I hope you understand that."

"I do."

"Your old bull probably knew how soft you are. He'd never have gone after a man with any backbone."

McGried strode from Will's room.

Catherine rushed through the bedroom door. "Oh, Daddy, I couldn't help but hear what that monster said." She threw her arms around his neck. "How could he say such things?"

"Maybe he's right, Catherine. Grandfather thought the same, now didn't he? It's the way I am. Maybe I am too soft." He shook his head vigorously to drive that thought from his mind. "I can't condone violence."

"I wouldn't want you hard-hearted." Catherine sat by her father, her head on his shoulder. "I love you just like you are, Daddy."

When she reached up to hug him, Will knew that a successful co-op wasn't the only thing worth living for.

124

After milking, Catherine brought Earl Roberts to the house. Before they entered Will's room, he heard his daughter say, "Mr. Roberts, just say hello. I know he'll be pleased that you've come to help. You must know how hard this has been for him. I worry about him, Mr. Roberts."

They entered the room together. "Daddy, Mr. Roberts wants to talk with you."

"Hello, Earl."

"How are you, Will?"

"I appreciate your help," Will said. "I don't know how I'd get along. We've missed you at the meetings."

"I was kinda harsh on you. Get too heated up."

"Earl, things are going to change. The war will decide that. And you'd better believe, we will be at war despite what most think. It'll be like the first war again. Prices will skyrocket. Someone has to feed the world, and we're all that's left. It's a terrible way to prosper, but mark my word, we'll all benefit. Won't you come back?"

"I don't know."

"Farmin's a hard way to make a living, but none of us would do anything else."

Will pried himself up, wincing. "I appreciate your coming today, Earl. I don't hold hard feelings against you. We all want to feed our families and maybe have a little left over to help make a more comfortable life. But I still believe that we have a better chance if we work together."

"I still have doubts."

"It'll improve, Earl. Just stick with us." Will reached his hand out.

Roberts squeezed Will's hand, shrugged, and, without another word, turned and strode from the room.

Will prayed things would turn for the better before everyone lost hope in their united effort.

23

Will sipped at his coffee.

Catherine played with her cereal. "Why is Ruby so stubborn?"

Mary heaped a ladle of cold fries on Will's plate. "If it's so wise, why doesn't everyone do it?" she said.

"I'm certain that soybeans are the wave of the future." He set his cup down. "Dr. Carver and others are developing new uses every year. Why, even Henry Ford's for them."

"What does Henry Ford know about soybeans?"

"He's making cars out of them."

Will heard a clamor on the stairs, and Ruby burst into the kitchen.

"No, he doesn't," Ruby said.

"Does, too," Catherine said.

"Whoa, girls," Will said. "What's this morning's dispute? It seems as if you're on a one-a-day plan. Sorta like those vitimins."

"It's that new boy in school. Catherine says he has eyes for me. No such thing."

"I haven't heard of a new family," Will said.

"He's up from Illinois to stay with his uncle," Ruby said. "A Kramer, I think."

"Larry Kramer? He farms downriver from Willow," Will said. "From Illinois?"

"Urbana," Catherine said.

"The government has a soybean industrial products laboratory at Urbana," Will said. "I read about it in the *Farm Journal.*"

"One or two eggs, girls?"

"Only one today," Ruby said.

"Worried about your weight, Ruby? He does have eyes for you. And you know it."

"Catherine!"

"Maybe I should visit that facility," Will said. "Not so far. I could get there in a day, and be back in three." He knew, with Petr away visiting friends in Iowa, this wasn't a good time to leave. "Why, I went farther south to see Dr. Carver."

"George Washington Carver?" Catherine said.

"A learned man if ever there was one."

"And a gentleman, too," Mary said. "A devout Christian."

"Dr. Carver's full of good ideas," Will said. "Did I ever tell you about my visit with him?"

"You talked to him?" Catherine said.

"I'd read the bulletins he's written for small farmers. 'Feeding acorns to farm animals,' and others, too."

"Is that why people turn their hogs out when the acorns fall?" Catherine said.

"And why they spend so much time mending fences," Will said. "He's written about alfalfa, soybeans, corn, poultry, dairying, and lots of things. But most of his work has been for the South, on cotton and peanut farming."

"What was he like, Dad?"

"He was the most humble man you could imagine. Dressed in an old, gray tweed suit with baggy knees, a beaten up cap, and a flower. He always had a fresh flower in his lapel."

"Most big shots aren't humble, are they Dad?"

"Well, they should be, Catherine. When things are going your way, you ought to have enough class to be humble, and when they're not so good, you ought to have enough sense to be humble."

"Was he a big man, Daddy?"

"Big in spirit. He talked softly, but you could hear a pin drop, even from the back of the room. He's won awards from all over the world. Even Stalin asked him to come to the Soviet Union to superintend their crops. But he wouldn't go."

"Were you near him?" Catherine said.

"As close as me to you. We talked about alfalfa and soybeans in the Corn Belt. How they enrich the soil. He's the one convinced me to grow them. He could be wealthy, but he refuses to make money on his ideas. He believes that food plants are a gift from God, not something to get rich on."

"We plant for money," Ruby said.

"I'm no Dr. Carver, and I'm sure you've noticed, my dear, we're not getting rich. Better get a move on. The cows must be bellowing for their hay."

The next morning at breakfast, Will fussed over his food. "I've been thinking about it, and I'd sure like to visit that Urbana laboratory. Would you come with me, Mary?"

"With Petr away, could the girls do the milking alone?"

"Sure we can," Ruby said. "Couldn't we, Cathy?"

Catherine nodded. "I wouldn't mind being alone for a while. My poetry anthology is about finished, and I've got to find a place to submit it."

"Maybe I could get James to come over and help. He milks his cows later, and if we start a bit earlier, he'd get back to his milking and the girls would get to school."

"Sharon is off school next week," Mary said. "I'll get her to come home and help. I'd like a trip, Will. It's been a long time. It could be—well, a second honeymoon."

Will noticed Ruby duck her head and snicker.

❦

Will bedded Fanny Too at the livery until their train returned three days later. When they drove up to the house, his girls were upon them before they stepped off the buggy.

"Oh, Daddy, you missed the excitement," Catherine said.

Will helped Mary down. "Tell me, what trouble did you and Ruby get into now?" he said. "But help us get the luggage into the house first."

Will could see that his girls hadn't spent much time doing housework. Unwashed dishes filled the kitchen sink and food littered the counter.

"When the cat's away the mice play," Mary said. "I expected better from my girls."

"Oh, Mom," Sharon said. "We were attacked in the night and Mr. Henning—"

"And I was scared," Catherine said.

"I wasn't," Ruby said. "Nothing bad happened. You two are just 'fraidy cats."

Will knew that Sharon could be a bit melodramatic and Catherine had a big imagination.

"Whoa," Will said. He turned to Ruby. "Let's go into the parlor and then tell me about it."

"You were attacked?" Mary said.

"We weren't attacked!" Ruby said. "Besides, Mr. Henning was here."

Mary frowned as she scanned the littered counters and sink. "Sharon, help me tidy this kitchen."

Will, Catherine, and Ruby slipped out of the kitchen and settled into the parlor's soft chairs.

Will knew that, under duress, Ruby was his most level-headed daughter, and she didn't seem much concerned. He opened the secretary and pulled out his Meerschaum and a pouch of tobacco. "I forgot my pipe and I'm dying for a smoke." He struck a match, held it to his bowl, and drew three times before he exhaled a spicy sweet aroma through the room. Will watched the smoke rings float toward the ceiling, and then slowly collapse into fluffy clouds that settled around the table and chairs. He settled back into his big horsehair chair. "Now, tell me your terrible tale."

Catherine began. "After we finished evening chores the first night you were away, Mr. Henning left for home, but he promised to come back the next morning."

"That night, when we were getting ready for bed," Ruby said, "we heard noises."

"It sounded like pounding on metal," Catherine said.

"We couldn't see anybody," Ruby said.

"The next morning we waited in the house until we saw Mr. Henning's car," Catherine said. "We told him that something awful happened during the night."

"You said that," Ruby said. "We didn't know what it was."

"You'll never guess what he found," Catherine said. "He found—"

"I'm telling this, Catherine," Ruby said. "He found our old wagon with a wheel knocked off. And—"

"Our cutter was up on the roof," Catherine said.

Ruby scowled at her sister.

"Mr. Henning said it must have been some kids," Catherine said.

"He thought it might be that Pickle McGraw and his gang," Ruby said.

"I heard they're real bad," Catherine said.

"And would you believe," Ruby said, "Mr. Henning came and slept in the barn that night?"

"Just in case they came back," Catherine said.

"And in the night, we heard a terrible racket out by the barn, but we didn't investigate because Mr. Henning had said, 'No matter what, stay in the house,'" Ruby said. "And when we went to the barn the next morning, we found Mr. Henning sitting with his shotgun across his knees and Pickle and two of his friends were doing our milking. And Mr. Henning said they'd come back to help that night. Better that than a visit to the sheriff."

"Pickle wasn't so scary," Catherine said.

"That boy has a reputation 'round here," Will said. "He has it pretty rough at home, they say. His father's one step ahead of the law." Will supposed that Pickle had heard he was away for a while. "But," Will paused, thinking about Henning and his shotgun, "I wouldn't worry about Pickle. We're not likely to see him around here again."

24

Will had laid the posts along the fence line the previous day, but he didn't have time to set them. Today he planned to finish this work and inspect his fields on the way home, so he had brought Fanny Too to the pasture.

Will raised his maul overhead and lowered it on the post with the power of sinewy muscles that had been forged by years of physical exertion. He thought about his father, and how he could set a post with three powerful strokes of his maul. Will couldn't do that, not unless the soil was uncommonly soft. He swung again and dust billowed into his face. He blinked rapidly to clear his eyes, spit out the grit, then pulled his handkerchief and wiped his face. This was the last post, and he was glad for that. He felt like he'd been hoisting full feed sacks all day, his muscles a flaccid mass. Two more good swings and the post was solidly in place. Will dropped the maul through a rope loop that he'd rigged to the saddle and mounted Fanny Too. He'd string the wire tomorrow.

Will looked up at fluffy clouds that, with a little imagination, seemed to morph into recognizable shapes. Will gawked at one that slowly drifted into a shape that looked like a fish lazing through a huge sky-blue bowl. He wished that he had more time to enjoy God's work, but he had to get home.

Mary had said that Marge Roberts was stopping over, but she wasn't sure about Earl. Will didn't know what to expect, but he tried to put it out of his mind. He inspected his fields as he rode toward home. He whispered to Fanny Too, "The Fourth of July's almost here and the corn's 'bout knee high. Best lookin' corn I've had yet, now isn't it?"

Fanny Too nickered her approval.

"Humid nights and a few thunder storms'll make a bumper crop."

Fanny Too snorted and tossed her head.

"You don't like storms, do you old girl?" He thought about Betsy and Mazy. "Makes me a bit nervous, too."

He rode alongside his oat field. The slender stalks' topmasts waved their greeting when a breeze picked up and blew through the fleet.

"See, Fanny Too, they're glad to see us."

Even though the grain wasn't mature yet, when he inhaled, he could smell its perfume in the air. "Filling out real nice, they are. They'll be golden-haired beauties within a month."

Fanny Too stretched toward the nearest clump.

"Oh, no." Will pulled her around. "Not yet, old girl. You'll get yours back in the barn."

Before his final push for home he detoured west toward his soybean field. When he dropped Fanny Too's reins and dismounted, she eyed the grass along the fence line but stood still when he called, "Whoa, old girl."

Will knelt and dug his fingers into soil that, near the surface, was as dry as a bag of flour. When he found a pointed stick and poked deeper, the ground felt cool and slightly damp. "There's a little moisture down there from last week's rains."

Prices had begun to improve, and although killing continued in Europe, it seemed that God was smiling on America. Will hoped they deserved it, but he knew their good fortune couldn't last.

After he watered, bedded, and fed Fanny Too her promised oats, Will checked to see that Petr had locked down the windmill blade, and then he walked to the house. Earl and Marge hadn't visited since he left the co-op. But it was good of Earl to help when he was flat on his back.

Will hoped that Earl would come along today. Maybe he knew about Will's efforts to expel McGried.

"Why, yes," Mary said, "I called Marge an hour ago, and she said they'd be over at eight. Said Earl'd come if she had to drag him by his ear, that this co-op business had stood between you two far too long."

Marge entered when Mary opened the door, but Earl held back until Will stepped forward and took his hand. "Come on in, Earl."

Mary motioned Marge to the counter. "I've just made a sponge cake, and I have some fresh strawberries and sweet cream. Would you help me dish them up?"

"It'll be the first strawberry dessert we've had this summer," Marge said. "It's Earl's favorite, you know."

"That's what I remembered," Mary said. "And there's homemade root beer in that pitcher over there." She pointed down the counter. "Why don't you men go to the parlor and get comfortable. We'll bring the food in a minute."

Will directed Earl to his big, soft horsehair. "Good of you to come, Earl."

Earl fished a corncob from his coverall pocket.

Will took his Meerschaum from his ash tray, and then he went to the secretary and reached for his Dunhill. "My favorite smoke." He handed the can to Earl.

Earl packed his pipe and lit it off Will's flaming matchstick. He took a long draw and sat back in his chair before exhaling. "Good tobacco." He drew again, exhaled, and cupped the bowl between his gnarled fingers. "Like old times."

They puffed in silence for a while.

Will wanted this to be a friendly visit, so he was leery about broaching the topic, but if he wanted Roberts back in the fold, now would be his best chance to discuss it when feelings weren't running high.

"We're both grade A," Will said. "We have the same needs and problems."

Earl exhaled smoke.

"I'd like you to come back, Earl?"

"McGried wouldn't stand for it."

"McGried's softening."

"I don't think I could sit with him. I still have the scars."

"Feelings ran too high. It got too heated."

"I know you stood for me. I appreciate that."

"Times are getting better." Will blew a smoke ring that first expanded, then faded as it floated across the room. "We've got to work together. Come on back."

"I'll think about it."

"Do that, Earl."

Mary and Marge brought four large bowls, each filled with a sponge cake that was covered with juicy, red strawberries and topped with fresh-ly whipped cream. "Don't wait until the cream sags. Start eating while I get the root beer," Mary said.

Earl took several bites, and then he took a deep breath and whistled softly. "Mary, I always said you made the best shortcake in Willow Town-ship. I've missed it."

"We've missed you," Mary said. She set the pitcher down and took Marge's hand. "It's good to have you here again. I don't know why we ever let these stubborn old coots keep us apart."

That night at bedtime, Mary said, "Do you think Earl will come back to the co-op? Do you think times will get better?"

"I think so." He reached for her. "On both counts."

"Do you think we'll be able to afford a few cows to replace those heifers?"

"I think we'll be in this war before we know it, before we're ready. I don't like to prosper from others' misery, but it's likely milk prices will go up. They did during the last war."

"What if we don't win?"

"Oh, we'll win it. We're a sleeping giant. But it won't be easy."

"Shouldn't we try to increase our production?"

"Probably so. And I will as soon as I get some money ahead. But I don't have it yet."

"I'll have to be more frugal," Mary said.

"I can't think of another thing you can do. You've already kept us afloat with your thrift." Will pulled her close. "And I do know how lucky I am."

◆─》》》◇《《《─◆

The day of the Fourth broke cloudy and misty. A bad omen, Will thought. He hoped that it would clear for the fireworks that night. And Senator Robert LaFollette Jr. was to give a noon hour address at the Willow square. Will knew that he'd speak against the war, against America entering to help England. He'd already opposed sending our liberty ships across the ocean. Will didn't like war, but he didn't like Hitler either. He was torn by indecision, but he wanted to hear all sides.

Will led Fanny Too to the house and helped Mary into the buggy as soon as she stepped out the door. After a thirty minute ride, they pulled into Willow's livery at eleven o'clock. He wanted to be sure that Fanny Too was watered, fed, and comfortable for the hot, muggy afternoon. They told the girls they could come to town, but to get home early so they'd be done with chores in time for the fireworks that night. Petr said that he'd seen enough fireworks in his homeland to last a lifetime, that he'd be happy to finish the milking.

As Will expected, the Senator railed against America entering the war. His words drew cheers from some and derision from others. James Henning, an ardent LaFollette supporter, shouted, "Give 'em hell, Senator."

134

Will didn't like the strident rhetoric on so important an issue. He knew that once in office, LaFollette, like most politicians, would find that it had been a lot easier to throw bombs than to catch them. Will's friends were split on war, even more than they had been over the co-op. Will wanted to avoid another heated argument, so he eased away from Henning and decided to avoid the Waterin' Hole, to stay on the park side of the street today. Besides, Mary had warned, "Will, I expect you to have a clear head for our trip home tonight." He was determined to appease her this time. He supposed he was a Neville Chamberlain at heart.

"Will," Henning called after him as he moved away, "come down to the Waterin' Hole. I'll buy you a drink."

"I'm eating ice cream today. I wanta stay away from the arguments. I got into enough hot water last time."

"Oh, come on. Just one."

"I'll buy you a cone."

"I'm having a Jameson. Sure you're not interested?"

Will started after his friend, but paused. "Better not, James."

Will confronted Mayor Stephens as he crossed through the square. "Mayor, I heard there's no parade today, how come?"

"The band director's out with the measles."

"Doesn't seem right, a Fourth of July without a parade." Will walked toward the green where several boys played football. Then he spotted Junkie Jenkins sitting on the curb banging a pail. That gave him an idea. "Junkie, go round up your friends and meet me down at the rapids, by the big willow tree. Tell them to bring pails and all the sticks they can find to bang with."

Will found Ruby and Catherine sitting under the village oak with some of their classmates. "Ruby, Catherine, follow me to the river." He rushed past. "Now hurry along, girls."

Ruby looked at Catherine and shrugged. "Why, Dad?"

"Bring your friends and meet me at the rapids," Will called back as he hurried down the path toward the willow tree.

He fished his knife from his pocket, sliced off several long, straight branches, and cut them into ten-inch lengths. Ruby, Catherine, and their friends arrived and watched intently as he crafted whistles from the willow pieces. Junkie, Jinks, and the younger boys came with their pails and sticks. Will handed the whistles to the older youth and told the younger boys to grab their drums and form a line behind the fife corps. He lifted a wooden baton that he had cut from a long willow branch, lined up his performers, and said, "Follow me, my fine fellows and ladies. Willow will not go without a parade this Fourth of July day."

They marched through town, and more youth joined the group. By their fourth go-round, most of the town's children were marching, and the adults stood at the streets and cheered them along. Henning and his friends watched from outside the Waterin' Hole and saluted as they passed. Afterwards, he told Will, "That's the finest parade I've seen since the university band came to town."

Later, Will rested under the oak and watched the boys play their football game. After a while, he ambled toward the action. He saw Jack Hornking talking to Billy O'Dell and hoped that Jack still didn't resent being let go. "Hey fellas," he shouted as they took a rest break, "can you use another player?"

"Not if you throw a football like you throw a baseball," Jack shouted back.

"My slow pitch?" Will laughed. "Naw, I'm a running back. Not very big, but I used to be fast."

"You can referee," Billy said. "We need a ref."

"Come on in," Jack said. "These guys can use a runner. Billy just doesn't want to lose his position."

Billy scowled, but Will laughed and said, "Don't you worry, Billy. I'll block for you."

The first down, Billy followed Will for five yards, but after the ball was grounded, Jack crashed into the pile, hard against Will's back.

"Whoa, young man," Will said, "this isn't a professional game, now is it? We wouldn't want anyone getting hurt."

Jack got up, wiped his hands on his trousers, and, as he walked away, said, "If you can't take it, don't play."

"Okay, Billy, let's get tricky," Will said. "When you get the ball, take a step or two toward the scrimmage line, then stop and pass it to me. Jack'll rush up to tackle you, and I'll run by him."

The play worked as Will hoped. He rambled down the lawn and past the picnic tables, the designated goal line. He felt like a kid again—except his back hurt.

"You'll pay for that, old man," Jack said.

Jack took the kickoff and brought the ball back to midfield. Will helped pull him down, but before Will could get off the ground, someone grabbed his leg and twisted hard. Will heard a pop, felt a sharp pain in his right knee, and limped to the sidelines. He knew that his football career was over.

Billy ran alongside and tried to prop him up. "I'm sorry, Mr. O'Shaughnessy. Jack did it. I saw him."

Jack Hornking took a step in their direction. "That's right, O'Shaughnessy. This time, it was my fault."

Will limped toward the tables where Mary was setting out their picnic lunch. She stood with a fork in one hand and a knife in the other, glared at him as he approached. "Will O'Shaughnessy, you promised you'd stay sober. I should skewer you." She pointed the knife in his direction. "Why, I've a mind to take Fanny Too and let you stumble home again."

"Mary." His hands pleaded his case. "I've not had a drop, I swear it, not a drop. I didn't go near the Waterin' Hole. I'm wounded, and I've come for your help."

Mary rushed to him and took him under the arm. "How'd you hurt yourself, Will?"

"I was playing football with the boys, and I—"

"Playing football?" She dropped his arm. "And you weren't even drunk? Who do you think you are, that athlete, Jim Thorpe? Who'll do the milking tonight?" Mary rushed back to the food and utensils.

Will limped to a picnic table at the far side of the green and flopped down. Should have gone to the Waterin' Hole with James, he thought. Mary would still be mad, but at least he wouldn't have gotten hurt.

25

The telephone rang.

"Will you get that, Mary?"

Mary lifted the receiver. "Yes? Right now? Thanks, Marge."

"Will, tune the radio to WGN."

Will knelt by the Crosley and tuned through the static until he heard, "Just one moment and the President will speak—The President of the United States."

Will and Mary leaned toward the radio's speakers. Will shivered as he heard Roosevelt say, "Yesterday, December 7, 1941—a date which will live in infamy—the United States of America was suddenly and deliberately attacked by naval and air forces of the Empire of Japan."

"I knew it," Will said, after the president's address. "I never thought we could keep out. But Japan? Pearl Harbor? The world will never be the same."

The telephone rang again. This time Will answered. "James?" His excited friend relayed the President's ominous message. "Yes, I heard. There'll be heck to pay now." Will had wondered, too, how soon there'd be a call for a draft. "We're lucky we don't have sons." Will agreed that Willow's little Methodist Church would be full this evening. "Better get there early. There'll be no empty pews."

Will reached for Mary and held her close. "We can't keep out of Europe either, not now. It'll be bad for our boys."

The call went out for a draft, but American boys volunteered in droves. Bobby McPherson. Snell's two sons. Ron Tyler's son. Jake McGried. Earl Robert's boy. Will was surprised when he heard that Jack Hornking joined the Navy. "Maybe he'll get some discipline there," he said. "But the price may be high." He hoped he wasn't being prophetic.

New and exotic names became commonplace in American conversation: El Alamein, Coral Sea, Savo Island, Kasserine Pass, Guadalcanal. Americans were enthusiastic about defending the nation, but the mood began to change when the casualty reports poured in. The first neighbor to go down was George Snell's oldest son, Franklin, in February, 1942 at the battle for Bataan.

Mary took her Bible and spent the evening with Lydia Snell. The next day, Mary had Catherine take a meat loaf and apple pie to the Snell's. When she got home, Catherine said, "It's so sad for George and Lydia, but they're thankful for their neighbors' kindness. Why, their tables were covered with food."

After the valley's first wave of patriotic volunteers, farmers entering the services slowed. The government recognized that someone had to produce food for the troops, country, and a dependent world, so draft boards were instructed to give deferments. Food prices skyrocketed, and Will began to see his small savings grow for the first time since the Depression began. All of America was at work.

Although rationing made life difficult, few complained. It was the least they could do to help those who risked their lives every day. Will told Mary that driving horses meant they didn't have to restrict their non-harvesting activities like the farmers who depended on fuel. "Aren't you glad that I stuck with Fanny Too? We don't have to show ration cards to keep her going, and she doesn't need rubber tires."

Will wasn't so sanguine about his sweet tooth. With sugar rationing, he learned to tolerate molasses cookies and fruit desserts instead of his favorite cakes and pies.

26

April 15, 1942

Will charged from the tool shed. "Catherine, have you seen that axe I bought last week? I put it inside the door, but it's not here."

"No, Dad, I haven't seen your axe."

"It's my new hickory-handled, double-bladed axe. Cost me five dollars."

"Where'd you last use it?"

"I haven't used it. I put it right inside the door."

"Did you ask Petr?"

Will rushed toward the house while Catherine turned toward the horse stalls. She hollered after him, "Dad, I'm going to take Fanny Too for a ride. We need the exercise."

Will knew that Catherine loved her time with Fanny Too, and he understood the feeling. "Be back by lunch. I want you and Ruby to shell corn this afternoon."

"Okay, Dad," Catherine called as she dashed toward the barn.

Will hurried toward the house to find Petr, but when he swore that he'd not seen the axe, Will turned to Mary. "Have you seen my new double-bladed axe?"

"Now what would I be doing with a double-bladed axe? I haven't seen it since you put it in the tool shed."

"That's what I thought, but it's not there."

Will seethed as he reached behind the crosscut saw for his old single blade axe. Having depleted his past winter's wood supply, Will decided it would be a good time, while the weather was still cool, to begin cutting for next year. He planned to spend the morning splitting logs that he'd already cut into stove length pieces. But his old axe was so dull that he had to sharpen the blade. "Who would have taken that new axe?" he muttered as he swung at the first log and winced when the blade stuck in the splintered wood.

By noon, worn to a frazzle, Will dropped the axe and headed toward the house for lunch. "Mary, hasn't Catherine returned yet? I told her to come back and help Ruby shell corn."

"I haven't seen her." She set a plate of potato salad and sliced ham in front of Will.

"That girl. She gets on Fanny Too and forgets everything. But it's not like her to be late when I've asked for her help." He piled ham on bread and spread some horseradish and mustard. "Are you sure that you haven't seen that axe?"

"If you'd bought me that carving knife, I wouldn't have to steal your tools." She flipped her dish towel toward Will's head.

After dinner, Will started back to the woodpile but remembered that he had planned to get Ruby started shelling corn.

"Where's Catherine?" Ruby said.

"She went riding." Will handed her the Little Speedy corn sheller. "I'll send her here as soon as she gets back."

A half an hour later, Catherine found her father and dismounted Fanny Too. "Dad, I'm sorry. I get out in the meadows with the birds, the butterflies, the small animals and I lose all sense of time."

Will wanted to be stern, but he couldn't chastise his playful daughter. He shook his head and puckered his face into his best imitation of an angry father. He wished that he had more time to ride, too. He pointed toward Ruby who leered at them as they talked. "Go help Ruby shell corn. She may not be so understanding."

◆◗◗◗◗◗◗◖◖◖◖◆

Catherine worked faster than usual all morning. Will knew she must have something on her mind. She didn't even carry on her usual conversation with Ruby while they scrubbed the cans and pails. He heard Ruby ask Catherine if she was angry because she had snatched the last piece of bacon, but Catherine answered, "No, Ruby, I didn't want that bacon anyhow."

"Well, you sure aren't very friendly this morning."

"I want to get the work done." She threw the sponge down and grabbed a pitchfork.

She had thrown half the soiled straw into the spreader before Ruby joined her, but Ruby didn't ask more.

Catherine finished the calf pen, raced out the side door, but took the pitchfork along. Will supposed she was headed to the loft to throw hay down the chute. She usually didn't do that until just before night milking. What demon possessed that girl today?

Then at lunchtime his youngest daughter caught him in the entryway. "Dad, I've got all my work done. Can I take the afternoon and go riding?"

Will wasn't surprised, but it seemed she was taking Fanny Too out more often than usual. "You're spending lots of time with that horse, now aren't you? I think your sister feels neglected."

"I just have to get away from Ruby, be alone for a while. And Fanny Too needs the exercise."

Will knew the feeling, and he supposed it did Fanny Too some good. She'd been inside all winter. "A little fresh air will be good for her. Get back before milking. You better not cross Miller's stream. There's lots of water flowing off the bluffs."

Catherine turned and ran toward the horse barn.

What could be wrong between his girls? He seldom saw them have serious disputes, not Catherine and Ruby. Will sighed. He supposed it was just a stage that teenagers go through.

When Catherine didn't return for dinner, Will called Ruby from her room. "Whatever is wrong between you girls? She should be back by now."

Ruby looked worried, too, but without a word, she brushed past him to the dinner table.

And when Catherine still wasn't home for night milking, Will grabbed Ruby's coverall strap and spun her around. "Ruby, tell me, are you girls having a fight?"

"I think she feels guilty."

"Guilty, why should she feel guilty?"

"I promised I wouldn't tell."

Will turned to his wife who busied herself over the sink. "Mary, talk to this girl. Something's wrong between her and her sister. What shouldn't you tell, Ruby?"

"Tell us," Mary said.

"I can't." Ruby pulled away. "You wouldn't want me to break a promise, would you?"

Mary took Ruby's hand. "Catherine should be back by now. Do you know where she went?"

"She didn't tell me."

Will knew the girls weren't talking before Catherine left. "I'm worried about her. Do you know anything?"

"Maybe she went to the county land, east of Miller's stream."

"I told her not to cross Miller's stream."

Ruby stomped her foot and looked defiant. "I promised."

"This may be serious," Will said.

"She told me she found her puppet man."

"Who?" Mary said.

"Remember that man we saw at Heinzelman's circus when we were little?"

"At Hinton?" Mary said.

"That was my brother Jesse," Will said. "What's this about the puppet man? Tell me, Ruby."

"He lives in an old shack on the county land. Catherine's been stealing food from the root cellar and taking it to him."

Mary grabbed her arm. "Why didn't you tell us, Ruby? Anything could have happened to that girl. Alone with an older man. Will, do something." She turned back to Ruby. "If anything happens to that girl, I'm holding you responsible."

"I told her you'd be angry, but she said he was a poor, injured war veteran who needed help." Ruby pulled away and ran up the stairs, but she turned back at the top landing and shouted down. "I told her she shouldn't be stealing." She started down the hallway but shouted back, "You always helped war veterans. Why shouldn't she?"

"Will, you've gotta find her. You said that Heinzelman sent Jesse away because he molested little girls."

"Mary, he didn't… " but it was no time to quibble now. Will rushed toward the horse stalls to get Lyda, but before he reached the barn, he heard hoof beats in the distance and saw Fanny Too lumbering down the lane toward the house, but with no rider. He ran to her and saw that she was mud covered. Will pulled himself up. "Let's go, Fanny Too," he called as he dug his heels into her side.

When he reached the end of the lane, he turned toward the marsh and hadn't gone another hundred yards when he saw them. Jesse staggered toward him with Catherine over his shoulder. Will slapped Fanny Too's neck. "Move it, old girl."

He hollered at Jesse, "What happened? Is she okay?" He could see they were both soaked and muddied.

"Will, get her to a doctor. She almost drowned."

Catherine moaned as Will and Jesse laid her across Fanny Too's withers, and Will grabbed her mane and pulled himself up. "Follow me to the house," he shouted back as he turned Fanny Too and kicked at her ribs. "Move it, Fanny Too. We gotta get this girl home."

Fanny Too seemed to know that speed was urgent. Will hadn't seen her move so fast since she was a colt. He balanced Catherine between his arms and held onto Fanny Too's mane. Mary must have heard them coming; she held the gate open when he got there. He pushed Fanny Too through and directed her toward the house. Petr ran from the house but pivoted back inside when Will shouted, "Call Dr. Snyder. Get him out here right away."

By the time he lifted Catherine off Fanny Too, Mary was by his side. "What did Jesse do?"

"She's been in the water and she's cold as an iceberg. Get some blankets."

Mary didn't protest further but held the door for Will to rush Catherine through. He took her to the divan where Mary removed her wet clothes, while he heaped blankets on her, then rubbed Catherine's arms to restore circulation.

They continued to work over Catherine until Will heard Ruby call, "Puppet Man's here. He's pacing outside the door like a mad man."

"Let him in," Will called.

"Will," Mary said, "do you think we should?"

When Catherine muttered, "Puppet Man? Please bring him here," Will called again, "Ruby, let him in."

Catherine smiled and held her hand out when he entered the room. She turned to her father. "I want to sleep, Daddy. I'm so tired."

"I don't think she should sleep," Jesse said. "One of our circus riders got kicked in the head, and they wouldn't let her sleep. Try to keep her awake."

They continued to work over Catherine, and they talked nonstop, did their best to keep her from dozing.

Mary talked as she paced back and forth in front of her on the sofa. "He should be here by now," she said.

"He said that he'd come right out," Petr said.

"He's slowed a bit, and he doesn't drive so fast anymore," Will said.

"He must be sixty years old, now, maybe more. He'll get here soon, you can bet on that."

When Dr. Snyder arrived, he rushed to the living room. "You fellas wait in the other room while I examine this young lady."

When Mary turned to leave, Dr. Snyder said, "Stay here and help me."

Will led Jesse to the kitchen. "I'll get some coffee," Will said. "Where'd you come from?"

"Fanny came alone to my shack."

"Fanny?" Jesse didn't know that Fanny was gone, Will thought.

"When I saw Fanny covered in mud, I knew she'd been in the water and I feared the worst. I'd seen the high water and knew the stream couldn't be crossed below your bean field. The current raged down there. But I didn't know that Catherine would come today."

"Where?"

"She's been visiting since last fall."

"You've been near here since last fall?"

"Even before, but I told her not to tell."

"Jess, it's been years. Why now?"

"It's a long story."

Will left the table and peeked into the living room. Dr. Snyder was examining his daughter but she seemed to be moving. He turned back to Jesse. "How'd you find her?"

"If she went into the water where she usually crossed, I knew she'd be swept downstream, so I started at the river and then worked my way up Miller's stream until I saw her." Jess lowered his head. "I was afraid of what I'd find. Afraid it was too late."

"You saved my little girl."

"At first, I thought she was gone, but my prayer was answered when she reached out to grab my hand. That girl's got some grit."

"Why'd you come back, Jess? How'd you know we were here?"

"Went to the Springs first. Bennie said you'd moved."

"Why now?"

Will tried not to be obvious. He paused a moment to scan his brother's terribly maimed face—the left side constructed of tin with a painted eye overlay, the right side with a sunken cheek and a depressed jawbone. Will hoped that the injured from the current war were treated better. He felt relieved when Jesse didn't seem to notice his momentary attention.

"I liked the circus, but small circuses are dying. I wandered around a few years but thought it time to come home." Jesse lifted his cup, sipped, then smiled. "Good coffee." He licked his lips before continuing. "I live in that fishing shack. Over east on the county land. No one ever comes there, no one but Catherine."

"She didn't tell me."

Jess sipped at his coffee. "I didn't want anyone to know. Not yet anyhow."

"You're her uncle."

"She doesn't know that."

"I came looking for you," Will said. "I went to see Heinzelman's in Cedar Rapids. You'd already left."

"Did you meet Mildred and Louise?"

Dr. Snyder called from the living room. "You can come in now. I think she'll be okay." He pulled a blanket tight to Catherine's chin. "Keep her warm and let her rest. This young lady is plumb tuckered out."

Mary left when Jesse walked into the room.

Will rushed to Catherine's side, but Jesse held back. "Can we move her upstairs, to her bedroom?" Will said.

"Sure," Dr. Snyder said, "if she'd be more comfortable."

"No, Dad, not yet." She smiled toward Jesse. "I want to stay here."

Will grasped his brother's hand and pulled him to the divan. "You should know, young lady, your puppet man is my brother. He's Uncle Jess."

"He's my uncle?" Catherine reached to touch Jesse's hand. "Even back then when I was only seven years old, I knew that Mr. Heinzelman was wrong about you. But I didn't know you were my uncle." She smiled toward Jesse. "Come live with us, Uncle Jess?"

Jesse smiled at Catherine, stammered, "I don't think so," then turned away.

Will felt relief when Jesse excused himself and stepped out the door. He remembered the last time he'd housed Jesse—the bloodied Mrs. Vanevenhoven and Mary's lost promotion. He didn't want to face that again.

Catherine recovered rapidly and was soon helping with chores. One morning she caught her dad in the loft after he finished throwing hay down the chute. "Why wouldn't Uncle Jesse come stay with us? Is it Mother?"

"Before the war, Catherine, Jesse frightened Mother when he was drinking. You know how she hates liquor. But the circus ladies, Mildred and Louise, said he doesn't drink anymore. And Mother's been sympathetic since he came home with those awful injuries. It's Jess who's reticent. I don't think Mother would object to his coming here."

"What happened to him, Daddy?"

"His face got shot away in the last war. They fixed him as best they could."

"Well, I think he should live with us." She stood a bit straighter and set her jaw. "I'm still going to help him."

"Could I keep you away?"

"Uncle Jess saved me twice."

"He's mighty fond of you. I can see that."

⦁》》》⦁⦓⦓⦓⦁

In June news came that Jake McGried was killed when the USS Yorktown was sunk by a Japanese submarine during the Battle of Midway. Mary packed food, placed a Bible in her bag, and, once more, left on a mercy mission. She called home at nine o'clock to say that Jackson and Eleanor were so upset that she thought it best to stay the night. And to Will's surprise, she said that Marge Roberts called, and soon after, Earl Roberts and Arnie Johnson showed up to do Jackson's evening chores. And they'd come back the next morning, too.

"I'll come over after I finish milking," Will said.

Will placed the phone in its cradle, slumped into his horsehair, and lit his Meerschaum. How small their co-op problems seemed now.

War news continued to fill the airways, casualties mounted. Will began to avoid the broadcasts. But soon, he felt compelled to listen, no matter how awful the news. "I think I'll tune to Gabriel Heater," he said to Mary. "He always has something bright to report."

And Heater didn't disappoint. As usual, he opened his August 10th, 1942 broadcast with an optimistic story. "Ah, there's good news in the world tonight. Our Marines have landed on Guadalcanal. Victory will soon be ours."

A week later, the good news turned bad when Earl and Marge Roberts received a telegram announcing that their Jimmie died in that battle.

Mary and Will left immediately for the Roberts' house. Jackson McGried was there when they arrived. Marge said that Jackson told Earl, "Stay with Marge tonight. I'll milk your cows."

Will joined Jackson in the barn.

147

"I never thought it would come to this," Jackson said. "I couldn't know how soon our boys would be gone." He slammed a pail against the wall. "How could I have taken my anger out on Earl? I'd thought that Jake's death was my punishment, but now—if I'd only known."

"Jackson," Will said, "there's many a time I'd have done things differently." He picked the pail out of the gutter and walked to McGried, placing a hand on his shoulder. "You're not responsible for anyone's death." Will remembered how he felt when Esther Nesbitt was killed. "But—you try to do better the next time." Will grabbed a pail from the milk house. "Let's finish these cows."

27

ill hurried through his chores. Reverend Rosner would be here by ten o'clock and the ceremony was scheduled to begin at eleven. Petr had begun milking, but Will wasn't quite finished spreading hay down the manger. The cows in their stanchions were bawling for their breakfast. He'd given Ruby and Catherine the morning off so they could decorate the living room, dining room, and parlor in preparation for the wedding.

Sharon, who was now twenty-one years old, had completed her teacher preparation and would now go to Ed Meadow's farm home near Logan Junction where she had taken a teaching position just outside of town. Ed had faithfully stuck by Sharon during her two-year teacher training at Platteville State Teacher's College.

Yesterday, he dutifully drove the fifteen miles from his home to Ashley Springs to pick up Thomas and Gertrude, then another eight miles to Hinton to get Grandma Tregonning. From there it was almost an hour drive down to Willow. Sharon was getting a good man.

The milking finished, Will and Petr hustled toward the house and slipped in the back door. "Mary said she'd hang our suits in the downstairs bedroom," Will said. "You go on and start dressing. I'm going to peek into the living room. The girls have been decorating the last two days."

Will knew that Petr was nervous. He told Will that he was honored but surprised when Ed asked him to stand up for him and to present the ring. He'd said, "I've never been in a wedding before."

Will had seen Ruby and Catherine picking roses from Mary's flower garden, and he supposed there'd be vases of yellow flowers placed throughout the living and dining room, but he was astounded to see the effort his youngest daughters had put forth to please their sister. In addition to roses placed strategically throughout the rooms, they had built a chicken-wire arch from floor to ceiling around the large doorway that separated the living room and parlor, and every square inch of that chicken-wire was filled with yellow roses. Will knew this arch must have been Catherine's idea. His Ruby would never have considered a thing so frivolous to be worth the effort. When Catherine had waxed eloquent about the splendor of a grand wedding, he'd heard Ruby say, "I'm going to elope."

When Will heard his mother's voice in the hallway, he ducked toward the back bedroom before Gertrude caught him and demanded he do some work. He remembered her frenzied activity and demands on the day of his own wedding, so many years ago, now. And she hadn't slowed down one bit.

Will had been surprised when Frank had called and said he'd be there. Maybe Frank was mellowing as he grew older. But he probably only wanted a break from his work. At first, he regretted that Jesse wouldn't be there, but then Will remembered the pain that Jesse had inflicted at his and Mary's wedding.

Reverend Rosner, Ed, Petr, Ruby, and Catherine stood under the rose-covered arch. Mary stood by the piano in the living room. And she was beautiful in her new dress. Although the hourglass figure of her youth had turned pleasingly plump, she looked splendid in her new red and yellow rose-flowered dress that complemented the yellow roses all around them. And it was the latest style. The padded shoulders extended past the edges of Mary's shoulders. The sleeves were puffed and gathered at the top but flowed downward to within an inch of the elbows. Her dress had a sweetheart cut neckline that stopped above her cleavage. The waistline was high, but unlike her older dresses, this one was daring: when Mary reached high, Will caught a glimpse of her kneecap.

He hadn't told her that he'd been saving his loose change to buy the dress that she'd deserved for so long. When Sharon announced the wedding, Will was still short money, so, unknown to Mary, he sold a young bull calf a bit prematurely; a calf that he thought would bring prime dollars in a month or two. With that money he'd had enough to buy Mary the finest dress in Willow's small department store.

Mary lowered herself to the piano stool. That was Will's cue, and when she began playing "Here Comes the Bride," he took Sharon's arm and guided her across the living room to those who waited under the flowered arch. The minister said the necessary words. Petr fumbled through his pocket, found the wedding ring, and handed it to Ed, who placed it on his bride's finger.

By the time Reverend Rosner said, "Now kiss the bride," Catherine looked so flushed and teary-eyed that Will thought she was going to swoon right there under the flowered arch. But she regained her composure when Mary began to play, "Blessed Be the Tie that Binds."

Before Mary had finished the last note, Gertrude burst through the kitchen door and demanded that all take their place at their name cards on the tables.

That night, after Mary had removed her new dress, she held it up and admired it once more. "Will, you can't know how much I love this dress." She reached for him. "But I love you far more. I couldn't have a kinder husband."

Will wished that he had more to bring to their marriage. But he didn't miss that calf—not one little bit.

○─**28**─○

June 2, 1943

Sharon lived with her husband, Ed, on his farm outside Logan junction. Ruby had graduated number one in her high school class and held that same position while attending nursing school in Milwaukee.

Sharon came home. Ruby came home. Thomas and Gertrude were there. Even Frank came. But Jesse was nowhere to be found. Today, Catherine would graduate from high school, and while everyone else lunched on chicken and ham sandwiches, potato salad, three-bean salad, orange Jell-O with grated orange peels, coffee, root beer, and milk, the girl of the hour hadn't made her appearance at her party.

Will knew that she was hidden away in the hayloft, practicing her valedictory address. And he knew that she was as scared as a rabbit with a fox on its tail. He slipped out the door and headed toward the loft.

"Catherine, are you up there?"

At first she didn't answer, so he walked up the ramp and stood a moment inside the loft, adjusting his eyes to the dim light. "Catherine," he called louder.

And then he heard a weak, "Dad?" from the far side of the loft, behind a stack of loose hay. Not knowing what he'd find, he walked cautiously in that direction. He knew this was hard for his youngest daughter, and he didn't want to embarrass her by catching her crying. And when he saw her, he saw that she was quivering and flushed, but she wiped her eye and attempted a smile when he reached for her hand.

Catherine took his hand and pulled him to the hay alongside her. "Dad, I'm so scared. I should have flunked my last civics exam. Then maybe Liz Roberts would have to give this talk. We were tied going into the semester."

"Have you memorized your speech?"

"I knew it perfectly last week. But the closer it gets, the less I remember. Right now my brain's so scrambled I can't think of a thing."

"You can use notes, you know."

"What I'd like is for Ruby to do it for me. She never missed a word in her address last year."

"Ruby can't always be your backbone."

"I know, Dad, but she's got enough for the both of us. I try to think about this fall, when we'll be together in nursing school." Catherine smiled for the first time that day. Then she frowned again. "I've got to get through this first."

"Just look at me the whole time, not anyone else. I'll be so puffed up that you can't possibly be scared." He rose, lifted his daughter off the hay, drew her close, and smiled his biggest smile. "You can't know how proud I am of you, my dear. Remember, keep your eyes glued on this big, old, ugly mug. Now, if that doesn't make you smile—"

When she pulled away he knew she wasn't convinced. He was about to remind her that this was the same advice he'd given her that day so long ago when she and Ruby sang "Playmates" at the Ashley Springs annual talent show. Then he remembered that day turned out bad.

"Dad? Is Uncle Jesse here? He said that he'd come."

Will took Catherine's hand and shook his head no. "I suppose he thought Frank might be here. I'm sure he wanted to come."

"I knew it would be hard for him," Catherine said. "The whole village will be there."

That night at the graduation ceremony, Will and Mary sat in the front row. Will smiled his broadest, most enthusiastic smile, and when Catherine faltered on a line, he furrowed his brows, wiggled his ears, and stuck out his tongue. Catherine stopped for a moment, stared at him, laughed at his antics, and then continued on with only a few stumbles.

Afterwards she grabbed her father's hands, pulled him close and whispered in his ear, "I'd never have made it if it wasn't for your big, old, ugly mug. But it was the most beautiful one in the house tonight." She kissed him on the forehead. "Thank you, thank you, thank you. I love you, Daddy."

Will felt warm all over. It was moments like this that made the hard times bearable.

29

Will slept little that night. He tossed and turned, thinking about his brother. Finally, he decided that he had to find Jesse, had to help if he could. It was time to throw out the old, soiled straw and lay down fresh bedding.

The next morning he saddled Fanny Too. Catherine had told him about the shack, and he turned in that direction, but he was nervous. Jesse had been gone more than ten years. And they had little opportunity to talk that day last spring when he brought Catherine home. After so long, Will didn't know what to say. Catherine had continued to visit, and from what she had told Will, Jesse was a different man. Will wasn't so sure, though. He remembered their past.

Will didn't mind that Fanny Too moseyed along. He loved riding his fields. Will smiled and tried to mimic the bubbly cry of a bobolink that floated toward him from the nearby meadow. Then he grabbed the saddle horn when a quail flushed from under Fanny Too's hooves and startled her.

The sun shined warm. A brisk breeze chilled the spring air. Will guided Fanny Too through the cow pasture to where the stream ran fast over the gravel bed that old man Barnes had laid down so his cows could cross to the other side. It was farther this way, but Will wasn't keen on an early morning bath.

Catherine said that Jesse's shack was nestled in the hardwoods east of the marsh, so Will turned Fanny Too toward the river and rode along the timber's edge until he reached the water, staying in the sun for as long as possible. How could a fifty-degree spring sun feel so warm, but the same temperature in August feel like winter?

Will knew Jesse wouldn't have come to the house if it hadn't been for Catherine. After all these years, would Jesse still want revenge? Will rode in silence until Fanny Too neighed. "You think that I'm neglecting you, don't you, old girl? Or do you know something that I don't?" Will flicked the reins. "You don't think he'd hold a grudge this long, do you, Fanny Too?"

Fanny Too nickered when she saw the shack ahead. That didn't surprise Will. Fanny Too always greeted her friends. And when he saw the crudely written no trespassing sign, Will was glad that Fanny Too called out their presence, thinking it best not to catch his brother unawares. He looked around, but there was no sign of Jesse. Darn, Will thought. He wasn't sure that he could get himself in the right frame of mind again. No matter, probably a fool's errand anyhow.

Will dismounted, snubbed Fanny Too to a sapling, knocked, and, when there was no response, he opened the creaky door. He could see that the frame and sills had been repaired, but not by a master carpenter.

When his eyes adjusted to the dark, he saw that the room was lit by one small window on the south wall. No electricity, no icebox, and no water pump. Jesse probably kept warm enough with the small potbelly stove in the middle of the room and a smaller cook stove at the wall. Not so different from Mary's kitchen. A face cord of split wood slabs insulated the shack's north and west walls. Although he didn't have much to work with, Jesse prepared well. And he kept it tidy. Everything seemed to be in place.

Will stepped out into the sunlight and unhitched Fanny Too from the ash sapling. She didn't nudge his shoulder, and she didn't nicker her usual greeting. She shook her head with fervor when Will approached. Then he noticed that he had hitched her over bare ground but within sight of lush grass in an open spot in the woods that some Irishmen called a fairy ring. Will wasn't so naïve as to believe in fairies, but he could see that Fanny Too didn't think him very bright at that moment.

Will heard footsteps coming through the brush along the river. For a moment, he wondered if he should be there. For all he knew, Jesse might have a gun. "Hey, Jess, is that you?"

"Stay away from my house. Didn't you see the no trespassing sign?"

Jesse burst through the underbrush, his cane pole thrust forward like a lance, his stringer, full of fish, held like a sling. He stopped when he saw Will. "Oh, it's you. When I heard the horse, I thought it might be Catherine, so I rushed back. Out fishing." He stood the pole against the shack. "I see you've been inside."

Will looked back at the entry and saw that he had been careless. The door swung outward on misaligned hinges. "I thought you might be sick, maybe down in bed, so I looked in."

"Oh?"

Will knew that Jesse wasn't convinced. "Jess, whatever you might think, I am concerned. I always have been. Years ago, when Catherine said you were with the circus, I went lookin'."

"Is she okay?"

"She just graduated number one in her class. She wanted you to be there."

"I suppose she'll be leaving." Jesse lowered his head. "I'll sure miss her."

"You must know that she's fond of you. She wants you to come up to our house." Will reached out, but Jesse ignored his hand. "She's afraid for you alone down here."

"I'm okay. I feel at home with the animals. They'll look me in the eye and never flinch. Most people wouldn't notice something like that, would they?"

"Don't you hunt them?"

"You think I'd have a gun? I like the animals. Better friends than most humans. I'll admit, though, I am gittin' tired of eating fish."

"I'll send some provisions down with Catherine."

"You'll let her keep coming?"

"Do you think I could stop her?" Will smiled his broadest smile, although he didn't reach out again. "And I wouldn't want to. I'll send some smoked meat down, something that'll keep awhile. And some canned sweets, too."

"Catherine's been bringing sweets: canned berries and pears, plum preserves, too."

"Ruby said that Catherine's been raiding the root cellar. And Mary blamed Sharon and me. Her sweet-toothed children, she calls us."

Jesse stepped through the open door, but he didn't invite Will inside. "I've got fish to prepare." He slipped the fish-loaded stringer off his shoulder. "Gutted them at the river. They'll spoil fast if I don't get them into my smokehouse. Tell Catherine I'm glad she's done so well."

"Jess, will you come live at the farm? Catherine will be gone soon. We can fix up her room for you. Catherine wants that."

Jesse closed the door before Will got "I do, too," out of his mouth.

30

The big Greyhound Silverside bus idled at the curb, but the driver must have been in the depot. Will took in every detail, from the blue and silver corrugated metal with a running greyhound dog painted over and behind the front wheel-well to the words "Greyhound Lines" springing from the back wheels and racing after the dog. To hold back tears he focused on what he could see, a cream colored top and the row of windows masked by a dark horizontal strip running along each side that reminded him of his cows moving single file toward their stanchions. Two luggage doors protruded from each side. A destination sign, "Milwaukee," assured him this was the right bus, and he felt reassured when he looked inside the open door and saw a restroom at the rear.

Will knew that Catherine was as excited as Teddy with a new ham bone, except she was a bit more restrained. And he knew she was nervous, too. He'd brought her to the depot at Spring Green, but she would leave alone. And it would be her first bus trip.

"Don't worry, my dear. You'll get on the bus here and you won't have to get off until Ruby meets you in Milwaukee."

"What if she's not there?"

"Has Ruby ever shirked a responsibility? She'll be there if she has to commandeer the taxi and drive it herself."

"Commandeer it? Ruby doesn't even drive." Catherine smiled. "I so look forward to being with her again."

"She'll be there."

"You're right, she'll be there." Catherine stomped her foot, picked up her suitcase, and grimaced. "Ruby'll be there." She kissed Will on the cheek, hesitated a moment, stood tall, took a deep breath, and stepped through the open door. Before she took another step, she looked back and smiled faintly. She waved once and disappeared down the isle.

His last child had flown the nest. Will wiped a tear. He was glad that Mary had said her goodbyes before they left home. He watched the bus drive away. Feeling empty, he turned and wandered in the direction of his buggy. He knew that Catherine could count on Ruby.

◆»»»-««««◆

Mary had asked him to help her pick blackberries up on the bluff, but he'd been too busy getting in his second crop hay. As he slowly drove home he thought about being alone with Mary for the first time after all these years. He decided that a good way to start this new life together would be to go pick those berries, and to bring a picnic lunch along, too. By the time he arrived home he was so excited about this renewal with Mary that after he unharnessed Fanny Too and put her in her stall, he walked off without feeding her oats. She wasn't going to let him get away so easy. Her loud complaints broke into his reverie.

Will rushed into the kitchen. "Mary, let's do it. Let's go pick those blackberries. I'll find the pails while you pack a lunch. We'll have a picnic up on the bluff."

"I was beginning to think there'd be no blackberry cobbler or pies this winter."

Will frowned at the thought of no sweets to look forward to at the end of a winter milking. Sometimes the thought of that pie was what fueled him through those last few cows.

"I hope the birds haven't eaten them all," Mary said.

They had walked across the tracks, crossed the road, and had started on the path that led to the top of the bluff when Will noticed that Teddy wasn't with them. "Where's Teddy?"

"I think he went to the field with Petr."

Will stopped walking. "Maybe I should go back and get him. There could still be rattlesnakes out on a sunny day like this."

"I haven't seen any for a while. I think we'll be okay."

Will took Mary's hand and started back up the path. He hadn't gone another hundred yards before he stopped again. "Mary, I'm going to get Teddy. Remember what happened to Junkie and Jinks up here. It's a good thing they had Teddy that day."

Will still shuddered at the thought of seeing Jinks stretched out, white as Will's newly painted tool shed, with Ruby working feverishly over him. "You wait here. I'm going to go get him."

"If you think it best. I'll go ahead and get the lunch out." She dropped the pails and took the picnic basket from Will. "Bring those pails when you come back up."

Will wanted to urge her to wait here until he got back, but decided that she'd be safe enough out in the open, preparing their lunch. He turned and trotted down the path.

Will hadn't gotten far into his bean field when he spotted Petr who was repairing a broken wire on the far fence. "Petr, is Teddy with you?" he called.

"He ran up the fence line after a rabbit. Do you want him?"

"Mary and I are going up the bluff to pick berries. I thought we should have him along. Rattlesnakes might be out."

"I'll get him." Petr hooked the hammer over the top barbwire strand and walked up the fence line, calling for Teddy.

Soon, his tail wagging, Teddy ran up to Will, plopped his backside on the ground, and extended a paw.

Will patted him on the head. "You're always the gentleman, now aren't you? Better come along. We may need you."

Will walked up the path to the pails, snatched them off the ground, and followed Teddy upward toward the top. As he got close, he called, "Mary."

He heard no answer at first. He stopped walking, listened for a moment, and thought he heard a muted, "I'm over here." It came from near the big rock at the bluff's edge. He started in that direction. When he paused again, he heard the voice speak in a loud whisper, "Don't come closer. There's a big snake coiled near me."

Will's panic took him a few quick steps in that direction. Then he stopped. He knew that he couldn't move fast or react rashly with a rattlesnake near. He crept forward to assess the situation. When he got close, he froze with fright. Mary kneeled on a half spread out blanket, and a big rattlesnake was within striking distance, singing his death song, a rattle that sounded like a million dry leaves protesting his footsteps.

Will's first impulse was to look for a rock to throw, but he knew he couldn't do that. What if he missed?

"Don't come closer, Will. I'm afraid it might strike."

Mary had kept her wits about her when she had frozen at the snake's warning. But he knew that she couldn't stay in that half kneeling position for long, that her muscles would cramp and she'd have to move.

The snake continued to rattle its death chant.

Before Will could think what to do next, Teddy took action. Slinking low to the ground, he edged toward the coiled snake, and then he circled and approached from the snake's rear, away from Mary. Staying within the snake's field of vision, he stopped beyond striking distance and began to claw the ground with his hind paws and growl at the snake's backside. The snake turned its head away from Mary, twisting toward the menacing dog.

Now that he had the snake's attention, Teddy slowly moved sideways, forcing the snake to twist around to watch him. Then Teddy lunged, but he stopped short of making contact. The snake struck, but twisted as it was, it was off target. Teddy retreated and continued to hold the snake's attention, enticing it into repeated ineffective strikes. Finally, totally frustrated, the snake uncoiled and slithered around toward Teddy. And then Will's brave dog charged forward, grabbed the snake in the middle, and shook it violently, like a gust of wind whipping a sheet on the clothesline. In a moment Teddy laid the dead rattlesnake at Will's feet.

Will hugged Teddy and then ran to Mary. "Are you okay?"

By now, Mary had rearranged the blanket and had started to lay out the lunch. "As long as we're up here we might as well eat our lunch," she said. "Then we'll go home. I don't think I'm in the mood for any berry picking today." She handed Will a sandwich.

Will had always known where Ruby's bravery came from, and it wasn't from his side of the family.

"I've wondered how Teddy did it that day with Junkie," Will said. "He's not only a brave dog, but a smart one, too. But I always knew that." He put his arm around Mary, pulled her close, and whispered, "I was scared. I don't know what I'd do if I lost you. Thank the lord that Barnes left Teddy with us when he sold us the farm. He's the best part of that purchase."

31

Either Will or Mary checked the mailbox each day, sometimes twice, to see if there was news from their girls. Two weeks after Catherine had left for nursing school, Will found her first letter stuffed between the newspaper and an advertisement for Carter's Little Liver Pills. Although he dropped the advertisement, he raced to the house with the letter firmly in hand. "Mary, a letter from Catherine." He thrust it toward Mary who was still at the kitchen sink.

"Well, open it, Will. Can't you see that my hands are all wet?"

Will grabbed a scissors off an open shelf and snipped the end off the envelope. He tapped the envelope on the counter so the letter fell to the opening, and then he fished it out. But he didn't have his glasses. "Mary, where'd you put my reading glasses?"

"Where'd I put them? I've got enough trouble keeping track of my own."

Will searched the living room, and after feeling down the side of his easy chair and under the cushions of their divan, he found his glasses tucked away in his writing desk drawer, right where they should have been. Why hadn't he looked there first? He supposed that searching the desk would have been far too logical. Besides, he seldom found them there. He walked back into the kitchen and read the letter to Mary.

"Dear Mother and Dad,

"I hate to be writing this letter, and I hope that you aren't too shocked. I've dropped out of nursing school."

Mary gasped. "She's dropped out? Why, she's hardly begun. How could she do this? Why did Ruby let her?"

"There's more," Will said.

"I just couldn't take the white walls, bedpans, and blood. I should have known—I did know, and, Ruby agrees, I did it to be near her. She

161

told me before I started that it might not be for me, that it took a strong stomach. I ignored her warning. And I shouldn't have. It's one thing to talk about it, but another thing to see a patient vomiting all over a nurse while he sits soaking wet in his own urine. I just can't do it, and it's better to decide now than wait until I've wasted the scholarship money. Miss Watkins, the administrative nurse, says if I drop out now they can still give the scholarship to another needy applicant. I think that my decision is best for everyone.

"Ruby says that I can stay here in Milwaukee with her for a while to think over my future—and to give you time to recover from my sad news. But maybe it's not so sad. You've told me, Dad, the one thing worse than making a mistake is to persist in it.

"I love and miss you both. I hope that you still love me.

"Catherine"

"Do I still love her?" Will said. "Why, I love her more than ever."

"I shouldn't be surprised, I suppose. She was always afraid of blood." Mary headed back toward the kitchen. "I hope she can find a career that will keep her independent. I don't want her to be forced to rely on a man, even if he is a good one."

❖

Before Will left for the field to cut soybeans, he told Petr, "Put fresh bedding down for the calves and horses and get the hay down for tonight's milking." He started to walk away, but stopped and turned back. "Don't go into the silo. It's beginning to look dangerous in there. Damp and crusted corn's built up on the sides. We'll pull it down when both of us are here."

Will hitched Ned and Ted to the binder and headed to his bean field. The binder had a reel that whisked the bean into a sickle bar, which sheared the stems and dropped the beans and their stems onto a canvas. The canvas carried the plant to a binding mechanism, which tied twine around the bundle. Will made sure to keep the twine's tension loose; when tied too tight, soybean bundles would mold under the twine. Once tied, the bundle was discharged onto the ground behind the binder. Later, Will and Petr would stack these bundles into shocks that resembled miniature Indian tipis, and leave them to dry in the sun until they were ready to haul to the barn or silo.

Will finished cutting his bean field shortly after noon. As he headed in for dinner he planned how he and Petr would return to the field to gather and stack the scattered bundles for drying.

Already late, Will rushed to the kitchen table. He was surprised that Petr wasn't there waiting; Petr always beat him to the table. Mary spooned cold fries and Spam onto his plate. Will wrinkled his nose, but kept his feelings about Spam to himself. He'd rather have ham, but knew that Mary was doing her best to save them money.

"Where's Petr?" Mary asked. "I thought he'd come in with you. I haven't seen him all morning."

"He wasn't in the field with me. I asked him to do barn work. You haven't seen him? He never misses a meal."

Will picked at his food. "He'll probably be here in a few minutes. He must have run into a problem."

After another ten minutes passed, Will pushed his chair from the table. "I'm going to look. It's not like him to be late for a meal."

Will hurried to the haymow and called up the ramp, "Petr." There was no answer. He hustled up the incline and stepped into the loft. "Petr, are you in here?"

When there was still no response, he feared that maybe Petr had fallen down a chute. The loft was full of first and second crop hay, so there was no place to hide. Will rushed to each chute, looked and hollered down, but still no response.

It wasn't like Petr to just up and leave. Will ran back down the ramp and around the barn to the milk house door. He rushed through the milk house and into the barn. He didn't see or hear a thing. As he hurried down the aisle, he hollered "Petr" toward the opening into the silo. There was no response from there, either. He headed toward the house to ask Mary to telephone their neighbors, said that maybe he went visiting. He knew there was little chance of that. Petr seldom left the farm.

Before he got to the house, Mary opened the door and Teddy rushed at him. "Mary, call Earl and James. Ask if they've seen Petr."

He was about to search the grain bin and machine shed when he heard Teddy barking in the barn. He ran back inside and found Teddy barking into the silo opening. He ran down the aisle toward Teddy. "What's there, Teddy? What do you see?"

When he looked into the silo, he saw it, too. Petr was buried past his neck, with steaming, loose corn silage filling his mouth. When Will muttered, "God help us," he saw Petr's eyes blink and his head move a little. Petr's left arm was buried, but his right was raised above the loose silage. Will saw those fingers beckon, as if Petr was motioning for help. Will knew that he had to act fast. He also knew that he couldn't enter that death trap without risking both their lives. "Don't move, Petr. Don't even wiggle a finger. I'll be right back."

Will raced toward the back wall of the barn where he kept a rope for moving his calves. He grabbed the rope off the hook and ran back to the silo. Petr's life depended on an accurate throw. "Petr, I'm going to try and hit you squarely in the hand so that you can grab hold." Will tied knots at the end of the rope to give Petr something to grip. "For God's sake, don't try to reach for it if I miss."

Will knew that the slightest movement could bring more silage tumbling down on Petr. Will tossed the rope. He missed Petr's open hand by a foot. Petr reflexively reached toward it—and Will's worst fear was realized. More silage tumbled down, but it fell against the back of Petr's head, pressing his face further into the wet mush.

"Stay still, Petr. Concentrate. We'll get this done. Don't move your hand or even twitch an eyelid. Not until the rope hits your fingers."

Will pulled the rope in and coiled it. "Dear Lord, let me get this right. Please, Lord, guide this to his fingers."

Will closed his eyes for a moment and took a deep breath. He felt a rush of panic as he inhaled the sweet and sour smell of the mass that was consuming his friend. Staring at Petr's hand, Will tossed the rope again. This time it dropped on Petr's fingers and slipped into his hand. Will could see Petr's eyes brighten with hope. "Petr, I'm going to wait a moment before I start pulling this rope. Concentrate on holding it tight. Clutch that rope like it's a pot of gold."

Will knew that Petr was as strong as anyone in the township, but could he do this? Could he hold the rope tight while the steaming mass beneath him gripped and sucked his body down toward certain death? "Petr, I'm going to count to three, then I'll pull with all my strength. I'll start slow. I won't jerk the rope. Just slow and steady. Are you ready?"

Petr blinked his eyes and flicked his fingers. "We're going to get this done, Petr. Here goes. One." Will paused. "Two." He paused again. "Three." He pulled on the rope. Petr's fist clenched the rope so tight that his fingers turned bright red. Will pulled harder and felt all the slack leave and the rope tighten. He kept the pressure on. Petr's arm stretched so far toward Will that it looked as if it was the arm of one of those circus rubber men, but Petr's body didn't move. Will didn't want to pull the rope from Petr's clenched fist, so he relaxed it for a moment. He could see fear creep into Petr's eyes. "Hold on Petr. I'm going to keep a steady pressure on the rope. When I feel you moving, I'll pull harder. Hang on Petr. We'll make it. You'll be out in a minute or so."

Will wasn't sure. He wasn't nearly as strong as Petr. And even with both hands on the rope and his whole body pulling, he wasn't getting anywhere, and he was beginning to tire. His fingers tingled with numbness, and his arms felt limp. He knew he had to keep up the pressure. He pulled a little harder. The tension in the rope relaxed a little. "You moved, Petr. Hang on." Will pulled harder but there was no more movement.

"God give me strength. Help me, please, help me."

The rope moved forward and Petr's shoulders emerged from the morass. Petr pulled his trapped arm free and reached for the rope. Will knew that with both hands gripping the rope Petr could endure. He wasn't so sure about himself. Will felt drained. "God, just this one more time." He wrapped the slackening rope around his hands, jammed his feet hard against the silo's floor, and pulled with strength that could only come from God's power in him. The rope squeezed his hand like a python squeezing life from its prey. Will's fingers burned, but, miraculously, Petr popped out and slid across the silage to the opening. Will reached inside and helped Petr through the door.

They sat on the floor trying to catch their breath, their backs against the outer silo wall. Will felt so exhausted he couldn't have said a word, even if he wanted to. For causing all this trouble, Will didn't know whether to hug or fire his man. Before he decided, Teddy reached up and licked Will's cheek. Will hugged his dog instead of Petr. "If it wasn't for you, Teddy, I'd never have known he was in there."

Will pushed Teddy toward Petr. "You'd better thank God that we have this dog. Without him, you'd have met your Maker, or, given the trouble you've caused today, more likely his horned adversary. I warned you, Petr. Why'd you ever go in there?"

When Teddy reached up to lick Petr's face, he ignored Will's question but leaned down and planted a kiss on the dog's nose. Then he looked up, stared into Will's eyes. "Will, I knew we needed the space in there for this fall's harvest. I just wanted to pull that old corn down to prepare for the new. I thought I could do it."

Petr looked so distressed that Will regretted his impulse to let him go. How could he be angry with a man who'd risk his life to make Will's life a bit easier? He reached over and placed his hand on Petr's shoulder.

"You're a good man, Petr. I was afraid I was going to lose you."

Petr flashed a wan smile, and then he turned and headed toward the milk house to change clothes and clean-up a bit.

When Petr came out in clean clothes, he looked a little recovered and refreshed. Will took his arm and guided him toward the house. "We've got a lot to be grateful for. Let's go give our thanks to God and get some food for our spent bodies."

Mary met them at the house. "I see you've found him. I was getting worried."

Before Will could explain, Mary shoved a letter at him. "This just came from Catherine."

As Petr headed toward the kitchen, Mary said, "You better get to the table. While you two were out there lollygagging, your food's gotten cold."

Lollygagging? He was about to tell her, but instead, he paused, glancing at the letter in his hand. "You start your dinner, Petr. I'll be there in a few minutes."

Will sat on the edge of the big horsehair in the parlor and read aloud:

"Dear Mother and Dad,

"I've decided. I'm going to be a teacher. Aunt Kate has said that I can stay with her while I attend teacher training courses at the County Normal School in Dodgeville. Professor Amundsen says that she'll take me a month late. I'm sure I'll have a lot of catching up to do, so I may not write again for a while. The professor's the superintendent of rural school programs in the county. They say that she's really good, but, don't tell anyone, she scares the bejeebers out of me. She's gruff, opinionated, and big. But I'd better learn to live with her. Not only will she be teaching me the next two years, but, if I take a country school here in Iowa County, she'll supervise me, too. So I'd better get used to her. I'll try my best. I promise, Mom.

"I'm sure going to miss Ruby. I don't want to think about it. I'll have to get used to that, too.

"With all my love,

"Catherine"

"You heard it, Mary," Will said. "Catherine wants to be a teacher, just like you."

"She'll not make much money. Still, it's an honorable occupation. There's nothing more important than our young people. I believe she'll make a difference in many students' lives."

"Just like her mother did. She can't go wrong following your footsteps."

Will settled into the chair and thought about his youngest daughter for a while before joining Petr at the table. He was grateful she'd found her calling. It was a new beginning for his daughter, and he was glad. The good news from Catherine overshadowed any intention he had of telling Mary about Petr's close encounter with death.

32

The war wound down in Europe, and victory over Japan was in sight when, in late March, 1945, the list of casualties at Okinawa arrived. And Jack Hornking was on it. His ship, the aircraft carrier *USS Franklin*, had been hit be a Japanese air attack that left more than eight hundred sailors dead—most killed by fire, others blown overboard.

Will O'Shaughnessy slouched in his horsehair chair and buried his face in his hands. "Mary, when he enlisted, I was glad. I thought the service might straighten him up."

"It's been a long ordeal, Will." She went to her husband and took his hand. "When will it ever end?"

⋙⋘

That night, Will attended another co-op meeting. He hoped they could move forward now. Earl Roberts and Jackson McGried were there, sitting side-by-side. McPherson called the group to order. "This is our first meeting in more than a year, and we have work to do. There's business that can't wait longer. Our co-op's profits are building at a pace that demands attention. Either we declare a dividend or we invest for the future. Maybe it's time to expand our operation. Before we decide, though, Will has something to say."

Will took the gavel from McPherson's hand. "When we started this co-op, I spoke of its many possibilities. We're having success with our marketing efforts, thanks to the improved economy and Jacob's shrewdness. I think it's time to expand, time to use our co-op's buying power as well as its selling power. Why, we could buy and sell gasoline, oil, grease, cattle feed, all kinds of farm supplies. And maybe do our own lending, too. We could save ourselves money on supplies and make money by selling to others. I've talked to Jacob, and—"

A call went up, "Swinstein, tell us what you think."

Jacob Swinstein stood before them. "Gentlemen, I've begun a position paper about how we can expand. I'll have it to you within the month. With the war nearing an end, I believe our potential for profit is greater than we've ever seen. Now's the time to be bold."

After the meeting, his neighbors stopped Will and thanked him for his persistence when things looked bleak, when blended pricing hurt him the most.

⬥⟫⟫⟫⟨⟨⟨⬥

Will wished that Ruby and Catherine could be here. Thrashing was their favorite farm work, too. He loved summer in the fields, when the breeze off the bluffs cooled the body and the meadowlark's song fueled the soul. Will walked Ted and Ned down the field, stopping at each grain shock to help Petr pitch them into the wagon.

They chatted as they worked. Will bent over and dug his fingers into the soil. He grimaced and sighed. "Hard as a rock." He loosened the soil with his pitchfork, and then kneeled down and scooped again. "There's a little moisture in there." He rose to his knees. "Not much, though. We're lucky we had ample spring rains."

Petr looked into the sky. "No rain in sight, either. If we don't get some soon, the corn cobs'll be bare."

Will climbed back into the wagon. "Giddyap, Ted, Ned. Move on old fellas. We've got more work to do." He flicked the reins over his horse's backs, hard enough to urge them into movement, but not so hard as to rile them. "Get along, fellas."

The wagon surged ahead for fifty feet to the next shock. "Whoa, Ted, Ned."

Will grabbed his fork and jumped from the wagon. They pitched in silence for a while. Now and then a gust of wind picked up the dry soil and blew it into their faces.

After they'd worked for a while, Petr said, "I haven't seen Catherine all summer. She's usually home for a week or so."

"Didn't I tell you? Now that she's earned her teaching certificate, she's taken a country school south of Logan Junction, up near Ed's farm. She's staying with Sharon this summer. She spends all her time writing work sheets and lesson plans. That girl's always been conscientious."

"Does she have a beau?"

Will knew that Petr was fond of his young daughter. Still, she'd never shown interest in him. "Catherine? She doesn't have time for a beau."

"She's sure a pretty girl. You know what they say about honey attracting the bees."

"In due time." He worried a little, though. She'd had plenty of chances, but his daughter never seemed interested in the young men. Will climbed back into the wagon. "Hop in. Let's get this load to the thrashing machine."

⬧⟫⟫⟫⟫-⟨⟨⟨⟨⬧

When his father called and said that Finian McCarthy was looking for a driver, Will hitched Fanny Too to the buggy and they left for Ashley Springs right after morning milking. "We're going home, old girl."

Fanny Too whinnied her approval.

The sun warmed them as it rose in a cloudless sky, as beautiful a summer day as Wisconsin could summon. Will hadn't been able to make telephone contact with Finian. He hoped the cattle dealer wasn't away with a load. But if he was in town, Will knew he'd most likely find him at Bennie's Bar.

When Will entered the bar, Bennie was chatting at a table, his back to the door. Will slipped onto a stool. "What's going on here? The owner doesn't attend to business anymore? He doesn't even recognize an old customer?"

Bennie whipped around. "Will O'Shaughnessy. I thought I knew that voice." He hurried behind the bar to face Will, and thrust out his hand. "Thought I'd gotten rid of you once and for all." Bennie clenched Will's fingers. "What're you doing in town, my friend?"

"I've got a terrible thirst. I heard you can help."

"Drove all this way for a drink, now did you? What'll it be, my man?"

"Do you still pour that good Springs' beer?"

"I thought you drank Jameson."

"Too rich for my pocketbook these days. I might be able to find a dime, though. I still have a taste for Ashley Springs' golden brew."

"Mineral Springs it'll be then, hometown's finest." Bennie grabbed a glass, held it under the open spout, and then tipped it at the last moment to add the frothy head.

"That long drive sure built up a thirst." Will swigged from the glass. "It's good, Bennie. Worth every mile for a drink of your golden elixir."

"You didn't come this far for a glass of beer. How can I help you?"

"I'm lookin' for Finian McCarthy. I heard he needs a driver. I might be able to help him."

"Farming's that bad?"

"It's for my brother, Jesse."

"Jesse's back? Thought we'd seen the last of him."

"I think he's changed. Maybe he'll take a job if I can find one."

"Finian's around. He usually stops in after supper, about seven o'clock. Can you come back then?"

"I made arrangements for a neighbor to help my hired man with milking. I thought that I might have to stay overnight. The girls used to help, but they're away now."

"It's hard to believe they're that old." Bennie picked Will's empty glass off the bar and dropped it in a sink of sudsy water. "I still remember you bringing baby Catherine around. You were so proud of her."

"She's a beautiful lass, Bennie."

"That's no surprise."

Will shook Bennie's hand and turned toward the door. "Don't you go running out of that beer. I'll be wantin' another glass tonight, maybe two."

"Let's see." Bennie tapped on the keg. "Half full, I think. Should be just about enough to do you and Finian the evening. He's drinking Mineral Springs, too. Had a rough go."

"Oh?"

"A bull knocked him down. Broke his right ankle, splintered it bad. Probably won't drive all summer, maybe longer."

"So that's why he wants help."

Will left the bar and unhitched Fanny Too. "What do you think, old girl? Should we go out to Grandpa's farm?"

Fanny Too nickered her approval as she turned up the street.

"Do you think Frank will be glad to see us?"

Fanny Too didn't respond.

Will turned into the yard and reined Fanny Too at his grandfather's cast iron hitching post. He didn't see Frank, nor did he hear any sound. "Where do you think he could be?"

Fanny Too remained silent, just flicked her tail and twitched her ears to discourage flies that flitted around her head.

"Maybe he's in the house." After knocking long and hard, Will decided to try the barn. "You wait here, old girl," he shouted toward his horse as he walked toward the big building. "Keep those flies at bay."

Will glanced inside the milking parlor. He called down the lane. He poked his head in the door of the shadowy machine shop. He thought of the day he couldn't find Grandpa, until he searched the hog pen. But Will wouldn't go there—not today, not any day.

Finally, a voice hollered from the loft. "Who's down there?"

Will shouted back. "It's Will. Come on down."

"Hold your horses, Will. Be there soon's I pitch this hay down the chute."

The buildings looked immaculate, not a bare spot on any board, no different than when Grandpa ran the farm. Will thought about the work it took to keep it that way. He'd give Grandpa and Frank credit for that. Not much else, though. Frank would never waste time running around the countryside trying to help a brother. Will walked down the lane toward the pasture, but the cows were nowhere in sight. He didn't need to see them. He knew they'd be faultless: well fed, full udders, and disease free. That's the way Grandpa kept his herd. He couldn't understand why Frank wouldn't go grade A. Certainly his cows produced enough milk.

Frank stumbled down the hay loft ramp toward Will. "This lumbago's getting the best of me." He stretched his back and wiggled his fingers. "Getting so that I hardly make it through a milking, these fingers get so stiff. Should quit milking, go to beef. What do you want now?"

"Have you seen Jess?"

"Why do you ask?"

"He's living down by me, in an old fishing shed on the river."

"He stopped here after he went to your house in Springs, before your place burned."

"I suppose he thought I still lived there."

"The woman threatened to call the police."

"He musta scared her senseless."

"I told him to get the hell outta here." Frank clenched and reopened his stiff fingers. "I've got enough problems without a good-for-nothin' brother underfoot. Grandpa wouldn't want him here."

"Grandpa's dead."

"I hear you're trying to form a co-op, doing grade A."

"That's right."

"Let me give you some advice. Keep it simple."

"Your cows don't produce enough for grade A?" Will said.

"I doubt yours give as much. You always spent too much time reading. Better to spend it in the fields. Grandpa said to keep it simple. Too many things can go wrong, and they always do."

"There are better ways."

"You think you know more than the rest of us, Will. Grandpa said so himself. Said, 'Your brother's smart as a fox in a hen house, but he doesn't have the sense of an ally cat.' You're bound to fail with your high minded ideas."

"S'pose you'd like that, Frank. S'pose it'd justify your opinion of me."

"Can't say I'd like it, but that's how it'll be. Grandpa always said you weren't attentive enough. Rather spend your time plowing books than plowing fields. You gotta keep things simple."

"You probably haven't noticed that I run horses. That's about as simple as it gets, I'd say."

"Horses are lots of work."

With a wave to show respect, although his brother didn't deserve it, Will mounted his buggy and clucked Fanny Too forward. "Maybe he'd be more kindly if he knew a good horse, don't you think, Fanny Too?"

Fanny Too neighed in agreement.

⚬⟫⟫⟩⟨⟨⟪⚬

Will entered Bennie's at seven o'clock. The bar overflowed with customers. "Looks like business is good these days," he shouted toward Bennie who scooted along the counter.

"I'm not complaining. Finian's at the back table." Bennie pointed. "You can't miss him. He's flashy as ever."

Finian was dressed in his usual bright colors: a brown, checkered derby hat with matching knee-length corduroy breeches; an emerald green swallow-tail jacket; a corn-silk-green shirt; and one bright red buckle-topped shoe.

When Finian saw Will, he hoisted himself off his chair and then, slowed only a bit by the large plaster cast on his right foot, sang and jigged his way through a crude version of the "Irish Washer Woman." When he finished, he bowed deeply in Will's direction and pronounced, "Gentlemen, fanfare please. Tah ta dah. My Wicklow cousin has returned." He motioned to Bennie who, along with all his customers, stared at this inflated facsimile of a Wichlow mountain leprechaun.

"Sir!" Finian beckoned toward Bennie. "Please, don't tarry now, bring this Irishman a drink."

Finian stepped toward Will. "How can I help you, my friend?"

"I heard you need a driver."

Finian thrust his encumbered foot forward. "And to make matters worse, the IRS is on my tail. Says I cheated on my taxes. Can you believe that? Cheated on my taxes."

Will believed it.

"Sheriff says if he catches me driving with this cast, he'll toss me in jail." Finian grabbed Will's shoulder and guided him to a hard chair. "He says I'm already too heavy footed. Do I need a driver? S'pose I do. You're here to help, Will?"

"It's my brother. He may be ready for a job. I best warn you, he tends to scare people. His face—"

"The one you went lookin' for? The brother with the circus? That was one fun trip. Never laughed so hard."

Will didn't remember it being much fun.

"I'm in an awful way," Finian said. "I got a big contract with Dubuque Packing Company and I can't get my cattle there. I'll need someone every day for a few months, then part time for a while. Can your brother drive?"

"He drove an army truck before they sent him to the trenches."

"Well then, get him up here. I need someone right now."

The easy part was over. Now, if only he could convince Jesse.

33

That night as Will and Mary got ready for bed, Will said, "With the war winding down, I think it may be the time to expand. I've never felt so optimistic about our business, about our future. I'll stay in after breakfast tomorrow. Let's sit for a while and plan how we can grow."

The next morning Mary fixed a large meal—fresh bread, eggs, bacon, cold fries—and when their plates were clean, she pulled warm cinnamon buns from the oven.

After clearing the table, she took out her pen, inkwell, and linen writing paper. "Let's do this right," she said. "We'll decide our priorities and record our decisions."

"You'll always be the scholar, won't you, my dear?" Will laughed. He was pleased by his wife's enthusiasm for improving their business. Now, after so many years of hardship, maybe they could prosper and put aside money. The war would soon be over, and their future looked better.

"Let's see," she said. "A tractor, milking machines, more chickens, new barn paint. What do you think? But first, we'll expand our herd."

"It makes sense to me. That's where we make our living. Maybe we can finally replace those heifers with some quality cows."

<hr />

Will edged through the trees toward Jesse's shack. He whispered to Fanny Too, tried to get her to signal their coming, but Fanny Too remained quiet. Will supposed that she sensed how anxious he was about this meeting. Could he convince Jesse to take this job, to step into the twentieth century and live like a human? His history with his brother was worse than bleak. Still, he wasn't about to give up, not now—not with possibilities in hand.

Will supposed that Jesse would be out foraging for food, but when he pounded on the door, to his surprise, he heard footsteps within.

"Who's there? Private property. Don't want no visitors."

"It's Will."

The hinges squealed as the door slipped open. It seemed they resented visitors, too.

"Come on in."

For a moment Will thought he saw a slight smile cross Jesse's face, but he wasn't sure, probably just a reaction to the half-eaten parsnip that he held in his hand. "Jess, why don't you come live with us on the farm? I promise, you'll get better fare than parsnips."

"Kinda like it here. I like the solitude and the animals."

"Why'd you come here, Jess?"

"Went home, but Frank sent me away. Not the first time. I don't know why I bothered."

"Bennie told you that I'd moved to the farm?"

"I was surprised you left your booming business and that grand house of yours."

"Bad years for business. You know that."

"Grandpa was right?"

"Grandpa—" Will's fists clenched.

"Hit a sore spot, huh?"

"Why'd you come here anyway?"

"I didn't plan to stay. Just passing through. Then your girl came by."

Will's anger wilted. He sighed and smiled. "Catherine."

"Got to likin' that girl. I looked forward to her visits."

"She misses you now that she's living in... ."

"You raised a fine girl."

"What'd you do all those years?"

"I liked Heinzelman's. Not him so much. It was the side show people. I felt right at home there. I sure hated to lose that job."

"I met Mildred and Louise. They were sorry Heinzelman let you go."

"I miss them. Was on my way to look them up, but I stayed here too long."

"They were fond of you, Jess. They knew you were treated badly."

"Story of my life. Grandpa blamed me for Grandma's death."

"He was a hard man."

"He was wrong. The wheel came off the buggy. I wasn't driving fast, no faster than he drove down that lane."

"You were drinking. That's all Grandpa needed to know."

"I didn't mean to kill Grandma, you know that. It's been hell ever since. I begged forgiveness. No one listened, not Grandpa or God."

"You don't drink anymore?"

"Not since Heinzelman's. I loved the children. I didn't want to leave. I miss Mildred and Louise. The only friends I've ever had."

"I've tried—"

"You? I expected Grandpa and Frank to hate me, but I thought better of you."

"I want to help."

"Every day in that prison camp, I prayed for your ruin. Every time I looked in a mirror, I cursed your cowardice."

"Jess, let me help now. I've talked to a trucker I know. He needs a driver. It'd give you a chance to earn some money, a chance to get on your feet again."

"I'm doin' fine. I don't need your sympathy." He turned away from Will. "You'd better go now. I've work to do."

Will wasn't sure whether to embrace his brother or grab him and shake some sense into his head. When he reached out and placed his hand on Jesse's shoulder, his brother moved away and said, "Goodbye, Will."

Will sighed, walked out the door, and mounted Fanny Too.

<hr/>

That night in bed, Will tossed and turned.

"What's the matter, Will?" Mary said. "What's bothering you?"

"I'll never understand why Jess blames me for his troubles. More than anyone, I've tried to help. Yet he resents me all the more."

"God knows you've tried."

"He always turns his back. He hates me for it."

"It's human nature, I suppose. Dependency makes a person feel inadequate. I remember the time I broke my leg. Although I depended on it, I wanted to toss that crutch as far away as I could throw it."

Will slept little that night. He couldn't get Jesse off his mind. Jesse could exasperate a saint, God knows, but Will wanted to make his brother more comfortable, to bring him back into the family. Sweet Catherine wanted the same. But how could he help Jesse and not be resented for it?

34

August 15th, 1945. V-J Day.

Japan's surrender came as no surprise to Will. This thing, this bomb, was a terrifying weapon. He didn't understand it. He'd read about the devastation to Hiroshima and Nagasaki. No country could take punishment like that for long.

Even though it was a Wednesday night, the village was full of people. Will and Mary joined their neighbors in celebration. Mary agreed that Will could visit his friends at the Midtown Waterin' Hole. "Only one drink," she said. And Will vowed to please his wife this time. He remembered the night that first war ended. He remembered the empty sugar bag, but he didn't recall much else.

Will paused before entering. Oh, Lord, give me wisdom—so much grief in the midst of celebration. He stepped boldly inside and looked around. James Henning was there. So was McPherson, Snell, Roberts, and McGried. It was good seeing his neighbors together again.

And to Will's surprise, Rich Turner, his friend from Ashley Springs, sat among his neighbors. "Rich, what are you doing this far from home?"

"Just passin' through, and when I heard the news, I decided to stop. I wouldn't miss a good celebration."

Henning jumped up. "Will, you old goat, come over here. I'm buying the first round. What'll it be?"

"A Jameson. What else on so glorious an occasion?"

"My namesake," Henning said.

"Namesake my rear end, James," Will said. "You've not a drop of Irish in that big Norwegian carcass."

Henning laughed and held his glass high as the bartender poured Will's drink. "A toast to victory."

"To victory," McPherson said as they touched glasses.

"Victory, yes, but a terrible one," Will said. "A toast to the boys who won't come home. A toast to Jimmie, Jake, and Franklin."

"Aye," Jackson said. But he didn't raise his glass.

The men sat silently, sipping on their drinks and absorbing the noise that bounced off the walls around them.

They drank until their glasses were dry—except Will's, who wanted his one drink to last.

Finally, Snell broke the silence. "What do you think of the co-op expanding?" he said.

"I'll be looking for some good milk cows," Will said. "Now's the time to grow."

Henning pushed away from the table and raised his empty glass. "Let me know if you find some. Bartender, over here."

"Your brother's selling his herd, didn't you know, Will?" Rich said.

"Frank? I knew his arthritis was hurtin'."

"Says he's going to beef."

The bartender approached and held out a bottle. "This one's on the house, fellas. The boss says I should 'liven your celebration. Our boys'll soon be home."

Earl Roberts looked away.

Will held his hand over his half empty glass. "Just this one, my friends. No more."

"Drink up, the night's young," Snell said.

"Did I ever tell you how I almost lost my good wife?" Will said. He stopped short—knew it was no time for levity.

"One more," McPherson said. "It's on me." He motioned to the bartender. Snell grabbed Will's empty glass and rushed a full one forward to take its place.

Will studied the full glass, clutched it, and then he unhooked his fingers and pushed himself from the table. "Goodnight, boys. I promised Mary I'd get into bed on my own tonight."

He started toward the swinging doors. After a step, he turned back. "I'm sorry, Earl. Jackson. A terrible cost."

◆》》》─《《《◆

Will was surprised when Jesse began hauling steers that fall. He hoped this job would give Jesse money to live a little better, would help reconcile the estranged brothers. He understood, as well, that the hostility may be seated too deeply, the gap between them too wide to bridge… a gap only God could heal.

35

Dear, Aunt Mary, Uncle Will, and the Girls,

I'm having great fun back here in Texas. Mother is so preoccupied with Aunt Marguerite that she doesn't have time to get after me. I do remember your sermons, Aunt Mary. I'm being a good girl. I wouldn't want to dishonor Daddy. Why, I've even got a beau. He's an older man, more mature and dashing than your Wisconsin boys, Ruby. You'd like him. He holds the door for me, says "yes ma'am" and "no ma'am," and—you'll like this, Aunt Mary—he takes me straight home after a dance. You can see why Mom doesn't holler at me. And he dances like Rhett Butler. A real Southern gentleman. I'd never marry him, though. He's too old. And I kinda miss those country roads. Just kiddin', Aunt Mary.

Well, I'm getting lots of riding in. Catherine and Ruby, you'd love riding out here on the prairie. You can ride all day and never turn around. 'Course, I don't go that far, but sometimes we ride to the Guadalupe and camp overnight. We had some excitement last weekend though. Lee Baldwin took his boots off but didn't check them the next morning. Stepped right onto a scorpion. He won't be riding with us next weekend. Don't let that scare you, Catherine. I still want you to visit me soon. Generally we avoid snakes and things. Most of us aren't so careless as Lee. Course, we've lived with these critters all our lives. Lee should have known better.

Do you ever see Jack? I feel bad that I was responsible for getting him fired. I don't think he left that gate open, but I'm not sure. I think he could have been a good worker, although he lacked some motivation. He didn't really want to be a farmer. He was always fascinated when I'd talk about the ranch. Said he'd like to be a cowboy. I don't think our foreman, Chester, would have been as forgiving as you, Uncle Will, even though you did fire him. If he'd lost a crop for us, that's probably not the only thing he would have lost. Chester's kinda mean that way.

Aunt Marguerite's beside herself over her family back in Hungary. I've never met them, but I'm sure getting to know them fast. They're having a terrible time under the Communist occupation. Aunt Marguerite says it wasn't this bad under the Nazis. Chester says he'd sure like to see those Communists come to Texas. He'd show them what a Texas pointed boot can do. I don't think I'd like them here. Aunt Marguerite sure'd like to get her son here, though, all of her relatives, but it's not likely, I guess.

I miss all of you more than I thought possible. I sure would like for you to come visit us here. We've got plenty of room, more than we can keep up right now. You could stay as long as you want. I sure would like to take you riding, Ruby and Catherine. 'Course, our Texas horses are a bit more spirited than Lyda and Fanny Too, but I think you could handle them. We could ride all day.

Please write when you get a chance. Tell me about things on the farm. Have you had a dance lately?

I love y'all.

Cousin, Gusta

36

Mary and Petr were only halfway through their supper when Will took his last bite and rushed his plate to the sink.

"Will, you're as antsy as a cat in a calf pen," Mary said. "Give us a chance to finish our meal."

Will returned to his chair and took his Meerschaum from his pocket. He tapped his fingers on the table top; his unlit pipe dangled from his mouth.

When Petr forked the last scrap from his plate, Mary said, "Will, why don't you and Petr wait in the other room. I'll be there as soon as I've cleared the table."

Petr ambled toward the parlor. Will stood, scowled at Mary, and then he turned away when she failed to look up. He threw up his hands and followed Petr, who'd already settled onto the scarlet settee. Will sat in his horsehair. "You'd think time didn't matter," Will said. "And I want more cows?"

"Calm down, Will. We don't need to start milking for half'n hour."

"The rate we're going, it'll be half the day." Will took a match from his coverall pocket, struck it on his pant leg, and touched the flaming stick to his bowl. He took three deep draws, filled the air with sweet smelling smoke, and sat back in his chair. "I always feel better when this Meerschaum heats up." Will drew again, mouthed it, and exhaled a fluffy donut that matured and faded as it wandered upward. "It's a big step for us, Petr. Maybe it's too soon. Maybe we shouldn't."

Mary entered the parlor and sat down. "Okay, Will, tell us your plan."

"The war's over," Will said. "Life will change for everyone." He puffed twice on his Meerschaum. "Our troops will return wanting all the things they've been deprived of these last years. They're young. They'll want families, and homes, and cars. They won't save for tomorrow. They've seen their buddies die young, so they know tomorrow may never come."

"How will that help us?" Mary said.

"They're tired of rations. They'll want to eat better. There'll be more children and more demand for milk. We're well positioned to serve Milwaukee, Chicago, Minneapolis, St. Paul. We'll all make money for a change. Especially those of us who sell liquid milk. It's time to expand, I think. I've got ten empty stanchions. Those I thought my heifers would fill."

"But, Will," Mary said, "that'll be thirty-three cows. How can you and Petr ever milk that many? Would you consider beef?"

"I never farmed steers and I don't want them now. No hogs either. Don't even mention them."

"It'd be a lot easier. More milking will put a strain on us all without machines."

"No beef cattle!"

"A bit edgy, aren't you, Will? Maybe we should talk about this another time."

"I'm sorry, Mary. If we can get by for a while, maybe we can save enough to buy machines. I've studied it a bit, and I like those Surge milkers. Not right away, mind you. I'll have to borrow to buy more cows. But, if we make enough—"

"How much will they cost?" Mary said.

"A good grade A cow? A hundred fifty, maybe more. Lots of farmers will be buying."

Will knew that if he ever wanted to prosper, this was the time to be bold, the time to expand. But he had a queasy feeling in the pit of his stomach. Too many things had already gone wrong.

Mary took a deep breath, walked to him, and grasped his hand. "Will, you've studied this. If you're convinced, I'm with you. Maybe God has better things in store."

Her touch lifted his spirits. When he was at low tide, Mary always made him feel better.

"I'll start looking for cows tomorrow."

⬦⬦⬦⟫⟫⟩⟩⟩

Will searched the river valley, but couldn't find the cows he wanted. When he drove to his brother's, he wasn't surprised at Frank's response.

184

"I'm looking to get out of milking. I'll sell you my cows, but don't expect me to give them away. I'll expect a fair price."

"I'll pay market. Are they healthy?" Will knew the answer. Grandpa never kept an unhealthy cow, and he knew Frank wouldn't either.

"Won't find better."

"Do you have production records?"

"Sure. They're down a bit. Startin' to dry up."

"A little early for that, isn't it?"

"I've been lettin' them go." He wiggled his fingers. "Can't keep up anymore."

"How much for ten cows?"

"One eighty-five each. I expect to sell all twenty-five at that price. It'll be two hundred if I break up the herd. I don't plan to do that, though. Plenty of buyers these days."

"That's a bit steep, and I can't use twenty-five cows. I don't have room for them."

"I won't sell them piecemeal, not yet anyway. Guess you'll have to look elsewhere."

Will was finding that difficult. "If I can get others to buy in, buy them all, will you take less?"

"I'll keep shopping them. If they're not sold by the time you get back to me, I'll take one seventy-five each, but no less. They'll not last long, I expect."

Will rushed toward his buggy, and then turned back before he unhooked Fanny Too from his grandfather's hitching post. "Will you hold them for a week?"

"Not if I can sell. And, Will, I expect you'll pay the delivery cost."

Will thought about the delivery cost on his way back home. He knew that Mary wasn't fond of Finian McCarthy, and he supposed he could find another hauler. But Finian's rates had always been reasonable. And with everything he could borrow going into these cows, he had to cut corners somewhere.

When Will arrived home, he found Mary in the kitchen. He explained Frank's offer and told her that Frank wouldn't pay for hauling the cows. When he suggested contacting McCarthy, Mary objected.

"I don't trust that McCarthy. He's a slick one."

"He can be tricky, still, there's not much damage he can do with the hauling, now is there?"

"I suppose not, but I've got this feeling that Finian could turn a honey covered sweet role into a smelly horse biscuit. With Frank asking so much, I suppose we must keep the cost down."

"He's always treated me right. His charges have always been reasonable. I think I'll call him."

Finian was as exuberant as ever. He told Will that he'd be glad to haul his cows, and that he'd come over the next afternoon to discuss prices.

Will called toward the kitchen, "Mary, Finian'll be over tomorrow afternoon. Do you want to meet with him?"

Mary wiped her wet hands on her apron as she entered the room. "No, I don't, but I'd better be here. It'll probably take the two of us to see through that man's schemes."

"Now, Mary." But Will knew her distrust of Finian wasn't totally unreasonable. He turned toward the front door. "I've got cows to care for," he said as he rushed from the house.

Finian McCarthy came down their drive in a new bright red Cadillac convertible.

"He couldn't be in too much trouble," Will said. "Looks like he's doing okay."

"Appears he's lost some weight since we last saw him," Mary said. "He looks kind of pale to me."

Finian was his usual jaunty self. Dressed in shamrock green slacks, bright yellow suspenders, and a lavender shirt, Finian, despite being hampered by a walking cast, bounded up the slope toward the house.

"Hello, Will. What do you have in mind?"

He crouched and pointed toward Mary. "And HELLO, Mary! I swear— you look better every time I see you."

He winked in her direction, took Will's hand, releasing it before Will clenched a finger, and moved toward Mary. She quickly stepped away and turned toward the house. "I've got some muffins in the oven. Come inside for coffee and a muffin."

When Finian offered to haul the cows for five dollars a head, two dollars less than anyone else, Will quickly agreed.

The next morning when he saw Henning at the creamery, Will explained his brother's offer. At first, Henning was hesitant to buy more because the cows that he owned didn't produce enough milk to justify the extra expense of grade A production. But when Will offered to help him turn horse stalls into stanchions and extend his air lines, Henning said that he'd think about buying ten cows.

Will knew that ten cows was all that he had room for in his barn, so he asked Earl Roberts to buy his brother's last five cows. Earl worried that with so many boys returning to their farms from the war, the market might be loaded with milk. When Will convinced him that Swinstein, being a better marketer than most, would get them a good price, Earl agreed to help get Henning on-board, too.

◆》》》◆《《《◆

Jesse drove down Will's drive with the first load of cows on September 20, 1945. Petr helped them unload. Will was surprised to see his brother because he thought Jesse was hauling steers to Dubuque.

"Finian didn't want anyone else to bring them. He told me, 'He's your brother.' Kinda surprised me. We're behind in our plant deliveries."

Henning took ten cows. Will had upheld his end of the bargain and had helped Henning get started with the whitewashing and converting the horse stalls to stanchions. Until Henning could meet grade A standards, he would have to sell at grade B prices, but with Will's help, it wouldn't be for long.

Mary didn't like the idea of Will being at Henning's when, with so many cows, they needed him home. But he could see no way around it. If James and Earl hadn't taken fifteen cows, then he couldn't have purchased his ten. Will had tried to convince Frank to hold the cows back until Henning finished his barn.

"Can't do that," he'd said. "I need that hay to feed my steers through winter. I won't feed someone else's cows, too. Grandpa wouldn't do it, you know."

Frank was so like Grandpa Duffy that whenever Will was with Frank, it was easy to forget that Grandpa was a quarter-century gone.

Will's herd now produced fourteen quarts per cow each milking. When Frank's cows freshened, he expected to average fifteen. Milk prices edged up, too. Will hired Junkie Jenkins to help Mary and Petr while he helped Henning.

When Petr questioned the neighbor boy's name, Will explained that

187

Junkie came from a large family, and when he was still crawling around, an older brother proclaimed that he was just another piece of junk on the floor. And he'd been Junkie ever since.

Three of the twenty-five cows were to freshen in spring, so Will agreed to pay a premium to take those cows and gain their calves. If the calves were heifers and their mothers proved to be good producers, he would use them to replace older cows.

Will became concerned when one of the cows aborted her calf. When it happened a second time, he called his vet, Raymond Callison, who came right out. Will pulled his herd into the barn, and after a lengthy inspection, Callison delivered his verdict. "Will, I'm afraid you've got a problem. It looks like brucellosis to me. We'll need lab work. I'll have to quarantine your herd until we know for sure."

Will grabbed hold of a stanchion. "Bang's Disease? Frank said they're disease free."

"Did you see the vet's papers?" Ray said. "They had to be certified before they were shipped. A state law, you know."

"Frank said they were clean. It's a good herd, from good producers. Grandpa and Frank only kept healthy cows." Will felt unsteady on his legs. "He's my brother."

"I don't know what could've happened. Don't get too excited, not yet anyhow. Let's wait for the tests. Have other cattle come in contact with yours?"

"Some went to Roberts and Henning."

"Afraid I'll have to quarantine them as well, at least until we know their cows are safe. If it's Bangs and gets out of hand, it can affect humans as well as cattle."

That night, James Henning and Earl Roberts pounded on Will's door. "What's this all about, Will?" Roberts screamed. "Did you buy sick cows?"

"Calm down," Henning said. "Can we come in?"

Henning stayed calm, but Earl's face was red and the veins protruded from his forehead. He pushed through the door and rushed at Will.

"Is Callison right?" he shouted.

"I'm sure this will turn out okay," Will said. "Just a few days and we'll know for certain. If you have losses, I'll reimburse you, but it'll take awhile for me to recoup, too."

"It's Bangs Disease!" Earl shrieked. "That'll ruin us, put us out of farming. We'll have to destroy our sick cows."

"Earl, Callison isn't sure. They'll do tests. It must be a mistake. It'll just be a few days, fellas. Those were my brother's cows."

Will couldn't sleep. He went downstairs, took out his Meerschaum, and slumped into his oversized horsehair. Frank could be an S.O.B., but...

He heard Mary on the stairs and knew he must buck up.

"Are you okay?" She sat on the large arm of the chair. "Your brother wouldn't sell bad cows. You know that."

"I don't think so, but he said his volume's down. It's not like him to let production slip. Not like him to let cows dry up early." Will set his unlit Meerschaum on the side table. "I know this: Grandpa wouldn't have slowed his output, not for any reason."

"He'd not do this to his own brother."

"Sick cows stop producing, Mary."

"Why don't you go see him? I'm sure he'll clear this up. It's probably all a mistake."

The next day, Callison drove up Will's long drive. "It looks bad, Will. The tests came back positive. We'll have to destroy the sick ones, and the rest will have to remain under quarantine."

"What about Henning and Roberts? I'll not be able to face them. I talked them into it."

"So far, only your cows test positive. We'll have to watch. We won't know for a while."

"Have you told them?"

"I stopped on the way here. Sorry, Will. Bangs is bad, real bad. We gotta stop it early. One good thing. You'll get reimbursed for each lost cow, about twenty-five percent, they say."

Will stopped in the entryway to remove his coveralls and shoes; then he stumbled past Mary who was canning pears in the kitchen.

"These are the best pears we've had yet." Mary reached one toward him. "Here, taste it."

Will ignored Mary's offer and slumped into his old horsehair. Mary followed him to the parlor. "Is it bad?"

"It's bad, Mary. Just when I'd gotten to where I can make ends meet, they've gone and moved the ends on me. What will we ever do?"

Mary sat beside him and took his hand. "We'll do like we've always done, my dear. We'll find a way."

Mary always stood by him when he needed her. Why hadn't he listened to her? If he'd not rented to Swartz, if there'd not been a fire, they'd

not be in this fix. He'd have his rent, and his heifers would be producing by now. Will's thoughts turned to a Dickinson poem that he'd heard
Catherine recite so often. It told about a door opening to wealth and
companionship. Then suddenly that door was slammed shut, leaving
only misery.

How could his brother do this to him?

37

Will charged into Frank's yard at midmorning. He didn't bother to tether Fanny Too, but ran toward the noise he heard in the milk house.

When Will pushed through the doors, Frank glanced up, and then he turned back to cleaning pails. "I thought you'd be busy with those new cows." He put the brush down, but didn't seem to notice that Will was angry.

"How could you do this to me?" Will yelled. "You've got some explaining to do."

"Are you crazy?" Frank stepped back.

"If I had a gun, I hate to think what I'd do."

Frank backed farther away as Will pressed into him.

"And I thought Jesse was the crazy one. What's eating you, Will?"

"Those cows you sold me, they're diseased. I'll lose the farm."

"The hell they are. I've got the records."

"And my friends may lose theirs, too."

"Will, those aren't diseased cows."

Will grabbed his brother by the collar and jerked him forward. "The vet says otherwise."

Frank slipped Will's grasp and rushed toward the door. "Calm down." He distanced himself farther. "Come to the house. I'll show you."

Will followed his brother into the kitchen.

"I'd give you a coffee, but you're already too worked up. Hold on a minute." Frank rummaged through the kitchen cupboard. "I thought I put those on the top shelf." He grabbed a packet of papers. "Here they are."

He thrust the pack into Will's hands. "Count them, twenty-five certificates, all healthy cows."

Will thumbed through the papers.

"Look carefully, Will." He thrust a chair at his brother. "You'll not find a bad one there."

Will read each report, shook his head, and handed the packet back to Frank. "Then who? How?"

"Are you sure they're diseased?"

"The tests came back with Bangs Disease."

"That's terrible."

"How could this happen?"

"Somebody must have switched them."

"Who'd do such a thing?"

"Jesse?" emerged simultaneously from Will and Frank's mouths.

"I don't think so," Will said.

"He always hated Grandpa and me," Frank said. "Didn't much like you, either."

"He's changed."

"A skunk doesn't change his stripe. He said that he'd see us in Hell. Looks like he got us both in one fell swoop."

"I don't think he'd do it." Who else then? Finian? Mary had always disliked him.

"Those were my cows," Frank said. "It's my reputation. I expect your sheriff to take action. I'll meet you at the sheriff's office, but, first, I need to shore up a pen for my new Hereford bull." He led Will out the door.

<hr />

Will approached Willow late afternoon. Along the way he decided he must seek charges. Henning and Roberts would be furious if he didn't take action. But hadn't Jesse suffered enough?

Sheriff Bates, whose attention was fixed on the papers on his desk, didn't notice Will at first.

Will cleared his throat.

"Oh, it's you, Will. I hate paperwork. If I'd known my days would be spent at my desk, I'd never have run for this office."

"I've never seen another Sheriff in that seat. Why do you stay?"

"Habit, I guess. What's on your mind?"

"I suppose you know I've got Bangs in my herd."

"Bad stuff. I heard that Jesse delivered the cows. What does he say?"

"I haven't seen him. I wanted to talk with my brother Frank first. He should be here soon."

"I'd heard they were your brother's cows. It's a crime to move diseased cows you know."

"All twenty-five of his cows were certified disease free. He's got the papers."

"Someone switched them in transit then. You think it was Jesse?"

"He delivered them, but… "

"Why would he do that to you?"

"I don't think he would. Maybe years ago."

"Roberts was in. He wants me to file charges."

"Against who?"

"He doesn't care. He says somebody should pay."

"Do you plan to arrest Jesse?"

"Not yet. We'll bring him in for questioning. I want that McCarthy first." Bates rose from his chair. "He's been known to cut corners. Nothing too serious, not yet. Nothing like this."

Will heard voices outside the door, where Deputy Smith held his brother back. The deputy stood aside when Bates beckoned Frank in.

"Will, I've mulled this over all the way from the Springs," Frank said. He rushed toward Sheriff Bates. "I want arrests. My reputation's at stake here."

"Calm down," Sheriff Bates said. He turned to Will. "This your brother?"

"Frank," Will nodded toward the sheriff, "Sheriff Bates."

"Sheriff, I want an arrest."

"And who are you accusing?"

"My brother Jesse. He hauled the sick cows, didn't he?"

"Maybe."

Frank turned to his brother. "He did haul them, didn't he, Will?"

"I don't think Jesse would do it."

"Lots of chances to make a switch," Bates said. "It could have been done before they were loaded." He glared at Frank. "It could've been done right in your own barnyard."

Frank slammed his fist on the sheriff's desk and shouted, "Are you accusing me?"

Bates threw his pen down and leaned into Frank. "Hold on. I'm not accusing you or Jesse. Least, not yet. I want to question McCarthy first." He walked to the phone on the far wall. "He owns the trucks."

After a short conversation, Sheriff Bates hung up the phone and turned back to the brothers. "Ashley Springs's Constable Stephens will bring him here tomorrow."

"He's arresting him?" Frank said.

"Bringing him in for questioning. We'll get to arrests later—if there's evidence."

"I want to be here when he comes in," Frank said.

"Might be a good idea. Both of you. Be here at noon tomorrow."

"I still think it's Jesse," Frank said to Will as he stepped into his Chevy. "The nerve of that sheriff. Accusing me."

"I don't think he's accusing anyone," Will said. "Not yet."

❖

Finian McCarthy sat on the sheriff's desk when Will and Frank entered the office the next day at noon. As cheerful as ever although a bit tattered, Finian wore his usual brown, checkered derby hat with matching knee-length corduroy breeches, emerald green swallow-tail jacket, field-corn yellow shirt, and his buckle-topped shoe a faded red.

Sheriff Bates peered around Finian, a frown on his face.

Constable Stephens looked befuddled as he dashed past the brothers toward the door. "That's the dangest trip I've ever taken. Gotta get back home to some sanity."

Finian pounced off the desk and grabbed Will's hand. "Good to see you, Will. Tell this man," he pointed to Bates, "that I'm an old friend. He thinks I cheated you. I wouldn't do no such thing. You know that."

Will jerked his hand free and remained silent.

"You know I wouldn't, Will. Not to a Wicklow man. Haven't I helped you find good cows?" Finian pressed so close that Will turned his head away from his foul breath. "Isn't that right?"

Frank grabbed Finian's arm. "Someone switched those cows. If not you, who then?"

Finian hung his head. "I hadn't meant to say anything. Your brother . . . . 'Course, I couldn't know for sure. I was doing business down in Dubuque when this all happened. But, who else could have done it?"

"That's what we're trying to determine," Sheriff Bates said. "Why do you think it's Jesse? Could have been Frank here. They're his cows."

Frank clenched his fists.

Will grabbed his arm.

"Don't know 'bout Frank," Finian said. "I do know that Jesse hated the two of you." Finian's pudgy face drooped and his lips tightened. "He complained to me how you cheated him, how it cost him his face and future. Why, you said so yourself that day we went looking for him. Didn't you, Will?"

Will's muscles tightened as he bristled at the memory of that day. He should have been more discrete.

"Well, didn't you?"

Will nodded.

"We better find Jesse and bring him in for questioning," Sheriff Bates said.

Finian snatched his hat off the desk and limped toward the door.

"Just a minute, McCarthy," Bates said. "I'm not through with you yet." He grabbed Finian's arm and guided him toward the cellblock. "I'm going to hold you a bit longer, until we get to the bottom of this."

Deputy Smith snarled, grabbed Finian by his grubby collar, and shoved him down the hall, Finian protesting at every step along the way.

"Take it easy, Smith," Bates called. "Wait until he's found guilty before you jostle him."

Bates turned back toward the O'Shaughnessy brothers. "Smith gets a little rough with our clientele at times." He grinned. "I tell him not to alienate my constituency. I don't mind after they're found guilty." He emitted a deep belly laugh. "They can't vote when they're in the clink."

A cell door clanged. Will heard Finian's loud protests, followed by a shrill yelp, and then ponderous footsteps preceded Smith's reentry into the room. "Glad to get rid of that man. He can scream his gripes at the walls for a while."

"Do you know where Jesse could be, Will?" Sheriff Bates asked.

"I saw Jesse enter the grocery store an hour ago," Smith said.

Might he have gone to the tavern?" Bates said.

"He doesn't drink anymore," Will said. "I've never seen him at the Waterin' Hole."

"I doubt that," Frank said. "Once they start, they don't stop. That's what Grandpa said."

"Smith, go see if you can find him. Bring him in. Go easy on him, mind you."

"Sure, boss." Smith sneered at Bates. "I always treat them right, now don't I?"

Will jumped up as Smith headed out the door. "Frank, I'm going with the deputy. Go to my house. Tell Mary I'll be home as soon as we find Jesse."

Will ran after Smith, but he couldn't keep up with the fast moving deputy. He heard Smith's call up ahead, "Have you seen Jesse O'Shaughnessy?" The voice came from around the corner of a building.

A gravelly voice called back, "Down by the river."

Will rushed onward, but people, drawn to the commotion, blocked his path as they raced forward on the heels of the agitated deputy. Will heard more calls from ahead. "He's running along the river bank." Will surged forward and pushed people aside. He had to reach the deputy before he got to his brother. He knew that Jesse must be insane with fright.

Then the crowd stopped and Will burst through. "Where's Jesse?"

Deputy Smith drew his gun, and people edged toward widow Wilder's house on the river.

"He ran through the front door," Smith said.

"Put your gun away," Will said. "I'll go in."

Deputy Smith began to holster his weapon. Then he rapidly drew it again when they heard screams from inside the house.

"What's he doing to her?" Smith said.

"The poor woman's scared," Will said as he ran into the house. He had no sooner pushed through the door when he heard shouts behind him. "He's running out the back."

"Stop. Stop or I'll shoot," Smith hollered. "Stop, I said."

Will heard a gunshot and feared the worst.

Will passed widow Wilder and her daughter, who huddled in the back entry and screamed like banshees but were apparently unhurt. He raced out the back door. As he exited the house, he heard another shot and saw Smith's gun pointed in the air. Jesse stood on the river bank. He looked back, and then he leapt into the water.

Deputy Smith raced forward with his gun leveled, but before he could fire again, Will shouted, "He's not a criminal. He's just wanted for questioning."

Smith turned toward Will who grabbed the gun from his hand and, without thinking, knocked the deputy head-over-teakettle into the rushing water, shouting, "Take that, Grandpa."

Will recoiled for a moment when he comprehended his action and words, but he felt good about it. Maybe he hadn't lost his manhood. He looked at the weapon in his hand, threw it into the water, stripped to his underclothes, and jumped in after Jesse. He sank deep, fought his way to the surface, and shook the water from his eyes. At first, he lost track of Jesse, but looked around while he treaded water. He saw hands reaching for the deputy who struggled in the water, but Smith's welfare didn't concern him. He whipped around and saw Jesse ahead, swimming toward a sandbar a hundred yards out. He wasn't sure Jesse could make it. Jesse had never been a good swimmer, and Will wasn't surprised to rapidly close in on his brother. He supposed that Jesse planned to run along the sandbar to where it spun off Turkey Island and then another mile up the island to where it rose less than thirty yards from the mainland. Will wouldn't try to stop him. This was no time for Jesse to face a frenzied crowd and an angry, wet deputy. Maybe he could hide Jesse away and go back to Sheriff Bates for help.

Will figured he was safe on the mainland side of the island where the water eddied and slowed before it reentered the main channel at the sandbar's end. He wanted to avoid the vicious undercurrents that swirled off the tip of the sandbar, awaiting the unwary. When he saw Jesse scramble onto the sand, Will treaded water and called, "Jesse, wait for me. Let me help."

Jesse turned and trudged up the sand. He didn't look back or respond to Will's call.

Distracted, Will had drifted downstream and now approached the sandbar from below. He felt the tug of the river and knew he could be in trouble. He swam with all the energy he could muster. He had to make the sandbar. He had to catch his brother. Will stroked hard against the rushing water. "Jesse, stop!" he screamed as he turned his head to the side for air.

He stretched upward and sank his fingers into the sand, but the river's fury grabbed hold of his lower body. Exhausted, he lifted his shoulders from the water and slithered onto the sand. The current sucked him back. He shouted, "Jesse, stop! Help me!"

And when Jesse saw Will's plight, he did stop. At first, he slowly retraced his steps. When Will slipped backward, Jesse ran and reached for his brother's hand as Will, completely spent, tried to pull himself up.

Jesse grabbed firm and pulled hard, but his feet slipped in the wet sand. He tightened his grip and stepped backward to gain leverage, but as he leaned back and pulled again, the sandbar crumbled under him, and he tumbled into the surging current. Jesse's fingers slipped from Will's hand. Will grabbed hold of his brother's shirt and they plummeted along together.

Will knew better than to fight the current. The turbulence swept them downstream, sometimes high like a schooner running before the wind, sometimes submerged like a broken derrick. Fighting to stay on top, Will tried to get an arm free, but he clung to his brother. "Grab around my shoulders," he shouted as he shifted under Jesse and held tight with one hand while he flailed the water with the other.

Jesse gripped Will's shoulders. Then he slipped as the water whipped about them. When his grip loosened, he shifted forward and, for a moment, stared into Will's eyes. "I didn't do it. Tell Catherine—"

When the water pulled them under once more, Jesse let go of Will's shoulders and he was gone.

Will started after him, but he couldn't hold his breath any longer. Water filled his nose, his throat, and he began to suck it in. His brain went numb as he kicked hard toward the light ahead, pulled at the water with the strength that remained, and popped into the sunlight at the river bank's calm. He gasped for air as hands pulled him up the slope and pumped life into his limp body. He spat muddy river water and it ran down his chin. He coughed a watery emission, again and again. "Where's Jesse? Did you find Jesse?"

⬦⟫⟫⟫⟫-⟨⟨⟨⟨⬦

Two days later, Will felt no physical effects from his ordeal, but he couldn't forget the look of despair on Jesse when he twisted back to look into Will's face before he slipped under the water. He had proclaimed his innocence with such fervor that Will had no doubts—not about Jesse.

When Mary asked about it, he told how Smith had chased Jesse, how he had followed, but his confrontation with the deputy was a muddle in his mind. He could only think about Jesse grasping his hand and the water that engulfed them. He could only think about their struggle against the relentless current that spun them in circles and dragged them under. He didn't want to talk about it, so he retreated to the barn and pitched hay in the loft.

When he and Petr had unloaded the summer's last hay crop, the pulley on the fork had frozen, so they dropped the last forkful in the center runway. To make room above for that spilled in the runway, Will climbed the stacked hay and began to pitch it toward the barn's far end. After fifteen

198

minutes of throwing forkfuls under the hot roof, sweat poured down his forehead and into his eyes. When he stopped to pull his handkerchief, he heard Petr's call from below.

"Will, you've been through an ordeal. Come on down. I'll do that."

Will wiped perspiration from his brow and shouted down, "I'll finish this. Get the cows up."

"We don't milk for another hour. I'll help."

When Will heard the crunch of hay under Petr's boots, he called, "Stay down, Petr. I'll do this job."

"Are you sure, Will?"

Will didn't answer. He shoved his hankie into his back pocket and furiously pitched hay toward the loft's far end. When the hay piled high, he moved forward and pitched more towards the back. He pitched until hay touched the track at the barn's peak. He pitched until his arms ached and his head throbbed. He pitched until all images of Jesse were erased from his mind.

After the last hay was cleared from the center runway and he had no more hay to pitch, those images returned. Could he have grasped his brother at that final moment—a brother who had saved his life at the sandbar and had rescued Catherine that day at the river? Could he have made one last attempt to save Jesse? Will mulled that thought over and over.

Roberts and Henning didn't wait for Will's grief to subside. They came to his house and demanded that he go with them to the sheriff's office.

"Will, you do the talking, but we expect action," Roberts said. "Let's get to the bottom of this."

Before Will could deliver his planned speech, Sheriff Bates was on him. "I was just sitting here trying to decide whether I should issue a warrant and go looking for you. Glad you've saved me the trouble. Tell me why I shouldn't throw you in that cell back there?"

"I—"

"Tell me why I shouldn't lock you up and throw away the key. You took my deputy's gun and threw it into the river." Bates pushed into Will. "You threw him into the river. I should charge you for interfering with the law in the line of duty. Assaulting an officer. Destruction of government property. Disorderly conduct. Let's see." He grabbed his duty book off the shelf. "I can probably find half a dozen things in here to throw at you."

Will had had enough. He jabbed his finger at the sheriff. "That man should be relieved of his job. He has no business being a lawman. Firing his gun at a man you wanted for questioning. He's incompetent. He has no business on the force. What's he think this town is—Dodge City?"

"He says your brother wouldn't stop. You were there. Why'd he run?"

"Your deputy shot at him! My god, man, he had his face blown away in the war. Wouldn't you run, too?"

"S'pose so." Bates dropped his duty book onto his desk. "Calm down, Will. There'll be no action." His shoulders drooped.

"We want to press charges," Roberts shouted.

"Against who?"

"Against McCarthy," Henning said.

"I released him," Bates said.

"You let him go?" Roberts screamed.

"We'll keep investigating, but there's not a shred of evidence."

"You think it was Jesse?" Will said.

"We'll never know, will we? It seems likely, though."

"He stared death in the face and swore that he didn't do it, Sheriff. He saved my life."

"Easy enough. T'wern't no Bible."

"Did they find his body?" Henning said.

"Not yet," Bates said. "They think he may have snagged on a dead-head. He may not emerge for weeks."

"It has to be Finian," Will said. "Pains me to say it, but years ago, I saw Finian cheat a man out of a meal."

"Lots of people cheated for meals in those days. 'Twas hardly a crime. Besides, that's circumstantial evidence. I can't arrest him on that."

"He had a motive, Sheriff," Will said. "People say he's cash poor. He could've netted a hundred fifty, maybe more, on each cow he switched."

"I can't prosecute on could'ves. His alibi's airtight. He was at the Dubuque Packing Company offices the whole week those cows were delivered."

"He was less than two hours from Frank's place. He might have slipped back."

"You could claim the man exchanged steers for prime bulls, but that wouldn't make it so. We'll keep looking. I promise you that. I'll let you know if we find something."

Roberts stepped past Will and stared the Sheriff down. "Why do I get the feeling you're not trying very hard? S'pose you've got better things to do than chase cow thieves. But someone's going to pay for this."

And Will had a pretty good idea who that someone was.

38

Will knew mechanical things, but he wasn't fond of them. They weren't as reliable as his horses. And besides, he couldn't talk to them. They didn't respond like his horse.

"Fanny Too, how'd we get into such trouble? It doesn't look good, does it, old girl?"

Fanny Too nuzzled Will's neck.

A machine wouldn't do that.

"I know. I know. You've done your best. It's me who's made the mess."

Will opened the gate, then paused before he left Fanny Too's stall. "It's okay, old girl. We'll see this through together."

Will walked slowly around the barn and up the ramp to the hayloft. He sat on a half-empty grain bag and placed his head in his hands. He remembered a tug-of-war competition when he was a boy. He'd slipped on the rope, and he and his friends lost the competition. He knew it was his fault, and he'd let them down. He ran all the way home and cried in his room. Over tug-of-war. It seemed so important then. He looked around the loft. The fork rope dangled to the floor. It hung limp, inviting… no, he wouldn't let Mary face the music alone.

Will reached around the milk house door and grabbed his fishing pole. The morning's dew sparkled in the grass. More than half his herd was gone. With so few cows, milking hadn't taken long. He'd hated letting Petr go, but he'd had little choice. Thankfully, George Snell needed the help. Will hoped that Snell would keep Petr on through the winter. He had enough cows needing milking.

Where could he fish undisturbed today? This may be his last chance before winter set in. Maybe the downed tree behind Earl Roberts's place. He hadn't been there since the summer. Did he really want to go near Earl's? Still, he felt drawn in that direction. He walked through his bean field, threw his pole over the fence, and slid under the bottom strand. He ambled through the hay stubble and turned toward the river. A slight cooling breeze blew in Will's face, and as he approached his largest corn field, the stalks bent to confront him. When he stopped to wipe his brow, he could hear their murmuring, could hear their whispered accusations.

Will turned toward the river. Should he go the long way or cut behind Earl's buildings? He decided to slip behind Earl's place. The shortcut saved a half-mile walk. From a distance Will saw Marge and their youngest daughter, Emily Lou, racing around the yard. He edged closer until he could hear a man's voice call from the barn. The words weren't those that Will would utter around his children. He moved closer. Emmy Lou saw him and ran in his direction. "Mr. O'Shaughnessy, Dad's having a terrible time. He can't get the machines working, and the cows are bawling for relief."

Will approached the barn door. He wasn't sure he should be there. "Earl, are you in here?"

Will heard a commotion inside the milk house. He hesitated but walked toward the noise. "What's wrong?"

"Will O'Shaughnessy, what are you doing here? I've got enough trouble as it is."

"What's wrong, Earl?"

"It's this damn pump. It's not working, not drawing air."

"Maybe I can help."

"Will, I swore if I never saw you again, it would be too soon. You've left me in a terrible fix. I'm lucky I haven't lost any cows, least not yet. Could lose my whole herd."

"No one feels worse than I do, and no one's lost more. You know I had no bad intent."

"We trusted your judgment. Now, I may not have enough income to pay my bills. I'll be in a terrible fix if I lose cows."

"It may not come to that. Let me look at your pump. Do you have a five-eighths socket?"

Will levered the piston. "Your rings are shot. It'll take a few days to get new ones."

"What'll I do for milking? The cows can't wait. I'm rusty milking by hand."

"I'll help. I owe you that. But I want to try something first. Bring your tractor over."

"Tractor?"

"I've got an idea. Always thought it might work."

Earl drove his Farmall tractor toward the milk house.

"Come as close to the door as possible," Will said. "A little more left."

Earl backed within two feet of the doorway.

"Whoa, that's close enough. I'll need a long vacuum hose, a spark plug wrench, and I'll need a petcock, too."

"What are you up to? I hope you know what you're doing. I don't know that I trust your judgment anymore."

"Fair enough, Earl. I don't know that it'll work either, but it's worth a try. It could save lots of squeezing."

While Earl retrieved the hose and wrench, Will inspected the milk line. He hoped the vacuum hose was long enough, but when he stretched it toward the tractor, he found that it wasn't. "Earl, we'll need something longer than this."

"It's the longest I could find. If it'll help, I have another just like it."

"Do you have a hose splice? Splicing'll cut the draw, I think. I hope the tractor's got enough vacuum to pull it."

Earl returned with the splice and handed it to Will, who'd just removed the plug from the manifold. "I don't understand."

"If I insert this petcock into the manifold," he fingered the shiny metal valve, "and then connect it to the milk line, I think your tractor can pull enough vacuum to run your machines." Will screwed the petcock's threads into the opening. "Keep your fingers crossed."

The hose didn't quite reach the milk line, so Will undid the connection and replaced the petcock with the plug. "Turn your tractor and come in from the side."

After several attempts, Earl jimmied the tractor in place, so tight to the doorway they couldn't get through. "Go round and work from inside," Will said.

Will removed the plug once more and reinserted the petcock. He stretched the hose, and this time Earl could connect it to the milk line. He shouted to Will, "Start the engine."

The engine popped and fizzled out. Will turned the crank again. The engine fired, coughed once, and then it settled into a hesitant, continuous popping.

Will slowly opened the petcock and heard the welcome sound of air rushing through the line. "It's working. Attach a milking machine."

Earl hung a canister under a cow's udder. "I hope this works, Will."

"I think it'll do," Will said as Earl attached the hose from the machine to the nearest petcock and then slipped the cups onto the cow's teats, one at a time. A steady rhythm of surging milk greeted their ears.

"Looks like you did it right," Earl said. "This time."

"Looks like you won't abuse your fingers," Will said. "This time."

Will strolled home, his fishing pole over his shoulder. He no longer felt the need to fish. Helping Roberts had been small recompense, and he felt better, but he wasn't sure why he should.

"Well, Fanny Too. Let's pull some of that brush that Petr cut last spring. I've been meanin' to do that all summer."

He hooked Fanny Too onto the stone boat and walked her through the gate, past his sparse herd, toward the far side of the enclosure. He knew a little exercise would do Fanny Too good, and it was good for him as well. It'd give him more time with his friend. "What do you think, old girl? Do you think I'll be able to recover?"

Fanny Too turned toward him and nickered softly.

"But how'll I make a living?"

They pulled brush across the pasture, through the gate, and into a large pile that Will stacked away from the barn. Will had seen innocent fires flare out of control and turn into monstrous beasts that consumed the farmer's buildings. He needed to be careful.

The brush reached upward toward a sun that was now high in the sky. "Fanny Too, I think we've done enough for today."

Will walked his horse to the water tank. When he released the brake, a wisp of wind sent the sail blades whirling, and fresh water gushed into the tank. Before the tank overflowed, Will pulled the rope which braked the flying sail. "No use wasting our precious water," he said aloud to Fanny Too. She turned away. He supposed she understood people better than conservation.

After she dipped her nose and drank long, Will said, "That's enough, Fanny Too. Can't afford to get you sick, now can we? We need each other, old girl."

Will led Fanny Too to her stall, forked hay into her manger and poured a scoop of oats alongside. He wanted to spend time with Catherine who was home for the weekend, so he turned toward the house, but not before he acknowledged Fanny Too's enthusiastic whinny with a tip of his cap. "Enjoy those oats, old girl. Let's hope there's more work ahead."

Will met Catherine as he stepped through the door. She ignored his greeting and ran past without a word. That's not like my girl, Will thought, so he followed her toward the kitchen. Will took one step into the room and saw Catherine, her head buried in Mary's bosom, crying her heart out. He retreated to his horsehair in the parlor. Whatever could be wrong?

After a few minutes, Will heard footsteps through the kitchen and then on the stairs. A moment later, Mary entered and sat across from him.

"What's wrong with Catherine?" Will said. "She didn't even say hello when I came in."

"It's a rough time for her, Will. She's in a dither, worrying about this first teaching position. She's worn herself to a frazzle, preparing all summer. She's hardly left Sharon's house. Then today, she went to Jenny Witherspoon's for an afternoon tea. She planned to stay into the evening." Mary looked so distressed that Will was alarmed. "The girls were so mean that she left and ran home. It's the cattle thing. One of the girls said that you've stolen their livelihood, and that it's all your fault."

"Jenny? Her father didn't lose any cows. Why, she's Catherine's best friend."

"No, Jenny tried to defend Catherine. It was Liz Roberts. She was vicious. She wouldn't let up."

"I helped Earl today."

"Liz probably didn't know," Mary said.

"It shouldn't affect our girls. They had no part in this."

"No, it shouldn't, but it does. You should know better than anyone that life's not always fair."

The sins of their fathers. Could it get any worse?

39

Now in 1946 the boys were home and America was booming, but Will was at the bottom of his barrel. All that he'd hoped for, all that he'd worked for, was over. He couldn't make his payments, so the bank called his loans.

Will snapped the reins. "Giddyap, Fanny Too." He'd been at the Midtown Waterin' Hole all afternoon and it was time to go home.

Buried in his misery and bleary-eyed from drink, he didn't notice the lone figure who strolled up the road. When Will got alongside, a voice called out, "Are you Will O'Shaughnessy?"

"What?"

"I'm looking for Will O'Shaughnessy. Might you be he?"

"I might be, young man." Will looked around. "Don't see anyone else. Must be me. Whoa, Fanny Too. And who be you?"

"I'm Jason McGraw. They call me Pickle." Pickle grabbed the back of the seat and pulled himself up. "Mr. O'Shaughnessy, you look plumb tuckered out. Want me to drive you home?"

"Pickle? Aren't you the fella who did the milking that time I was away? You live down by the slaughterhouse, don't you? Your dad—"

"Yeah, he's Sam McGraw." Pickle turned red. "Suppose you know he's in prison. My fault."

"How's that?"

"He didn't like the crowd I ran with. Ben stole from Dad's best friend. Dad beat the crap out of him. Hurt him bad, so they sent Dad up. I'm lookin' for work."

"I had to let my man go. I couldn't afford him. How old are you, Pickle?"

"Almost eighteen." Pickle dropped to the road. "Had a couple jobs. Not for long, though. Never farmed but I'd try." He kicked at a toad that he spotted in the grass. "Git outta here horny toad. Don't want your warts."

"I don't do much farming anymore. Maybe you heard. The bank's closing me down."

"Need some money to help my mom. Aunt Tessie's helpin' Ma and my little brother, Tom, while Pa's up the river. Aunt's a pain in the backside. Always readin' from the Book. But she's good to Tom."

"Doesn't your aunt live over near Spring Green, in the Valley of the Almighty Joneses. Tessie Wright? She spoke at our church last fall and gave a big donation to our missionary fund."

"That's her all right. She has land that she doesn't farm since Uncle Ruben died—some money, too."

"I'm allowed a little money to get ready for auction. I could use some help cleaning the machinery and buildings. I can't pay much though."

"Meals, too?"

"We can do that. Mary's a good cook, even when provisions are short." Will extended his hand. "Come on up." Will handed the reins to Pickle and slid across the seat. "Here, you drive."

Will sat in silence as Pickle guided Fanny Too along. "Gotta clear my head a bit. Too much drink. Not good for you, lad. Don't you do it."

"Dad was drunk when he pounded Ben. I like white lightning when I can get it."

"It's not a good idea while you're with us, young man. Mary doesn't like alcohol. She'll not be happy with me today."

"Do you have many horses?"

"Fanny Too here. Then there's Mabel. I run her with Fanny Too. There's Ned and Ted, as sturdy a team as you'll find in this county. They pull my heavy loads."

Pickle waggled the reins. "Gitup, horse. Whatta you call her?"

"Fanny Too. She's a good horse, boy"

"That's a funny name for a horse. Gitup, Fanny Too."

"Her mother was Fanny, and when this one came along, my daughter, Ruby, called her Fanny Too, and the name stuck. Sometimes I forget that old Fanny is gone."

Pickle smiled as he flicked the reins over Fanny Too, but not hard enough to slap her back.

Will could see that the boy liked horses. "I can't forget Lyda. When my daughters were home, they rode Lyda. She's too small for heavy work. Gotta get rid of them all now, even Fanny Too." Will removed a flask from

207

his shirt pocket and took a swig. He didn't offer any to Pickle. "It's not fair to take them all. I've had Fanny Too and Mabel a long time now. I haven't told them yet. It'll break the old girls' hearts."

"Lots of people lost their places, Mr. O'Shaughnessy."

"When times were bad. Rotten luck, I guess." Will took another swig from his flask. "I bought sick cows. Wiped out my herd. Maybe others, too. That's the bad thing, son. Hurt other people."

"Some have the demon on their shoulder. That's what Aunt Tessie said."

"And some don't have the grit for it. That's what Granddad said."

When they turned up the driveway toward the buildings, four horses raced across the pasture toward them. "They think they're being neglected," Will said. "I usually give them oats midmorning."

"Can I feed them, Mr. O'Shaughnessy?"

"Well sure, boy. Help me stow this rig, and I'll show you the grain shed. You can refill the bins and feed the horses. Fanny Too's earned hers today."

After Pickle helped push the buggy into the shed, Will led him to the granary. "Hoist that sack of oats and carry it to the barn. It should refill the bins."

Pickle bent over, grabbed the sack, and planted it on his shoulder.

"Hold on there. You'll hurt your back lifting like that. Put it down, and I'll show you the right way."

Pickle dropped the sack to the ground. "I said I didn't know farmin'. I've been liftin' all my life. I'm not wet behind the ears, you know."

"Certainly not. You're a strong boy, stronger than me, I'm sure. Yes you are. But you'll be stooped at a young age if you lift that way. Bend your knees, son. Here, I'll show you."

Will dropped his butt, grabbed the sack, lifted it to his shoulder, and straightened back up. "See, I can hoist a sack now as easily as when I was young."

Will lowered the sack. "Now, you do it."

"If you say so, Mr. O'Shaughnessy." Again, Pickle bent at the waist and lifted the sack to his shoulder. "Where do you want it?"

Will shook his head and sighed. "Take it to the barn. I'll get the horses."

Once the horses were in their stalls, Will searched for his grain scoop. "Let's see, where did I put it? That's another thing. Always keep your tools in one place. Try to anyway. Saves time that way." He moved some grain sacks. "Not here."

Pickle walked the line of horses. Each leaned across the rail, straining to receive a share. He inched his hand forward and patted one on the nose. Fanny Too stood away from the rails, acting as if she understood that her grain would arrive in due time.

Will muttered as he searched for the missing scoop.

Pickle climbed onto the bottom rail and leaned toward Fanny Too. She stood quietly, resting her back leg. He climbed to the second rail and reached out. "Mr. O'Shaughnessy, over here. Your scoop's in Fanny Too's stall."

"Must have sprouted legs." He retrieved the scoop and motioned Pickle to the feed sack. "First, empty the oats into that bin over there." He pointed toward the side of the horse barn. "Then feed one scoop to each horse, in the end of their manger."

Pickle grabbed the feed sack, as stiff-legged as before, dumped it, and seized the scoop. He walked past the eager horses to Fanny Too's stall and pushed the hay aside.

"Don't worry too much about the hay, Jason. They'll search for that grain like we'd search for gold in a sluice."

Pickle continued to brush the hay away.

Will wasn't sure if he was concerned about Fanny Too or just being difficult. Give him time.

Pickle scooped grain to each horse. He stopped at Mabel's stall and watched her longer than the others. "Isn't she kinda heavy, Mr. O'Shaughnessy? Should we be givin' her grain?"

"Good eye, Jason. She's with foal. I think she'll deliver before the auction. You may see new life on this farm. Give her a little extra."

Pickle dropped a second scoopful into her manger.

"Not too much now."

"I've never seen a newborn, not when they're wet from their mother."

That night before supper, Will asked Mary if she had any angel food cake left over from the night before.

"I planned to take that to the church meeting tonight." She glared at Will. "Looks as if we could use a little piety around here."

"Now, Mary. For the boy. He worked hard today."

"Maybe I could spare a piece, just one, mind you. For the boy. Put him in Petr's room. You'll find fresh linens in the closet."

Pickle ate like he hadn't seen a meal for days. "That's sure good chicken, Mrs. O'Shaughnessy. Could I have another piece? Please?"

"Pickle, may I call you Jason?"

209

"Sure, Mrs. O'Shaughnessy. Don't much like Pickle anyhow."

"We have little money, but we don't go hungry, with the garden, animals, and all. Eat as much as you'd like. Don't forget, there's a big piece of angel food cake for dessert. Thick frosting, too."

After Mary left for her meeting, Pickle said, "Mr. O'Shaughnessy, don't you like angel food cake?"

"Well, yes I do. Mary wanted the cake for her meeting tonight, and I ate mine last night. Besides, I think she's sending a message. Women do that sometimes, you know. She doesn't like my drink."

"I don't know much about women."

"You'll learn."

"I'd rather learn about your horses."

"We can't rush things. When you're ready, I'll make you my horseman. But there's more pressing work now. Tomorrow, I'll start you cleaning machinery."

The next morning, Will called toward Pickle's room from the bottom of the stairs. "Time to get up, son. Looks like a bright, sunny day ahead."

No answer.

Will wasn't surprised. He trudged up the steps. "Jason, there's work to do."

Still, no answer.

Will entered Pickle's room and shook him hard as he called, "Get up, boy. We've got work ahead."

Pickle rolled over and squinted. "It's the middle of the night." He turned away.

"If we wait much longer, it'll be middle of the day. It's after five already."

Pickle stared at Will. "Five o'clock? In the mornin'?" He groaned, and then he slid a leg from under the blanket.

Will started down the stairs. Then he called back, "If you're going to work here, you'll have to get used to it. We start early. Milking won't take long, but there's plenty of other things to do."

Will was pitching feed to the cows when Pickle, bleary-eyed and lethargic, caught up. "Go to the milk house and get two big cans and a pail off the rack." Will pitched another forkful down the chute. "Put them on the aisle. But stay back from the cows. They sense strangers and they'll kick. And if they hit you, they'll leave a dent."

Will was pleased to find the cans and pail in the center aisle away from the gutter, just as he had asked. "I don't expect you to do the milking. It takes practice. Go grab a five-tined fork," Will pointed toward the back, "and start cleaning out the horse stalls. Pitch it into the spreader, but turn the horses out first."

"Ugh," Pickle muttered.

"Part of farming, lad. If you want to be a horseman, you gotta do the dirty work, too."

"Can I ride one?"

"Have you ever ridden a horse?"

"A little."

"You'll get your chance, Jason, but I better give you a few pointers first." He handed a manure fork to Pickle. "I learned the hard way and made many a mistake. You can learn from my mistakes. You won't live long enough to make them all yourself."

"Shucks," Pickle said as he grabbed the fork and turned toward the stalls.

"Just pitch it into the spreader. I'll take it away when I get done here."

Forty minutes later, Will joined Pickle at the horse stalls. "Milking doesn't take long these days. I lost half my herd." Will grabbed a manure fork. "When we get this done, I'd like for you to start cleaning machinery. I'm going to the south forty to repair a downed fence."

"Will there be time for riding?"

"Don't be in a hurry, young man. There's enough machine cleaning to keep you busy for a while. And then we'll clean and whitewash the buildings." Will threw three forkfuls into the wagon while Pickle watched. "I'm lucky the bank's paying for cleanup. It's the only reason I can take you on, son. Remember, you're here as a worker."

Pickle tossed a forkful. They pitched manure for half an hour, and then Will set his fork down. "It's getting hot. I need to work on those fences." He motioned forward. "I'll start you on the machines."

Pickle hesitated.

"Hustle now, son. Help me pull the plow and cultivators from the machine shed."

After they removed the equipment and parked it under a tree near the water tank, Will left to get a putty knife, a brush, and a hose. He sank one end of the hose into the tank and sucked through the other until water flowed freely. He showed Pickle how he wanted the machines cleaned, and then he left to hook Fanny Too and Mabel to the wagon.

Pickle dabbed at the mud on the plow shears while Will headed out to the south field.

When Will returned late that afternoon, Pickle wasn't with the machines. Will looked in the barn, through the sheds, and behind the house, but saw no sign of his helper. He asked Mary if she had seen him. She shrugged. "I haven't seen him since milking. I thought he'd be in for lunch. When he didn't show up, I supposed he'd gone with you."

"He must have decided that farm work's too hard. Probably set out for home."

Will went to the barn to finish the manure job they'd begun that morning. He had worked no more than half an hour when he heard horse hooves outside the building. When he went to look, he found Lyda standing at the door. Her saddle hung under her stomach, and she bled from scratches across her side and belly.

Will released the saddle and raced to the house as fast as his stiff knees would allow. "Mary, something's wrong. Lyda's outside, all cut up, her saddle hanging loose. That boy must have tried to ride her. Maybe he's down and hurt. I shouldn't have left him alone."

"Stay calm, Will. You search the lane. I'll get on the phone. Maybe someone's seen him."

Will rode Fanny Too toward the river. Why'd he ever take a chance with a strange boy anyhow, and one with Pickle McGraw's reputation? Why did trouble find him whenever he tried to help? Maybe Grandpa was right, maybe he wasn't wise enough to make tough decisions.

He hadn't ridden two miles when he saw a bloody Pickle limping toward him. "Jason McGraw, I trusted you, and look what you've done. You could have killed yourself, and Lyda, too." Will slid off Fanny Too and put his arm under Pickle's shoulder. "Are you okay, son?"

"It's that old saddle. It slipped and threw me into the barbed wire. Darn horse. Darn saddle."

"Jason, you've got to learn how to fit a saddle. First, you need a blanket under it, and then you have to tighten the cinch properly. Lyda sucks air when you tighten down. That leaves the saddle loose." Will boosted Pickle onto Fanny Too's back. "You've got to pull it tight when she exhales. I told you to wait until I could teach you. It's not the saddle, lad, it's your impatience. I can't keep someone who won't listen. It's far too dangerous."

Pickle winced as he turned away, and Will saw the pain in his face

He probably shouldn't keep him. The boy had lots to learn, but, despite his rashness, he was beginning to like this Pickle McGraw.

40

Will saw the dust before Frank's Chevrolet came into sight. He had called Frank and asked him to come, but he wasn't sure what to expect. A year earlier, Will would have been astounded by Frank's interest in his welfare. But Frank had changed. Maybe he had some of their father's tenderness after all. Maybe he wasn't all Grandpa Duffy. The transformation seemed to have followed Jessie's disappearance. Maybe death was on his mind these days. Or maybe—who knows—but he liked the new Frank better.

Will walked to the drive as Frank pulled into the yard. "I wasn't sure you'd come."

"I thought I'd inspect your equipment before the auction. Might be something I can use."

"I keep my machinery in good repair. It's not the machines I'm concerned about, it's the horses. It's Fanny Too. I'd like for you to buy her."

"I'd not want her if you gave her to me."

"I can't give her away."

"Don't know how I'd use her. I got two tractors now."

"Come to the house." Will grasped Frank's arm. "Mary'll make a cup of coffee. Maybe she's got an English muffin, too."

When Will reached for the door, it rushed at his fingers, and Pickle brushed him on his flight out. "Sorry, Mr. O'Shaughnessy. Gotta feed the horses."

"Hold on, Jason. I want you to meet my brother Frank. This is my new man, Jason McGraw."

Frank nodded.

Pickle said, "Hi," but he didn't pause in his rush toward the barn.

"The most horse crazy kid I ever saw," Will said.

Coffee aroma filled the entryway.

"That sure smells good," Frank said to Mary. "Worth the trip for a cup of good coffee. Makes an old batch think he should have a woman."

"Git on with you. No woman would have you." Mary hugged Frank. "What brings you?"

"Didn't you hear, woman, I said your coffee. Maybe an English muffin, too."

"You'll not get an English muffin in this house." She frowned at Frank, and then she broke into a smile as she grabbed his arm and pulled him into the kitchen. "I might find a Cornish one someplace."

"That'll do just fine. How're the girls? Haven't seen them in ages."

"Well, Sharon finished teacher training and she's married now. Living up near Logan Junction, on a farm. She married Ed Meadows, Earl's son. And Ruby's taken over the Dodgeville hospital. She's head nurse there. That girl's a hard worker."

"How's little Catherine? Always had a soft spot for that girl."

"She's not so little anymore," Mary said. "She finished teacher training, and now she's a teacher. Like Sharon. Like me."

Will was surprised to hear that Frank had ever noticed his youngest daughter. He led his brother to the parlor and directed him to his old horsehair. "Won't you consider buying Fanny Too? I raised her as a colt, you know."

"A horse is expensive to keep. I don't need a pet."

"She's not just any horse. You know how I feel about her, how I felt about her mother. Will you do it for me?"

"I'll think on it. Money's hard to come by. I thought you couldn't afford a man."

"I can't. The bank's paying for it. They know the buildings and equipment will fetch more money if they're in good shape."

Mary brought two cups of fresh, steaming coffee.

"I can't pay him much, but he needs the money. He's getting to be a pretty good worker, too. Now my girls are gone, he kinda fills an empty space."

After Frank left, Will joined Pickle in the barn. "I'll pull the disc harrow out of the shed. I'd like for you to clean it today."

Pickle forked the last bit of soiled bedding off the stall floors. "Soon as I get fresh straw down, Mr. O'Shaughnessy. Okay?"

"Sure, Jason. Finish with the horses, then get at it."

Will wondered how the horses would fair with new owners. Sad thing, losing old friends like this. "I'm going to hitch Fanny Too and Mabel and

214

bring in a load of corn. I should be back before you're finished. If I'm not, give Mary a hand in the garden."

"Okay, Mr. O'Shaughnessy."

Will hitched the horses and headed towards the field. When he returned two hours later, he walked past the machine shed on his way to the house. He circled the harrow. *The boy works hard. It looked new. The bank's not getting short-changed here.*

He found Pickle husking a pile of sweet corn. "Jason, that sun was hot out there today. I'm going to take a nap. Will you feed and water Fanny Too and Mabel? Walk them a spell first. They're pretty heated up."

Pickle sprinted two steps toward the barn. Then he stopped and turned back. "Mr. O'Shaughnessy, thanks for lettin' me tend them. I sure do love horses."

"I know, son." Will sighed as he watched Pickle race toward the animals. *He knew the feeling.*

Will sensed trouble when he woke from his nap. Maybe it was because he couldn't find Mary. Maybe it was a sixth sense about his horses. He knew something was wrong. He hurriedly pulled on his coveralls and rushed toward the barn. Mary kneeled in Mabel's stall and Pickle looked down from the rail. "She's sick, Mr. O'Shaughnessy. Somethin's terrible wrong. She won't get up."

Will recognized the problem as soon as he saw his downed horse. She was bloated and breathed hard. "We've got to get her up," he said. He tied a long rope to her halter and handed it to the boy. "Jason, you pull from the top of the rail. Mary, help me lift from behind."

Pickle pulled while Mary and Will lifted, but they couldn't get her fifteen hundred pounds off the floor. Will knelt beside his downed horse. She neighed softly, and her pupils rolled. "Come on, Mabel. You've got to help us." He lifted her head and tugged harder, tugged until she got to her knees. "That's it, old girl. Pull, Jason."

With a lunge that almost toppled her forward, Mabel staggered to her feet. "Good girl. Now, let's walk. Jason, come down and take her outside. We need to keep her upright if it takes us all day."

"Will she be okay," Mr. O'Shaughnessy?"

"I hope so, but if she goes down again, we'll have to call the vet fast. He'll have to stick her."

"Stick her?"

"Puncture her belly, let the gas out. She's badly bloated. It could kill her."

Pickle grimaced as he led Mabel from her stall. "That's awful. Is it my fault?"

"After you watered her, did you feed her fresh alfalfa?"

"Well, yes. I thought she deserved new hay after she worked so hard. Fanny Too wouldn't eat any."

"Fanny Too's a wise old girl. She knew better. It's not your fault, Jason. I didn't think to tell you. They've been on grass all summer. I don't feed the alfalfa until it's thoroughly dry, and then I blend it with timothy at first. Their stomachs can't take the change, especially when they're hot and watered."

"Oh, Mr. O'Shaughnessy, I could have killed her," Pickle said. "I could have killed her foal."

"Yes, but you didn't. I think they'll be okay, son."

⋅⟫⟩⟩⟨⟨⟨⋅

The days passed quickly. Pickle cleaned machinery while Will harvested the crops, sometimes assisted by a neighbor. Mabel recovered and seemed ready for the harness, but Will delayed placing her in the hitch. Instead, he used Ned and Ted more than usual. He didn't want to put the colt at risk. And Fanny Too deserved a respite, too. He wondered what her new owner would demand. Will shivered. He hated to think she would end up with someone who'd whip the last mile out of her.

The auction was two weeks away when Mabel gave birth. It was a strapping young colt that Pickle instantly adopted as his own. Will had difficulty keeping Pickle at the machinery, he was so enamored by the new foal. But he was ahead with his work, so Will didn't keep him and his sweetheart apart more than was necessary.

Will and Pickle were sweeping the barn's walls when Will heard the sound of an automobile. "Now who could that be?" he said. "I wanted to get the barn whitewashed this morning. I need to get to the field this afternoon. Maybe it's Saul. He said he'd come over to help harvest corn."

A voice called, "Will, are you in here?"

"Why, it's Frank," Will said to Pickle. "What could he want?"

"Will?"

"Over here, Frank. By the horse stalls."

Frank ambled past the stanchions to where Pickle and Will mopped the sidewalls. "We're getting ready to whitewash. You come to help?"

216

"The lime makes me sick. I hire mine done."

"You can afford it."

"Will, I want to see you alone for a minute. I've got something to show you. Mary wouldn't happen to have some fresh brew, would she?"

They walked to the house, but couldn't find Mary. "She must have gone outside," Will said. "Should be back in a few minutes." Will checked the coffee pot. "Empty, but she'll make a pot when she gets here. It's better fresh, anyhow."

Frank dropped his cap on the chair and pulled a crumpled envelope from his pocket. He handed it to Will. "Got this from your boy."

Will inspected the scrawled address before he dug out the letter. "It's his writing. He hasn't had much schooling."

He read aloud.

"Dear Mr O'Shaughnessy. Im the boy you met at your brothers last month. Will has been mitee good to me but I'm worreed bout his horses. Them gitin sold and all. You no how he loves Fanny Too. She's a good old horse. I think it may kill him lossin her. I no he asked you to buy her and Id be much obligd if you wood. He cod visit her at your farm and no shes ok. I dont have much mony but Id help pay her keep. I coud send a dollar a month or whatever I can scar up. I promise, Ill try. Please do this for Will.

"Jason McGraw."

"He doesn't make much money, does he?" Frank said.

"Very little, and besides, he needs it for his family. He does love the horses, though."

"Will, I think it's you he cares about," Frank said.

Will was only a little surprised. He'd sure miss that boy.

"I'll take a rain check on that coffee. Gotta get back." Frank snatched his cap off the chair. "There's work to be done."

Will watched as Frank rushed toward his car. He still had a lot of Grandpa in him.

◆◆◆◆◆

Pickle cleaned machinery each day. When he suggested they paint the rusty old plow, Will said he didn't think it would bring enough to justify the work. When Pickle insisted, Will said he had a gallon of red metal paint in the machine shed, and that he'd look for it after breakfast. "You'll have to scrape the rust first."

Pickle scooped the last cold fry from his plate and rushed outside. "The boy's obsessed with getting things ready," Will said to Mary. "He keeps so busy that he neglected the horses this week."

"It's too painful, I think. He knows it's almost over."

Will didn't want to think about it either. He'd not only lose the farm and the horses, but the boy, too.

Pickle worked two days on the old plow, and now it looked almost new.

"You've done fine work, Jason."

"I'll miss the farm, Mr. O'Shaughnessy."

"I've been thinking, son. You've earned your pay, deserve more, but I don't have it. I want you to have the colt. Do you think your Aunt Tessie will let him feed in her pasture, maybe help with expenses? If she'll agree, I'll hold him out of the sale."

"Oh, Mr. O'Shaughnessy! Can you do that?"

"Probably shouldn't, but I will. You deserve it, son. I don't know what I'd have done without you."

On the day of the auction, Will smiled when he saw his brother's Chevrolet among the early arrivals. By now, he wasn't sure what to expect from Frank. Attendance was always dependent on the weather, so Will was glad for the warm, sunny day. He was surprised to feel so keen about the auction's outcome. He supposed it was a matter of pride.

Pickle hadn't been around all morning, but Will knew where to find him. He stopped for a moment to let his pupils adjust when he left the intense sunlight. "Jason, are you in here?" Will shaded his eyes and looked toward the horse stalls.

"Mr. O'Shaughnessy, over here."

Will entered Mabel's stall. He was glad the bank agreed to let him hold the colt from the auction, but the cost was high: Will offered a sum that was surely more than the foal would bring. Still, Will believed he got the best of the deal. He was sure of it when he saw Pickle's tenderness and love for the youngin'. He thought about the day that Fanny Too was born, and knew how the boy felt. Pickle had seldom left the colt's side.

The bond was good for the colt as well.

The bank also agreed that whoever bought Mabel must allow the colt to stay with her until he was weaned. That could be a problem. The little one wouldn't be ready to leave his mother for several more months. "Well, Jason, take good care of the little darlin'. Pretty soon, you'll be all he has."

Pickle looked up with a wan smile. "Mr. O'Shaughnessy, I'll miss the farm." He averted his eyes. "I'll miss you."

"We both need to move on, now don't we, son?"

Will stepped toward Mabel's stall, hesitated; then, he turned toward the sunlight. It was a dark day.

⋘⋙

The auction began with the machinery. Will knew they wouldn't get much for his horse drawn equipment, now that most everyone had tractors. Will was glad to see enough bidders to compete, and they bought more than he had expected.

Will was anxious about attendees' fear of brucellosis in his herd, but the cows he'd brought to auction had all been certified healthy, and he pressed the auctioneer to make that clear to the crowd. He'd even invited his veterinarian there to answer questions, and, at the last moment, he convinced Callison to make a statement to the bidders before the first cow was brought to the block. Will hoped that his cows would bring premium prices.

And they did. The best ones brought more than he'd paid Frank for his cows, and the others brought as much. To be selling now when good cows were hard to find was a stroke of luck. Maybe there'd be a little money left over after the bank got its dues.

Then the auctioneer's assistant led Fanny Too to the front. "She's got some miles on her but she's been well kept. You can see that, gentlemen," the auctioneer chortled. "Lots of hours left in her. What am I bid? Fifty dollars?" He looked over the disinterested throng, then back at Fanny Too. "Clint, bring that other gray out."

Clint led Mabel into the arena, and the auctioneer shouted to the crowd, "A great matched pair. Buy one, buy them both. I'll sell the team."

Frank placed a hand on Will's shoulder. "Is this your idea?" Did you tell him to sell those as a pair?"

The auctioneer called out, "Who'll give a hundred for this fine pair of animals?"

Most of those nearby walked away to inspect other items.

Half a dozen men stayed and eyed the two horses that stood before them, Fanny Too resting one hind leg.

Frank appeared disinterested as he slowly circled the men who gathered around the horses.

Will took pride in seeing there was interest in his matched pair, but he hated the thought of losing his friends. Maybe no one would bid.

When a voice called, "I'll give a hundred," Will felt emptiness. He looked toward Frank who slowly backed away from the action.

Another voice called out, "One fifty."

Will turned away and started toward the barn. He couldn't bear to watch any longer. He heard a voice behind him shout, "Two hundred."

The auctioneer called, "I've got two-hundred. Two-fifty, do I hear two-hundred-fifty?"

There were no more bids.

"Going once," the auctioneer called. "Going twice."

Will's face burned, and, as he stepped into the barn, he steadied himself by grabbing a nearby stanchion.

He heard the auctioneer shout, "Last chance, at two hundred it'll go to—"

Then Will heard a familiar voice call, "Two hundred-fifty."

There was a long pause and the usual summation of "going once, going—"

Will was out the door by the time he heard the auctioneer cry, "Sold!"

He raced toward Frank who stood hands on his hips with a sour look on his face.

"Darn you, Will. What'll I do with two broken down nags?"

Too choked to speak, Will grabbed his brother and hugged him. This wasn't at all like Grandpa.

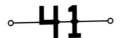

41

ow in 1947, at almost sixty, an age when many farmers had accumulated enough to leave the farm work behind, Will O'Shaughnessy had retired, too. It wasn't because he could afford a life of leisure. He hadn't even saved enough to buy Mary a new apron. Grandpa had been right all along. He didn't have what it takes to manage a business.

All he had left was Mary and the girls. And if it weren't for the generosity of his son-in-law, he wouldn't have a house to live in. Sharon and Ed Meadows resided on the family farm one mile east of Logan Junction. Ed owned his deceased parents' house in the village, and that's where Will and Mary lived now that he'd lost everything. He couldn't even afford a rent payment, and without Ruby and Catherine's help, they wouldn't have food money.

Ruby had completed her program at Mount Sinai School of Nursing in Milwaukee, and, even though she'd worked twenty hours a week at a local laundry, she had graduated at the top of her class and was now head nurse at the Dodgeville General Hospital, seven miles to the west of Logan Junction. She'd been offered higher paying jobs out east, but she came home to help her family.

After leaving nursing school, Catherine completed a preparation program at the Iowa County Normal School and was now in her third year teaching at a country school two miles south of Logan Junction. Catherine was fortunate to board at a farm home near her school. Nevertheless, she walked the two miles to her parents' home each Friday after school, where she could wash and iron her clothes in preparation for the next week.

Catherine arrived one cold winter afternoon glowing with news to share. That afternoon, Jonathon Hays, the Logan Junction principal, had called to her as he was leaving his schoolhouse. After introducing himself, he surprised her with a request that she accompany him to the next school dance. She told Will that she was astonished by this handsome young man's boldness. "Why, we were never even properly introduced," Catherine had said. But she couldn't have been too offended by his brashness, Will thought. They'd been dating ever since.

Will knew that he couldn't get by without his daughters' help. And to make matters worse, Mary, with little money to spend, worked harder than ever to make ends meet. Except for his flower gardens and some yard work, Will found little to do. So he filled his days with visits to Kelly's Bar, a short walk up the street to Logan Junction's small business district.

Sharon had quit teaching and stayed busy helping Ed on the farm. Ruby worked long hours at the hospital, so she was seldom home. Will's solace through these lonesome days was his time with Catherine. They worked together in the yard when she was home for the weekend. And when she was out at night, he sat in his big horsehair smoking his Meerschaum and waiting for her return. He'd discovered long ago that he was the family's designated worrier.

Will lifted himself off his chair when he heard voices on the front step. The door squeaked open and Catherine's footsteps floated toward him in the parlor. He tapped his Meerschaum against the table leg and dumped the ashes into his tray. He pulled out his pocket watch. Eleven forty-five.

Catherine peeked into the room.

"So my Cinderella's back from the ball."

"I knew you'd be in here."

"Was he a prince or a frog?"

"It was wonderful. I felt like a puppet in his arms."

"My little girl's in love."

"Oh, Daddy, Jonathon wants to see me again tomorrow."

"So soon? This must be serious."

"He wants to show me something. I have no idea."

"You've gotta be careful of these older men, my dear. You know the trouble your mother got into."

"He wants to meet after church. For only an hour. He is a bit strange."

As Will got to know her beau, he was delighted by his daughter's choice. Jonathon was a tall, handsome man. He looked like Gary Cooper, Will thought, but was far more loquacious. And when Will went riding with Jonathon in his wonderful Bugatti, he forgot all his troubles. What a beautiful car! Will had never seen anything quite like it. It sure put his

Model Ts to shame. Jonathon said that cars like his had won fame on the race circuit, but he drove sensibly when Will was aboard. Still, Will couldn't keep from shouting "Whoa" whenever they approached a stop sign.

Sometimes, with little else to do, Will sat on a hard chair in the kitchen and watched his family at work. Today, Mary and Catherine were at the kitchen counter, making bread for the week. Mary mixed flour, yeast, water, egg, and honey for a new batch, while Catherine kneaded the last batch of dough, getting it ready to set out to rise.

They were so busy at their work that they didn't notice when he slipped out the door. He wasn't of much consequence anymore. He walked to the small tool shed out back. After fifteen minutes of sharpening his scythe, he hung it back on the wall and looked for more tools to sharpen. It seemed that was about all that he did anymore. He must have the sharpest cutting tools in town. He strolled through his yard to see if he'd missed any weeds during his cutting foray the day before. He could see that scything today would sever nothing but air. He had garden work, but he'd promised Catherine to save it until tomorrow when she could help.

His brief expedition brought him back to the front sidewalk. He couldn't think of a thing more to do, so he turned up the walkway on that familiar path toward Kelly's Bar.

Will pulled a stool to the bar and called, "Kelly, pour me a golden brew, will you please?"

"A Mineral Spring?"

"Is there any other kind?"

Will hadn't taken his first sip when Pete Baumgartner approached, slung an arm around Will's shoulder, leaned heavy against him, and slurred, "I hope you're in a generous mood today, Will O'Shaughnessy."

They called Pete, the town drunk, "Bum." At first they called him that because of his name, but now "Bum" described his favorite pastime: bummin' drinks.

"Will, I'm dry as that desert over there in Africa." Bum's breath, which smelled like a newly tapped beer keg, put the lie to that claim. "How about just one drink?"

Will signaled to Kelly to pour another glass. Buying a beer was worth it to get the bum off him. To avoid another assault, Will hurriedly finished his drink and slid off his stool. "Well, Kelly, I better get on home. My woman's not too happy these days."

"Never seemed like a complainer to me."

"Oh, she doesn't say much. She works so hard that she doesn't have the time. But she must be unhappy. Can't blame her, I guess. Living with a failure. She deserves better."

⟫⟫⟫⟨⟨⟨⟩

Will placed the lily in the hole, spooned dirt over its roots, and poured water into the loose soil. Catherine looked up from her weeding. "Daddy, I love your gardens. It'll be the prettiest yard in town."

"Well, my dear, it's all the farming I have left. It'll not provide a livin', but it does feed the soul. I never had time for it before."

A robin bounced across the lawn, searching for its morning meal. Catherine laughed and recited:

"A bird came down the walk:
He did not know I saw;
He bit an angle-worm in halves
And ate the fellow raw."

"You and your Dickinson," Will said. "You always have a ditty to tell."

Catherine's smile turned to a frown. "Daddy, why doesn't Ruby like Jonathon?"

"Hard to say, my dear. I'm sure she wants what's best for you. Doesn't think it's Jonathon, I guess. Why? I have no idea. I like the young man myself."

"She won't even ride in his wonderful Bugatti."

"Now, that's some car. I've never seen anything like it. Maybe she's jealous. Jealousy's awful, my dear. It can do horrible things to a person."

"I try to include her, Daddy."

"But she doesn't have a beau."

Will hated to see this fine young man come between his two youngest daughters. He knew that Ruby was so busy at her work that she didn't have time for men. Fresh from nursing school and being charged with managing older, more experienced nurses was a heavy burden. Her dislike for Jonathon surprised him. He had never seen Ruby show jealousy before. But maybe this clash was a good thing. This time, his little girl didn't let Ruby make the decision for her. Catherine was showing some spunk.

Will knew that he had to get hold of himself, had to tame his drinking. He thought about Jesse during their youth, how Jesse had ruined his wedding day, how he had intruded on their home. All because of the liquor. And Will couldn't resist either. When he began stewing over his desperate situation, his feet led him toward Kelly's.

Kelly poured a beer. "How're your gardens coming? I hear they'll soon take over Logan Junction."

"The neighbor's aren't complaining, are they?"

"Haven't heard complaints. They do talk about them, though."

"I miss farming, Kelly. I miss my horses and the smell of sweet clover. Why, I even miss the darn milkin'."

"Must be some farmer could use your help."

"My brother Frank needs help. He asked if I'd come over for thrashing. I'll probably help him out. But it's not the same, Kelly. There's nothing like your own land and your own animals. It's like you owning your bar, instead of just being bartender."

"There's lots of headaches. Can't wait till I retire."

"You'll miss it, Kelly."

He felt depressed as he slowly walked toward home.

Every cloud is supposed to have a silver lining, Will thought, and this cloud's silver was yard time with Catherine. She told him she'd help when she got back from her date, so he began weeding the lily bed while he waited.

Will was beginning to think she'd forgotten when Catherine raced around the house toward him. Now, what could be bothering that girl? Will levered himself off the ground. She's like a whirling dervish since she met that man.

"Daddy! It was terrible! I've never been so scared! He saved my life! We coulda been killed!"

"Slow down, girl. Make some sense."

"We went to see our old farm. When we walked across Temby's pasture to get fresh water, his bull chased us. Jonathon saved my life. He whooped and hollered to draw the bull away from me, and then he went racing across the pasture, the bull hard on his heals. I thought he was a goner. You should have seen him, Daddy. He's my hero."

"Your Prince Charming, now is he?"

"Just like my story books."

"You're in love with that young man."

"I think so, Daddy." Will saw her frown, and then she looked up at him. "I'm not sure."

"Do you want to talk about it?"

"Later Dad." She reached up and kissed him on the cheek, then turned toward the house. "We're going to a movie. He'll be here in fifteen minutes. I've gotta get changed."

Will watched Catherine race into the house. Seemed as though he'd been replaced in Catherine's hierarchy of affection, but he didn't mind. He'd never seen his youngest daughter so energized.

•◦◦◦◦•

Will knew he should go home. Supper would be on the table. "Just one more, Kelly. Then I gotta go."

Kelly poured a beer. "People are talking about that new principal. Running around in that blue bomb of his. Pretty car. Some people like it. Some don't like it so much. It rattles the glassware and assaults the ears. Your daughter's beau, isn't he?"

"Jonathon Hays? Nice young man. I've heard the kids like him, too."

"That they do. They also like boogie-woogie, and their parents don't like that either."

Will hustled toward home. He'd made plans to enjoy this day in the yard with Catherine. Dressed in denim work trousers and one of his old long-sleeved shirts, she met him at the front walk, took his arm, and led him around the house. She didn't say a word about alcohol on his breath. Mary would have noticed.

"I'll get the clippers," she said as she turned toward the tool shed. "I'll meet you at the flower beds."

Will was on his knees, inspecting his roses, when Catherine arrived with the shears. She reached them toward him. "Show me how to prune the roses."

He took the clippers from her hand and tried it. "First, you cut away the damaged wood." He spread the bush and reached deep inside the plant to clip an old branch. "This one was stressed by winter. You can see it's dead. Just cut down to the green shoot." He clipped away a few more darkened branches. "Now, I'll cut the healthy branches to about half their length, maybe less for the mature ones." He cut each remaining branch. "If you do it right, they'll come back more beautiful than ever."

Will handed the shears to Catherine, grabbed a shovel, and walked to his lily beds, which made up his rainbow garden. "If I loosen the soil, the rains will soak the ground but not run into the grass. I don't need more water there. I've already got too much mowing."

Catherine reached for a spade and dropped to her knees beside him. "No one in town has gardens so lovely. I love helping you make them beautiful. Maybe it's better than farming. We've got time to talk."

"It's an ill wind that blows no good," Will said.

"Why do people look down on farmers, Daddy?"

"I suppose it seems we're grubbing in muck most of the time. Like it doesn't take brains. Maybe it's because the farmer's been subservient through the ages, not his own master. Why do you ask?"

"Jonathon's father—he's a professor, you know—seems to think we're backward. I gave him a piece of my mind. Ruby would have been proud."

"So my little girl stood up to him. You've developed some spunk, my dear. And I like it. How'd your Jonathon take it?"

"I think he was surprised. He didn't complain. Maybe his dad intimidates him a bit, too. But Jonathon admires him."

"That's good. A son should respect his parents."

"Daddy, Jonathon's getting serious, I think. I don't know what to do."

"Not sure, are you now?"

"No, I'm not. I love being with him, but he wants to go back to the city, and I'm not sure about that."

"Farmers are leavin' for the city all the time. I'm afraid we'll see lots more. They'll never be happy. I may be impoverished, but I'll die in the country. I wouldn't have it any other way."

"I'm not cut out to be a city girl."

"Sometimes we're afraid of things we don't know. If you love that young man, you've got to trust your heart, my dear."

He wanted to hold his daughter and tell her it'd be okay. He didn't want her to go. He didn't want to lose her. But he wouldn't say that. She was beginning to show some spunk, and that was a good thing.

Will clanked his glass on the bar. "Fill 'er again, Kelly. Might swell drink into a stupor. I'm good's dead, anyhow."

"Will, you've had enough. How 'bout a cup of coffee? I don't want your old lady after me. She'd like to shut me down."

A voice called down the counter, "Over here, Kelly. Take care of your customers."

Kelly hurried down the bar.

"Pour me a Potosi, Kelly. Who's that down there? He's two sheets to the wind."

"Oh, that's O'Shaughnessy. Will O'Shaughnessy. Havin' a tough time these days."

"Ed Meadows' father-in-law?"

"That's right."

"The old souse, living off a man who's going broke. Doesn't he know that Ed's in financial straits?"

Will hated the thought of hurting his daughter. He staggered out the door, his last drink untouched. He stumbled toward home. He hadn't reached the end of the block when he tripped over an up-heaved edge of pavement and tumbled over the curb onto the road. He felt blood running down his forehead. With some effort he pulled his handkerchief from his back pocket and pressed it against the cut with one hand while he pushed himself to a sitting position with the other. He reached toward the curb. He reached again and came up empty. The cement slab wavered before him. He shook his head vigorously to remove the cobwebs and, when he reached out again, someone grabbed his hand.

As Bum pulled Will to his feet, he said, "Will, you've had too much booze. You've got to go easy, man. It's not good for you."

Bum eased his arm under Will's shoulder, lifted him, and helped him home. Although Will pleaded his innocence, saying that he was a bit unsteady because of the blow to his head, he knew that Mary wasn't one bit convinced. And he knew better, too. Preached to and carried home by the town drunk. He couldn't go on this way.

42

Will knew he couldn't continue to burden his family. But he had no idea how he could earn a living? He would earn a little money helping Frank with his harvest, but that wouldn't last long. Then the letter arrived.

Dear Aunt Mary and Uncle Will,

I sure wish I could find a way to earn additional money. As you know, Mother's worried sick about her nephew in Hungary. He's gotten in serious difficulties with the Communist authorities, and if caught, he'll probably end up in prison, or worse. He's in hiding, but for enough money, there are people who will get him out. And to make matters worse, his family is suspect and under surveillance, too. They've lost their jobs and are almost destitute. It's the Communist way, you know.

Aunt Marguerite begs Mother to help, and she'd like to, but Father's money is about dried up, so there's not much left to help family. Mother let two wranglers go last month.

The oil business is booming down here in West Texas. New workers stream in every day. The merchants get rich the fastest. There must be some way that I can get my hands on the money that's all around. But I can't think of any, except maybe rob a bank—but Aunt Mary wouldn't condone that. You're a smart man, Uncle Will. Think of some way to help your favorite niece. I've still got some inheritance money left and Mother's got enough money to get by for now. The crops haven't been good, so she's mighty worried about next year. And there's Aunt Marguerite.

Tell the girls—

Will didn't continue reading. His thoughts spun as he pushed the letter back to Mary. An idea had been percolating in the back of his mind for some time. He remembered how Gusta loved Wisconsin cheese, and he thought that others might enjoy it as much—and with West Texas flooded with workers and money—maybe that was the answer. He rushed to the telephone. "Mary, what's Gusta's telephone number?"

A few moments later Will heard, "Hello."

"Is that you, Gusta? I do have an idea for making money. See what you think. I remember how you liked our Wisconsin cheese, especially the Swiss. I remember you saying how it was almost worth staying in the North a mite longer just to eat that cheese. If I could get it down there, do you think you could sell it to those oil field workers?"

Mary smiled as he hung up the phone.

"You heard me," Will said. "Gusta's enthused and wants to ask around to see what interest is out there. She'll get back to me next week."

At first, Will was excited when he considered the possibilities, how he could travel Iowa County and visit the many cheesemakers to get their best prices. The thought of spending time with Fanny Too brought a smile to his face. Then he began to have doubts. He thought about Grandpa's admonition. Could he ever succeed in a business? When Gusta didn't call back the next week, Will began to lose hope and decided that his failure in another business would be more than Mary could take.

His hopes surged once more two weeks later when Mary called him to the telephone and said it was Gusta. He could hear the excitement in Gusta's voice.

"Uncle Will, you're a genius. I've got merchants within a hundred miles eager to take any cheese I can get down here. I'll need a buyer up there, someone who knows good cheese. Someone to pick it and ship it. And you're the man for it, Uncle Will. With your co-op experience, you must have lots of contacts. It could be quite profitable."

His niece's enthusiasm was uplifting, but he was hesitant. "Are you certain there's an interest?"

"There sure is. I've even inquired about buying a refrigerated truck for hauling cheese to the stores, and as soon as you give the word, I'll place the order. If the business blossoms, I'll keep the ranch and get Mother's family out of Hungary, too. Tell me when you're ready to go, won't you, Uncle Will?"

"I'll have to talk with some cheesemakers to see where I can get the best price. I'll do some road time, and then I'll get back to you."

This was moving faster than he'd expected. Was he ready? Would his family agree to a new venture?

Will put the phone down and told Mary about Gusta's enthusiasm for his idea.

"So Gusta wants to go into a business?" Mary said. "She's got spunk. I think she can do it."

Will, too, thought Gusta could do it, but what about him?

Will got up from the kitchen table and paced the room. "Maybe I'm too old." He walked to the parlor, to his big horsehair, and sat down. He couldn't make it in town. He couldn't make it farming. Could he make this go? "I thought it was a good idea, but—what do you think, Mary? Are we up for something new?"

"You know cheese as well as anyone, but—" She went back to her sink.

⚬⚬⚬⟫⟪⚬⚬⚬

Then Gusta called again.

"I want to get started, Uncle Will. I'll need some cheese for this weekend. We've got a rodeo and a dance, too. I promised to give out samples to introduce Texans to Wisconsin cheese. I'll pay for you to fly it down. There's not enough time to ship by mail. I want too much cheese for that, anyway. And there's another reason that I want cheese now, but I'll tell you about that when you get down here. And, Uncle Will, can you bring a cheesemaker's outfit? One that'll fit you."

"Fly it down? I've never been in a plane. I don't know how I'd do it."

But Gusta was adamant about him coming, and she needed the cheese now. Will said, "Let me talk to Mary about it."

Will pulled Mary and Catherine into the parlor to tell them about Gusta's plan. "She wants me to fly cheese samples down next weekend." He knew that Jonathon Hays had a flyer friend. He turned to Catherine. "You don't suppose Jonathon's friend would fly it down for me, do you? Gusta said she'd pay."

"Brayton Edwards? He does fly for hire."

"I'll find the cheese if he'll fly it," Will said.

"You've decided to help Gusta?" He could hear fear in Mary's voice. "You're going back into business?"

231

"I'll help with the samples, but I haven't decided. Catherine, will you ask Jonathon about Brayton?"

The next day, Catherine returned with the news. "Dad, Brayton agrees to fly your cheese. He said that he needs to go to Corpus Christi anyway, but he has to be back after three days." She poked at her dad's ribs and laughed. "And Jonathon says that if you'll do it, he'll go along to keep you on the straight and narrow. He says that he's always wanted to take a trip with Brayton."

43

West Texas winds buffeted the plane as it approached over the prairie. Its wings waggled like a wounded duck. The fuselage dipped, leveled, and then dropped toward the runway. Will's stomach churned, and he grabbed his seat to hold on. He felt like Pecos Bill riding a Texas twister.

Until now the ride had been smooth and pleasant. Will had watched the scenery as it changed from a checkerboard of greens, browns, and yellows in Wisconsin and Iowa, to a tan canvas in West Texas that stretched to the Guadalupe Range, and he'd been spellbound. There were scenes below like he'd only seen in pictures—winding rivers that appeared to rest motionless between their banks, villages with buildings that were no bigger than the snow-covered houses he'd placed under his tinseled tree each Christmas, and cars that seemed to stand still on long ribbons of highway. Now, here in West Texas, he could see the broad prairie dotted with objects that looked like black specks on a tan polka dot dress. As the plane dropped lower, he could see arms slowly moving up and down, and knew these were the oil wells that Gusta had talked about. He'd never imagined there could be so many.

The wings waggled again, and then the plane settled onto the macadam runway.

Will unhitched his seatbelt, pushed forward the seat in front of him, and stepped from the plane. He wasn't sure that his wobbly legs would hold him, so he grabbed the hand grip for support.

Once on the runway, he saw Gusta and a big man running toward them. "Thank heaven you made it," Gusta said. "For a moment there I thought I was going to lose my cheese."

Gusta hugged her uncle and turned to her companion who had held back. "This is Chester, our ranch foreman."

Will could see that Chester—dressed in a Stetson hat, Big Daddy Joe Justin boots, an unbleached osnaburg shirt, and Levis—was a working cowboy. Although Jonathon was six foot and athletic, Chester dwarfed him. Will thought about Gusta's letter, about how Chester would give those communists the boot. Looking at this hulk of a man, Will could see why they might not want to visit Texas.

"Mr. O'Shaughnessy, Gusta says you need some help with that cheese."

Chester grabbed the wheel of Swiss that Jonathon pulled from the back compartment and lifted the two hundred pounds to his shoulder as effortlessly as Will hoisted his saddle each morning. "Here," he reached out his free hand, "let me grab that smaller one, too. No sense takin' extra steps."

He strolled toward a pickup that was parked alongside the runway and eased the treasure into its cargo box.

Gusta, Will, Jonathon, and Brayton removed the rest of the cheese.

"I didn't know you'd be bringing all this," Gusta said. "But I think I can use it. No telling how much we'll give away at the dance. I promised we'd have fresh Wisconsin cheese to go with their wine." She grabbed Will's arm. "You brought your cheesemaker's outfit, didn't you, Uncle Will?"

"I'll look like I just stepped out of the factory."

"For a minute or two at landing, I was afraid we'd underestimated our weight," Brayton said. "I didn't anticipate this wind."

Gusta sidled up to Jonathon. "So you're Jonathon Hays? Catherine has written so much about you that it seems I almost know you."

Jonathon took Gusta's hand. "And I've heard lots about you, too, Gusta."

"I bet you have."

"Just what do you have in mind?" Jonathon said. "Why'd you want all this cheese now?"

"I think it'll sell like candy down here. And I want to introduce it this weekend. With Uncle Will's help, we'll do well." Gusta covered the cheese with a sheet of canvas which she weighted down with two-by-sixes. She turned to her uncle. "Poor Aunt Mary, I doubt she'll ever recover from my visit. I suppose she thinks she failed her long-dead brother, but she influenced me more than she'll ever know."

"She misses you, Gusta. We all do."

"What's your plan?" Jonathon said.

"I'll tell you when we get home. We've gotta get dry ice on this cheese. Chester bought slabs on the way here."

234

"Is there a motel nearby? Brayton's flying to Corpus Christi tomorrow. He'll be back Sunday."

"If these winds don't blow me into Mexico," Brayton said.

"Just down the road a bit," Gusta said. "They pick up and deliver, too. Cater to air travelers." She waved him to the truck. "They say it's the wave of the future."

"They're right about that," Brayton said. "I appreciate the lift."

"You'll have to ride in the back," Gusta said. "Will, you ride up front with Chester." She grabbed Jonathon's hand. "I'll ride back here with Jonathon."

Jonathon slipped out of Gusta's grasp and hopped into the cargo box alongside his pilot, making sure there was no room left. "I need to make plans with Brayton. Besides, you wouldn't think me so ungracious as to make a lady ride the boards." He nodded at Will. "There's space enough up there, isn't there, Will?"

Will heaved a sigh of relief. "Gusta, we need to talk about this plan of yours," he said as he grabbed Gusta's arm and pulled her into the cab. She hadn't changed, not one bit.

Gusta shouted back to Jonathon as she scrunched next to Will, "I'd be surprised if Catherine said I was a lady. I'm sure she has her doubts."

⊷∙∙∙∙⊶

They dropped off Brayton at the motel. An hour later Chester drove up a long, dusty driveway and slid to a stop in front of a large, rambling, country craftsman-style house. Its front patio area and its covered entry with two doors, one leading to a screened-in porch—the other into the big house, looked inviting to Will.

Jonathon coughed and spit grit while he jumped from the back of the truck.

"I'll help unload and ice down this cheese," Chester said, "then I'm going to the bunkhouse. Need my sleep tonight." He winked at Gusta. "Because tomorrow night we'll howl at the moon."

"Go on, Chester," Gusta said, "get your beauty rest. I'm sure Jonathon will help us with the ice." She touched Jonathon's arm and, in a purring voice, said, "Won't you, Jonathon?" Gusta turned to Will. "Chester rides in the rodeo tomorrow."

Jonathon continued to wheeze while he brushed dust off his shoes and trousers. He spit out a mouthful of Texas dirt. "I'll help in a minute, soon as I catch my breath."

"He'd like to draw Satan, the buckingest horse in Texas. Be a sure winner if he can hold that saddle. No one's stayed on him all year, have they, Chester?"

"Not this year—or ever." Chester hopped into his cab, and then he looked back at Gusta and Jonathon. "No hanky-panky now, you two."

"Get on with you," Gusta said as she waved him away.

Gusta turned to Jonathon. "He thinks he's got a lasso on me, but no one'll rope me anytime soon." She threw a stick after the departing truck. "Let's get this cheese on the porch and wrapped in ice. This Texas heat'll turn it to mush."

"Some like it soft," Will said. "It's more pungent that way."

"We'll hold some out for Saturday. I'll ice the rest. I won't need most of it until next weekend."

Will started, "How's that—"

"Let's get this done," Gusta said. She handed gloves to Will and Jonathon. "You'll need these to handle the dry ice. It can give a wicked burn."

Gusta laid a tightly woven blanket over a wedge of brick cheese and then covered it with a slab of dry ice. Vapor floated around the cheese. "Put the cheddar on those grapefruit crates." She pointed to the other side of the porch. "I'll introduce you to Mother and Aunt Marguerite as soon as we get this cheese iced down." Gusta covered the cheddar with blankets and ice. "You may not understand her. She's Hungarian, and her English isn't too good."

Will and Jonathon carried the Swiss wedge to a large board that Gusta placed in the center of the porch. "Help me unfold this blanket, Uncle Will. Do we have enough ice?"

Jonathon layered the remaining slabs of dry ice on the Swiss cheese, careful not to touch them to any bare skin. A fog spread across the room. "These slabs should last a long time," he said. "Cover them with additional blankets and the cold will settle around the cheese. You shouldn't need more before next weekend."

Gusta turned when footsteps came from inside the house. "Oh, Mother, where's Aunt Marguerite? I wanted to introduce her to Uncle Will and Catherine's friend." She grabbed Jonathon's hand and pulled him forward. "Jonathon, this is my mother, Allie Tregonning."

Allie nodded at Jonathon and hugged Will. "It's been too long, Will. I do appreciate what you and Mary did for my young lady here." She grabbed Gusta's arm. "She grew up a bit in that year." Allie hesitated. "I think."

"Grew up?" Gusta exclaimed. "I wasn't an inch taller or a pound heavier than when I'd left Texas—well, maybe a pound."

"You know what I mean," Allie said.

Will doubted if Gusta would ever change. But he'd never tell Mary that he kinda liked her spunk and sauciness.

"Marguerite went to her room," Allie said. "She received a letter from her son today. He had to sneak it out through Austria. He's still in trouble with the authorities, and afraid they'll pick him up for sedition. He says the Russian influence is stifling. Marguerite's beside herself, she's so worried. Lots of people have disappeared and not been heard from again. Hungary's a terrible place these days."

"Can I help get the food ready?" Gusta said.

"You can help Angelina get supper on the table. Tell her to bring ours to Marguerite's room. I'm sure she'll feel more like socializing in the morning."

Gusta took Jonathon's hand and led him toward the sitting room. "Come along, Uncle Will. Now's a good time to tell you about my plan. Selling Wisconsin cheese will be a pretty ambitious undertaking."

"How'll you market it?" Jonathon said.

"That's why I needed it now, this weekend. I know it must have been a terrible burden on so short notice, but—"

"Lucky that I know a pilot."

"This weekend there's a rodeo and dance. You'll get to see firsthand how Texans love your cheese. It's too bad you can't stay on because next weekend there's a food convention over in Harvin. All the vendors will be there. I rented a table and plan to give out cheese samples, introduce Texans to Wisconsin cheese. I just know they'll love it."

"Brayton has to get back," Jonathon said.

"This is only a start, Uncle Will. With your help, we'll both make a ton of money."

"I hope you're right, Gusta."

"How can we possibly fail?" Gusta grabbed his arm, pulled him close, and hugged so tight that Will turned red. "Why, you and lil' ol' me will make a strappin' good team now, won't we?"

The same old Gusta, Will thought.

"I'm sure I can convince lots of West Texas store keepers to sell Wisconsin cheese. And with you buying up there, we'll do really well." Gusta stared out the window into the West Texas darkness. "I'm looking to buy a cold storage building. I'll need lots of money to help Aunt Marguerite."

Later that night, Will settled into a soft feather tick bed with his head full of contrary thoughts. Gusta's excitement was contagious. Could he do it this time? Once more, Grandpa Duffy's admonition came to mind. But he didn't feel so antagonistic anymore. Will smiled to himself. You can't say that I'm not persistent, you old curmudgeon.

※》》》※《《《※

The bull took flight and when, stiff legged, he returned to the ground, the rider collapsed over his shoulder like a flimsy feed sack. A quick spin introduced the bull's nose to his tail, and a return in the opposite direction introduced the rider to the ground.

Eureka the clown grabbed the bull's tail and twisted hard. As the bull spun off the downed rider, he threw the clown through the air, then with the agility of a cat, Eureka landed running, the bull close behind. Scooter, Eureka's partner, ran at the bull and distracted him for a moment, enough time for Eureka to jump into a barrel, not to emerge until his enclosure had been battered, gored, and left for dead by the enraged animal.

"And I thought Wisconsin bulls were mean," Will exclaimed.

"These animals are bred for chaos," Gusta said. "Three quarters of a ton of ill temper."

"You couldn't pay me enough money to play hide and seek with that beast," Jonathon said.

"They don't do it for the money. They only get ten or twenty dollars a night. If they weren't rodeo clowns, I think they'd be stunt men, cycle jumpers, or some other dangerous and exciting occupation. They're a different breed."

"I can see they're good athletes," Will said.

"Have to be or they won't last long," Gusta said. "Still, they spend as much time in the hospital as out. Bronc riding is about to start. I wonder what horse Chester's drawn."

"Is bronc busting as dangerous as bull riding?" Will said.

"Some say worse. Broncos are leaner and quicker, a more agile animal."

"Is Satan that bad?"

"He sure is. No one's ridden him to the horn. Eight seconds, is all, but it's an eternity when you're jolted, twisted, and flung in every direction.

238

There's six riders today, so there's one in six chances for Chester to draw Satan."

"I bet he's nervous as a mouse running from a kitten," Will said.

"You can't be scared, but it's a bit unsettling. You're confident in your abilities or you shouldn't be out there. And you can win if you draw the best horse, but you know the odds are against you when you get Satan."

After a rip-roaring ride during which his mount pitched like a small craft on a violent sea, the first rider made the horn and jumped into the clown's arms as his horse, now free of the cinch, spun away. The second and third riders didn't make the eight seconds. Still no Satan or Chester.

"Maybe he'll draw Satan, after all," Jonathon said.

"I hope not," Gusta said, "I've got a bad feeling."

The fourth rider's hat showed above the chute, and a loud squeal emerged from the enclosure. A head popped up, and hooves banged against boards. "That's Woody," Gusta said, "and he's on Satan."

The horse screamed and reared. This time a tormented cry came from the chute, and attendants reached down from all sides to grab a cringing Woody off the angry beast. "It must be his leg," Gusta said. "They're always vulnerable in the chute."

A few minutes passed. Satan remained in place. Then a black Stetson emerged from behind, and a Big Daddy Joe Justin boot swung over the sideboard. "They're going to let Chester ride Satan. He could have passed on it. I don't feel good about this," Gusta said as she folded her hands in front of her mouth.

Satan broke from the chute with four feet off the ground and landed stiff legged. Chester sagged and then bounced high, the cinch taut within his clenched fist.

A spin right, then left, and the enraged animal erupted once more before he reacquainted his feet with the ground.

Chester lurched sideways but regained his balance, his gloved fingers welded to the rig.

Satan spun once, twice, and leapt for the heavens.

"How can he possibly stay on?" Will said.

"He's a fine rider," Gusta gasped through her fingers, "I think he'll do it."

Another spin, and the horn punctuated the screams and cheers from the crowd. But it wasn't over yet.

"His glove's wedged under the cinch," Gusta said. "He's having trouble. He can't get off."

And Satan didn't believe it was over. He spun and doubled up, his hind hooves intersecting his front ones as he tried every move in his repertoire to dislodge the thorn that dangled sideways off his back. In those few seconds, the horse twisted, spun, and jumped, all to no avail.

Chester, although half off the horse, couldn't get free.

Eureka ran alongside the enraged animal, and, after jumping astride, he reached around Chester and grabbed the cinch release, which loosened the entangled glove so that Chester could yank his fingers free. They tumbled to the ground together. Then one last spin and kick caught Chester in the midsection, and he collapsed on the ground while Satan surged away, victory his.

Chester lay still on the dirt.

Doctors raced from behind the chute.

⊷⊶

They walked down the hospital corridor toward the intensive care unit. After an hour of sitting in the waiting room with no word, Gusta looked drained.

"Does he have family near?" Jonathon said.

"I'll call them when we know more, but they live in San Antonio, too far to get here fast."

The doctor met them at the door. "You can go in now, Miss Gusta. He's sedated, so don't stay long. He's pretty sore, but he'll be okay. Three busted ribs, and several cuts and contusions. We bound him up. That's about all we can do. It'll take time."

"Hello, Gusta," Chester whispered. "Didn't think I'd ever get off."

"You did it this time. You rode Satan. You won."

"Yeah. Guess I did. It sure do hurt. I don't feel like a winner." He winced as he adjusted his pillow. "Sorry 'bout tonight, Gusta. Guess we'll not be howlin' at the moon, after all."

"Oh, don't you fret about that, Chester. I'm sure Uncle Will and Jonathon will take your place. Just this once, mind you. You'll be back on your feet in no time. Don't you worry, Chester, they'll take fine care of me." She turned toward Jonathon. "Now, won't you, Jonathon?"

Jonathon flashed a weak smile.

Chester looked worried.

Will worried, too.

Before they'd left the rodeo for the hospital, Gusta had given cheese samples to Eureka, Scooter, and the rodeo crew. "I've asked Eureka to stand for pictures that I can use in my advertising, maybe use on my packaging. He's a celebrity around here, but he hasn't agreed to an endorsement yet."

"Do you think he will?"

"He sure liked your cheese."

That night, when they got to the auditorium, Gusta, Jonathon, and Will set up the table, covered it with white butcher paper, and filled it with plates of cheese samples. Gusta pointed Will to the men's room. "Go in there and get your cheesemaker outfit on, Uncle Will. They'll think this cheese came straight from the factory."

As Will pulled on the outfit, he was worried that he couldn't answer all the questions. He even felt slightly angry with himself for being drawn into this charade. He'd never even helped make cheese before. He looked into the mirror and smiled. It was too late to back out, so he returned to the dance floor and approached Gusta and Jonathon who had just caught the band leader's attention. Gusta introduced Jonathon to Bob Wills.

"Mr. Wills came all the way to Wisconsin to bring me back home." Gusta said. He's my favorite musician. I wouldn't have missed this dance for anything. Don't you just love his music?" She turned back to Will. "You remember him, don't you Uncle Will?"

Will couldn't wait to hear more from the Texas Playboys. His own fiddle playing had never sounded as good.

Gusta grabbed Jonathon's arm and pulled him toward the dance floor, leaving Will alone. Dressed in a white shirt, white trousers, and a leather apron that covered him from his chin to his knees, Will circulated with plates of cheese and discussed each kind and the process for making it.

Dancers crowded around him. "Mr. O'Shaughnessy," one lady said, "did you make all these cheeses yourself? I've never tasted anything so good," she said as she fetched her third piece. She dribbled her drink across his apron as she gushed over him. Will could see that she liked the wine, too.

Will felt like a celebrity. He'd never had so many compliments on his own dairy products before, but he'd never met his customers face to face before either. This was kinda fun.

Except for the two dances that Gusta saved for her uncle, she and Jonathon danced every set. "Why, Mr. Hays, Catherine said you were good." She clutched his arm tighter and stared into his eyes. "I never dreamed a Yankee could dance like this. You weren't born south of the Mason Dixon, now were you?"

"Arthur Murray taught me all I know."

"I doubt that Arthur Murray knew western swing, Mr. Hays. I think you have a talent. I'll bet dancing's not the only thing you do well."

Will blushed. He hoped that Catherine wouldn't get wind of this. But he felt better when he saw Jonathon frown and pull his arm away from Gusta's grasp.

⊶⟫⟫⟩⟨⟨⟨⊷

The bright southern moonlight illuminated them as they walked to Gusta's car. "Why, I think Texas has put its best foot forward, Uncle Will. Just for your pleasure. Let's drive around the reservoir so I can show you the sights on the way home. You'd like that, wouldn't you, Jonathon?"

"That's mighty kind of you, Miss Gusta," Jonathon said, "but I'll take a rain check this time. Braxton's flying in at daybreak and it's been a long day." He winked at Will. "And besides, Chester's not here to drive us in the morning, so I'll have to rely on your generosity. I'm sorry that we'll have to get you out so early, but I don't think Will's up for a walk back to the airport."

Will didn't mind being the excuse for early retirement. In fact, he was feeling better and better about this trip as time ticked down to his departure.

44

Will set his empty glass on the bar.

"Another one?" Kelly said.

"No, Kelly. I've gotta keep a clear head. When the girls get home, we've got some talking to do."

"Oh?"

"Whatta you think? Can an old man start over?"

"They say you're never too old, but… I don't know. I'm lookin' forward to retirement myself."

"And you're a young man."

"I don't feel so young. Shoulder's gone." Kelly rotated his arm and winced when he raised it above his head. "Lifted too many kegs."

"It's tough to grow old," Will said. "It's not for sissies, that's for sure."

"Better than the alternative, I suppose," Kelly said.

"You're right on that score. I don't look forward to that eternal underground rental."

Will eyed the uneven walk as he rushed toward home. This was no time to be helped through the door. He felt excited but a bit apprehensive, too.

When Will stepped into the living room, Mary sniffed the air. "You've been in Kelly's again. Will, don't you think it's time to get hold of yourself?"

"I only had one." When she shook her head and frowned, Will could see that she wasn't convinced.

"The girls will be home soon. Supper's almost ready."

"I thought Catherine would be out with her young man."

"She put him off for tonight."

"She must think this is serious."

"And you better be, Will. Why else did you want this meeting?"

243

Their supper finished, Mary and her daughters cleared the table and stacked the dirty dishes in the sink. "We'll do these later," she said.

"Girls, did I ever tell you about the last time your mother left the dishes undone?"

"Will, you didn't call us together to tell one of your stories," Mary said. "Let's go in where the chairs are soft."

They walked silently to the parlor. Will sat in his big horsehair, and then he turned to Sharon and Ruby who sat on the sofa.

"Mother and Catherine know that Gusta and I are planning to start a cheese business," Will said. "The more I think on it, the more I think this may be opportunity calling. I want your opinions. It'll affect us all."

"Tell us more, Dad." Ruby said.

"You know that Gusta needs a middleman up here. To buy cheese and send it down there. I think that's a job for me."

"Are you up for it?" Sharon said.

"Do it," Ruby said. "It'll be a chance to recover."

"I don't know," Sharon said. "You can stay here. The yard's gorgeous with all your work. What do you think, Catherine? You've helped outside."

"Yes, the yard's been good for Daddy," Catherine said. She reached for her father's hand. "Good for us both. The work softens the loss. I've grown to love the flowers, and Daddy has, too."

"Sharon, my dear," Will said. "I know you need the income. It's time I pulled my own weight."

"It's been kinda rough," Sharon said. "But Ed just got another loan. He thinks that lead mining will be profitable again. Why, maybe we'll get rich. You can stay on here; surely you know that, Daddy?"

"What's this talk about staying," Mary said. "I don't know that the decision affects our staying one way or the other. We'll have to live someplace, and it won't be Texas."

"Mary, do you think I can do it?" Will said.

"Let's get this on the table right now," Mary said. "A few people think what happened with those cows was your fault. I don't." Her voice shook. "You're too good a man to be wastin' away at Kelly's. I'll admit, when you first proposed this to Gusta, I was unsure, but I'm glad you're getting your gumption back."

Mary dropped her head into her hands.

Will rushed to her side. "Oh, Mary." He put his arms around her.

She looked over his shoulder. "I'm sorry, girls."

Ruby stood and faced her father. "Mother's right. You may be a bit older, but you've still got your brains. You can make this work."

"No one knows dairy products better than you," Catherine said. "Besides, if it's successful, you can spend the coldest weather in the Texas sun. You can cultivate your clients, teach them about Wisconsin cheese."

Will liked that part of it. He smiled. "It looks like we're together on this," he said. "What do you think, Sharon?"

"Where'll you get the money?"

"Gusta said she'd bankroll the venture," Mary said. "She says she'll take out the loan, put up the collateral."

Will returned to his horsehair. "And there's no problem finding good Wisconsin cheese."

Gusta called the next night. "Hold on a minute, Gusta." He set the receiver down and turned to Mary.

"Gusta's pushing for us to get started. What should I tell her?"

"Seems to me that you're ahead of her, don't you think?"

"I guess so."

He picked up the receiver. "Gusta, I'm ready to go. I'll get on the road right away. I'm sure I can get good prices. You send the orders, and I'll fill and ship them."

The next morning, Will sat with Mary at the breakfast table. "I'd sure like to make amends for the trouble I caused at Willow. If only they made a Swiss cheese down there. It'd be closer and more convenient than buying in Monroe or New Glarus. Though, I must admit, they do make good cheese in those towns."

"Will, you needn't feel guilty. But if it'd ease your mind, why don't you go talk with Swinstein?"

"I think I will."

That afternoon Will called Frank and asked if he'd send Fanny Too and the buggy over. He said he'd made arrangements to board her with a farmer who lived near Logan Junction. Frank agreed to send her with his hired man.

When he heard a horse's hooves on the road—an uncommon sound in 1947—Will knew it must be Fanny Too. He hailed Frank's man, Lester, when he jumped off the buggy. Then Will forgot the man and rushed to his horse. Will grabbed her halter and patted her neck. His heart thumped as he ran his fingers through her mane.

"Well, old girl, we're back on the road again."

Fanny Too nickered softly and nuzzled Will's shoulder.

"Maybe we'll have a few more years together."

Fanny Too whinnied loudly.

"It would be nice, wouldn't it? I didn't think we'd get the chance again."

When Will offered to drive Lester back to Frank's, he shook his head and said, "I made arrangements to ride back with a neighbor when he comes through from Madison. I'll meet him downtown." He turned up the walk.

Will knew that Lester had little time away from Frank's supervision and that Kelly would see a new face today.

Will and Fanny Too spent the next two weeks driving Iowa County, bargaining with the best cheesemakers. While Fanny Too moseyed along the roads, Will took pleasure in surveying the countryside. The grass had never looked greener, the corn ears never so full, and the sky had never been bluer. Life was good. "Fanny Too, this is the most fun we've had since you were a colt. This work's not too hard, now is it?"

Fanny Too tossed her head and whinnied softly as she looked back toward Will.

Will drove past his old farm on the way to Willow. He couldn't forget how hard it had been, but also how much he'd loved it. He winced when he looked toward the buildings, now radiant in new red jackets. His soybeans had been replaced by a cornfield. It was a good farm, full of potential. But he couldn't think about that now. He drove on to Willow and hitched Fanny Too in front of Swinstein's office.

"Hello, Will," Swinstein said when he came through the door. "It's good to see you again. What brings you back to these parts?"

"I want to talk business, Jacob."

"I thought you were out of business."

"I'm getting back in."

"You were good to me. You hired me to manage the co-op when things were tough, and I'll always be grateful."

"I guess my name's mud in these parts."

"Most don't blame you. Bangs disease is a terrible problem. Roberts—"

"I heard that he was quarantined the longest. He was my friend."

"He's still bitter. It almost cost him his farm."

"It was a bad time for us all," Will said. "I'm sorry, Jacob, terribly sorry. That's why I'm here."

Will explained his Texas cheese business. "My niece Gusta believes that we can sell tons of our best cheese. If she's right, I'll take all the cheese that our—your co-op can make. Maybe more."

"I'll see what the members say."

"I can buy your cheddar now. Then if the business prospers, I'd sure like for you to get into the Swiss business. Swiss seems to be the favorite cheese down there."

"I'd have to hire another cheesemaker."

"Maybe I can make it worth your while. Either way, cheddar or Swiss, I'll pay you ten percent over market. I owe my friends that, even if it comes outta my profits."

"You're a decent man, Will. Too bad what happened here."

"I appreciate that, Jacob."

Will drove Fanny Too toward James Henning's farm. "I haven't talked to James since I left," he said. "I hope he'll see me."

Fanny Too remained silent but plunged ahead with renewed vigor.

Will reined Fanny Too toward the tool shed when he saw James in the doorway. "Hello, James. Passing through. I thought I should stop."

"Good of you, Will. How's life treating you these days?"

"It's getting better." Will explained the Texas cheese venture and his conversation with Swinstein.

"I've missed your guidance on the board."

"James, I've never apologized properly for your troubles. It was my fault. I should have known better."

"I never did trust Finian. I'm not blamin' you, Will."

"There were signs, but I was blinded by opportunity."

"Some still think it was Jesse."

"It wasn't Jesse."

"I don't think so either, but that's water over the dam now." He closed the shed door. "Come to the house. I'll brew a pot of coffee."

"Good of you, James." Will stepped from the buggy, led Fanny Too under a large elm, and looped the reins over a low hanging branch. He turned to Henning. "I'd like a cup of your brew. It's good and strong, if I remember right."

⊷∙∙∙∙∙⊶

A week later, a large purchase order arrived with a letter from Gusta. Mary scanned the page and handed it to Will.

Dear Uncle Will,

This is for Aunt Mary, too, but I wanted especially for you to know how I feel about you and doing business with you. You didn't have to take me in. I was no kin of yours. You treated me like a daughter. Better than some fathers treat their daughters. But then, that's your way. You said that some people think you're too gentle for your own good. Don't you believe it, not for one minute. I didn't like the North, especially its weather, but I love you and Aunt Mary. And the girls, too. Remember that as we go ahead with our venture. We'll make this work. And I'd sure like to see you come down here to visit. You're always welcome. You know that.

With my steadfast love.

Gusta

"How about that? Would you believe it? Our little Texas cowgirl. This is going to succeed, Mary. I know it will."

"Let's go to bed. We've got work ahead."

Will didn't go to his horsehair chair. He didn't take the Meerschaum out for his nightly smoke. The stars would shine bright tonight. A new beginning, and just when he thought he was at the end.

THE END

LOOKING AHEAD

Will O'Shaughnessy didn't know all that happened during his farming years. Did Gusta and Ed do shameful things on the back porch the night of the welcoming dance? What really happened the day Gusta played strip poker with Pete Simmons, Adam Baxter, and Henry Laurie? What happened to seven-year-old Catherine at the circus that weighed heavily on her for the rest of her life? Did Jesse survive the Wisconsin River? And did Catherine's romance with Jonathon last? Catherine will tell this and more in *Sugar 'n' Spice*, the next O'Shaughnessy Chronicle story. Coming soon.

ABOUT THE AUTHOR

Harold William Thorpe grew up in Southwest Wisconsin and lived on farms for brief periods when he was very young. He spent many happy hours at his relative's farms, and during his teen years he detasseled corn, worked two summers as a live-in farm laborer, worked one summer as a Surge milking machine sales and service man, and worked part of another summer as a United States Department of Agriculture field man.

After high school, he graduated from UW-Platteville with an education degree. He worked for eleven years in Janesville, Wisconsin — first as a general education and special education teacher, then the last four years as a school psychologist. During these years he started a business and earned a masters degree in educational psychology at UW-Madison. Afterward, he left Janesville for Utah State University where he earned a doctorate degree in education.

Upon returning to Wisconsin he took a position at UW-Oshkosh where he initiated a program to prepare students to teach the learning disabled. For the next twenty-five years he taught classes, supervised student teachers and graduate students, and served in administrative positions as a graduate program coordinator, a department chairperson, and a college associate dean. But his first love was conducting research that produced more than twenty-five publications in education and psychology journals.

After retirement, he decided to learn how to write fiction. The award winning *Giddyap Tin Lizzie* was his first book in the *O'Shaughnessy Chronicles* series. *BitterSweet Harvest* is his second.